Stealing Fortune's Brick

The Audacious Tea Heist

STEALING FORTUNE'S BRICK

A novel

Stephen Foehr

Föhr + Son

The Audacious Tea Heist, Stealing Fortune's Brick is a compilation historical fact, myth, and the author's imagination. The characters, places, and incidents are used fictitiously. Any resemblance to actual events, locales, or persons, living or dead, is entirely coincidental.

ISBN: 978-0-578-66720-1 (paperback)

Published in the United States by Föhr + Son.
Cover design by Berger & Föhr

Also by Stephen Foehr

Fiction

Water War, Snake Valley Okies vs Las Vegas
Killer Love
Storyville, The Eternal Triangle of Love, Sex, and Money

Nonfiction

Waking Up in Nashville
Dancing with Fidel
Jamaican Warriors (Waking Up in Jamaica)
Taj Mahal, Autobiography of a Bluesman
*On The Heart's Edge, A Powerful Story of Love and
Adventure in Africa*
Eco Journeys

` CHAPTER 1

CHALLENGE

"I want you to find and steal Fortune's Brick for me," the old man demanded.

Until that moment, Tom Edelson, twenty-five, had never met his mysterious grandfather. As a five-year-old, he had sent a Christmas card to "Dear Grandfather" in China. A stern reply came back: You are never to call me grandfather.

So he was suspicious on receiving a handwritten invitation to call at Hong Chen's Mayfair house. Nevertheless, he couldn't pass up the opportunity, if for no other reason than to challenge Hong Chen for the sorrow he had caused Tom's mother. When she married Tom's California father three decades ago, Hong Chen accused his daughter of tainting the family's bloodline and disowned her.

Tom waited a day before he phoned the number on the invitation. A crusty British voice answered. Tom introduced himself. "Ah, yes, Mr. Edelson. Would this afternoon at three o'clock be suitable?" Tom said it would. "Very good, sir. Do you know the address? We're near Berkeley Square."

Tom had never been to London. Before leaving the hotel, he consulted a street map and discovered Berkeley Square wasn't far; Grosvenor Place to Hyde Park Corner, take the underpass to Piccadilly, then turn at Berkeley Street. The walk would give him time to sort out how he felt about meeting Hong Chen. He didn't consider himself a vengeful person, but the chance to cause his grandfather pain—payback—brought a smile. Second thoughts raised a caution flag: How did his grandfather know he was in London? And the hotel where he was staying?

Berkeley Square gave the first clue of how little he knew about Hong Chen. The quietude of the elegant rectangle, two blocks off noisy Piccadilly, spoke of privilege. Tall trees with full canopies and neatly trimmed grass lent the attitude of a private garden. The Bentley dealership, the stately facades of the buildings, the gallery of antique art—by appointment only—spoke of wealth that could afford the privilege. Tom circled the square to Bruton Street and started looking for Hong Chen's house number. High-end women's clothing stores and other smart shops lined the street. The short block led to New Bond Street, with more expensive stores, but no residences.

Confused, Tom slowly turned in a circle and noticed a passageway to the right, which led to a small street anchored by Bellamy's restaurant. He checked the invitation and realized his mistake: Hong Chen lived not on Bruton Street, but Bruton Place, this exclusive tucked-away narrow street. No parked cars or sidewalk or trees or flowers cluttered the austerity. Façades of the two- three-storied buildings edged the pavement. Discreet signage, rather than big display windows, informed of bespoke shoemakers and tailors for those who could afford to know. An occasional doorway with a buzzer indicated residences on the upper floors. He nearly walked past Hong Chen's recessed doorway before noticing the glint brass numbers on the black lacquered door. Taking a deep breath to calm his nerves, Tom pressed the buzzer. An Asian man opened the door.

"Hong Chen is expecting me," Tom told the man, dressed like a butler with the attitude of a bodyguard—not hostile but frosty, with the added intimidation of a bouncer.

The bodyguard/butler nodded, motioned for Tom to enter, and shut the door. Tom followed the man up stairs barely wide enough for his shoulders. *This is a defile easily defended,* Tom thought.

The butler led him down a corridor, knocked twice on a door, and ushered Tom into a room with a cluster of silk-covered settee and chairs in front of velvet curtains on the street-front windows. He sensed, rather than really saw, accoutrements of wealth and culture: ink-wash paintings of landscapes, hanging scrolls of calligraphy, a jade horse in a lighted shadow box, the intricately carved lacquerware.

Hong Chen stood ramrod stiff behind a large desk, hands tucked in the wide sleeves of his brocade *changshan*, the style once favored by Manchu officials. A drooping mustache framed his mouth, as if a bracket to physically prevent a smile. Tom's mother smiled often and warmly. The eyes were haughty with none of the humor Tom so enjoyed about his mom. Hong Chen had her small and trim body shape, but had none of her softness. He reminded Tom of an ornamental sheath concealing a deadly sharp blade.

Protocol called for Tom to bow in respect to his elder; he remained stubbornly unbent. Ignoring the slight, Hong Chen asked, in his native tongue, "Do you speak Mandarin?"

"Yes." Tom grew up speaking Mandarin with his mother. "How did you know I was in London?"

"The doorman told me," Hong Chen replied, as if it were so obvious no further explanation was needed.

"Why have you contacted me after all these years?"

"I want you to find and steal Fortune's Brick for me."

"Why would I do that?"

"Because rescuing that priceless heritage will secure our family's legacy."

Tom knew the rumors that had swirled for decades around Fortune's Brick. Robert Fortune, a Scot botanist, committed one of the, if not *the* greatest acts of industrial espionage in history. Fortune had been sent to China in 1850 by the East India Company to steal tea plants and seeds, the secrets of how to manufacture black tea—imperfectly understood at the time outside of China—and the process of curing green tea. The penalty for stealing those state secrets was death. As a disguise, he covered his red hair with a wig of black Chinese hair. His Mandarin was good enough to pose as a tea merchant. To hide his six-foot-two-inch height, he traveled about the countryside in a sedan chair.

His success shifted the center of the tea industry from China to the British colony of India. The sabotage ruined thousands of small Chinese tea farmers and caused poverty and hunger for their families. The Chinese regarded Fortune as a criminal, a black-hearted man. In Britain, he was hailed as a celebrated plant hunter for procuring the many species previously unknown in England. British gardens are rich with Fortune's finds.

He had also reputedly stolen the ornate brick of tea created to commemorate the coronation of Xianfeng, the ninth emperor of the Quin Dynasty. According to legend, Fortune sent the rare tea brick to Queen Victoria—and it hadn't been seen since. To find Fortune's Brick would be the equivalent of locating the score of a missing Mozart's mass; notoriety from the discovery would jump-start Tom's academic career. He was in London to research his doctoral thesis, "Ancient/New Chinese Icons and Their Importance in East/West Relationships."

"I know nothing of finding and stealing," Tom said, in English.

Hong Chen gave him a don't-play-dumb-with-me stare. He flipped open the folder on his desk and handed Tom a press clipping. Tom scanned the news-paper article that praised the University of California, Berkeley, Tom's alma mater, for generously returning a thousand-year-old jade Quan Yin figurine, a treasured cultural artifact, to the Chinese people. The statue, sto-len from China by traders in the mid-1800s, had been a prized item in the university's museum.

"This private report," Hong Chen handed Tom a sheet of paper, "tells me that you are a man capable of bold action and proper spirit."

Tom read the three paragraphs, startled at the details never publicly revealed: the thief had broken into the dean's third-story office by rappelling off the roof and opening the sash window. Even more alarming was the note verbatim that he had left on the dean's desk, along with the Quan Yin statue: "Return this to the Chinese people or else."

Tom hadn't known what the "or else" would be, but imagination is more powerful than a specific threat.

The stunt had been a dare to himself three months before earning his master's degree. He wanted to give his inner nascent hero a chance to shine before begin-ning the slog to a PhD. Tom had never been questioned about the statue, although he was the dean's gradu-ate assistant. How did Hong Chen know about this? Obviously someone linked to Hong Chen had made the connection.

Hong Chen opened a drawer and set a Quan Yin figurine on the desk. "This is the statue you repatriated. She's always been my favorite, the goddess of mercy and compassion who hears prayers and sees with a thousand eyes." Hong Chen lifted the eight-inch statue of Quan Yin to his cheek as if nuzzling a baby, a show of emotion Tom found as unsettling as he did tender. "Like Quan Yin, I hear and see many things. Old, dear friends, secret friends, in China consider me the protector of our nation's precious icons, like this statue, and Fortune's Brick. That pound of tea is a national treasure, a direct link to our ancient heritage. I must possess it before greedy pissants destroy it to enrich themselves."

"How do you know Fortune's Brick exists?"

"My supporters in China have reported that it will be sold at a private auction, here in England. Others are searching for Fortune's Brick."

"How many?"

"Four, maybe more. Some may have already arrived in London."

"Where and when is this auction?"

"That's what you have to find out, and then steal Fortune's Brick."

"Why steal it? Why not place the winning bid at the auction?"

"Because I need to be invisible. There are people who would stop me from having Fortune's Brick. I am a danger to them. You are family. I can trust you, and no one knows you are connected to me. When you bring me Fortune's Brick, I will acknowledge you as my grandson, and heir to my fortune."

Hong Chen saw the flash of hostility—no, he realized, naked hatred—in Tom's eyes at the bribe made without offer of grandfatherly love. Good. Personal revenge is a stronger motivator than greed.

"I don't even know where to begin." Tom had never acted with heart-wrath vengeance, so had no idea how to make Hong Chen suffer.

Hong Chen noted his confusion and offered misdirection. "Robert Fortune lived and worked in London. He sent the tea brick to London. Perhaps you will find clues in Fortune's London."

The opportunity to give the old bastard payback was too tempting for Tom to turn down. Reach for the golden ring, and make it a noose; he had no idea what that meant, but it accurately expressed his sentiment. Get in the game, and then figure out the play. "I'll give it a couple days. If nothing pops up, I have better things to do."

Hong Chen carefully placed the Quan Yin figurine back in the desk drawer and handed Tom a slip of paper. "My private line. Time is short. Forces are already in motion."

After Tom left the library, Hong Chen summoned his loyal employee Ling. "Put the American under surveillance."

CHAPTER 2

THREAT

The next morning Tom made a list of places in London connected to Robert Fortune. The East India Company, which had sent Fortune to China to steal the tea plants and manufacturing secrets, was a logical starting place. Would there be a ledger of Fortune's tea account forgotten in a vault or an archive? Perhaps a private diary? A receipt for a pound of tea from Robert Fortune to Queen Victoria?

Tom flipped open his laptop and queried East India Company. Google told him the site was now the headquarters of Lloyd's of London insurance. Forty minutes later he emerged from the Monument underground station and walked down Gracechurch Street, looking for a building dating back to the 1800s.

A 30-foot archway flanked by ornate columns caught his attention. Tom walked through and into a warren of cobbled streets and passageways lined with shops and restaurants. The green, maroon, and cream painting scheme, brightened by dabs of red, gave a patina of an older era to the place. A dome hovered sixty feet above the junction of the four main walkways radiating in the cardinal directions. Head tipped back for a full look, Tom thought, *Suitable size for a cathedral, and the shape of a behemoth Marie Antoinette's tit*. He loved the historical tidbit, true or not, that the Queen of France had a coupe glass for drinking champagne molded in the shape of her left breast. She wanted her court to toast her health by drinking from a glass in the form of her bosom. Her mother's milk being the bubbly, perhaps.

Knots of men in suits—the look of insurance men and bankers—stood outside pubs hoisting pints and adamantly talking. Wandering about the space, Tom thought, *Rather grand; suitable for Lloyd's of London*. But he found no sign for the insurance company. He walked past Naturally Fast Food, the Mexican Grill, and the Regis Snack Bar. Ling, unnoticed, stood in the shadows as Tom stepped out one of the four arching entrances. Turning to reenter, he saw a plaque: Leadenhall Market, built in 1881. Right look, wrong place. From the corner of his eye, he caught sight of a pastiche of stainless steel tubes and cubes that reared up from the curb.

He walked onto narrow Lime Street, eyes fixated on the construct. Distracted by the startling building with growths and plumbing pipes climbing its walls, he bumped into a woman sketching the building. "Excuse me, excuse me," he apologized, bending to pick up the pencil he had knocked from her hand.

"Bit rude, don't you think," she said. He apologized again. "No, I mean *that*." She pointed to the building. "Lloyd's headquarters. Known as the Inside-Out Building because the elevators and utilities are pasted onto the exterior. Looks like an oil refinery mashed with a condo building posing as art, don't you think?

"And that," she gestured to the three silver pipes the size of an industrial sewer line leading up the building to a huge finned silver box, "ghastly, utterly ghastly. And those flat tower-like bits and the turrets curling around give a vague medieval castle feel. The mutation of old and new is astonishingly confusing. No wonder we live in a mess, being surrounded by such architecture."

Tom was not looking at the building. The woman was tall and slim, long dark hair pulled away from her forehead. Her right eye was a deep soft brown, a doe's eye. The left eye was blank, a depressed socket, possibly a birth defect or the result of a vicious punch.

"Yes, a mess," Tom managed, flustered, not knowing where to look—the bare eye socket, the alive eye, her breasts, her teeth. He sneaked a look at her sketch. She had softened Lloyd's building with latticework shaded to give a simulacrum of tall narrow windows in strict ranks, a feature of Victorian architecture.

Tom gave another awkward apology and quickly stepped away to find the entrance to Lloyd's, tucked under a canopy on the sublevel fronted by glass doors. As soon as he entered, a man in a suit stepped forward. "May I help you, sir?"

"Yes, I'd like to look around," replied Tom.

"Sorry, sir, the public is allowed only by special permission arranged in advance. I could show you some photos, if you'd like."

Tom declined. Back on the street, he observed men, with a sprinkling of women dressed in the same somber colors, take a street escalator to the first floor and tap what must have been an entry credential at the turnstile. He approached a young man hustling to the escalator. "Excuse me. Excuse me." The man stopped. "I need a huge favor." Tom flashed his University of California, Berkeley I.D. "I'm a visiting professor here on a research project. I'm afraid there's been a screw up with the paperwork. Is it possible I can go in with you?"

"Sure, mate. Come along."

Inside, Tom stood in the 120-foot atrium, head tilted back, like a turkey in a rainstorm, amazed. The whole place looked like a giant erector set bolted together with lug nuts on the support columns. A stitching of escalators linked the upper floors. In the center of the atrium stood an information desk curved around an intricately carved ciborium of four dark-wood Corinthian columns topped by a four-sided clock. A shiny brass bell with a pull cord hung beneath the clock.

Tom inquired at the desk about possible East India Company archives on site. "This is Lloyd's," the officious deskman told him.

"Yes, I know this is Lloyd's, but at one time the East India Company occupied this site."

"Surely not in living memory," the man replied.

Tom explained about the East India Company, a trading company—tea, spices, furs, all sorts of things. "Perhaps that bell," he said, pointing, "came from an East India Company ship."

"That's the Lutine Bell, rung to announce news of overdue ships. Ships insured by Lloyd's."

Tom started to explain about Robert Fortune and the emperor's tea and Queen Victoria. The man stared over Tom's shoulder until his indifference brought Tom to a halt.

"Perhaps, sir, you should try the British Library archives, or some historical society."

Tom turned away from the desk and nearly walked into the woman he had bumped on the sidewalk. "Hello, again," he said, surprised to see her in the building. "How did you get in?"

"I know the right people." She glanced at his jeans and sneakers. "Nice trick you played, to gain entrance in your American clothes."

"I, uh, am doing research."

"Are you researching apiculture? This is an industrial beehive." She waved a hand at the floors of people stacked and stacked upon each other, busy with their tasks. "Notice the sound, a low hum."

Tom pointed to the atrium's curved glass roof. "A beehive with a skylight."

"Influenced by Joseph Paxton's Crystal Palace of Kew Gardens. Paxton was a gardener by trade, an innovator of greenhouses."

Kew Gardens was on Tom's list of places linked to Robert Fortune.

"I'm interested in Kew Gardens. Perhaps you can direct me?"

"I'm on my way there now. I'll show you the way if you'd like." The woman stuck out her hand. "Rosemary Eleanor Hocks."

Tom was impressed by her firm grip. "Tom. Tom Edelson."

Ling watched from the other side of the information desk. His street name in China had been Ghost for his ability to be unseen in plain sight.

As Tom and Rosemary crossed the street from Lloyd's, she stopped before a massive black building of glass sloping up and away. "This is fondly known as the 'Cheese Grater,' obvious from the shape. It reminds me of Darth Vader, with those foreboding girders forming the entrance, bit like a mouth ready to chomp, don't you think? And those things," she said, gesturing to two twenty-foot-high white ovals with red screens, "air vents disguised as speakers. But overall I like it for the clean line and seemingly simple design."

A block on she stopped him. "Look at that."

Tom followed her pointing finger to an attractive church of beige sandstone with a modest tower that reminded of a castle. What appeared to be a thick spaceship on a launch pad loomed in the background. "The Gherkin, also known as the Eggplant. Actually, it's the Swiss Re Headquarters opened in 2004," Rosemary said. "It's the landmark building that began the transformation of London into a new era of architecture."

She turned to Lloyd's and the Cheese Grater and four or five other hulks of buildings in the neighborhood. "I like the Gherkin because it doesn't intimidate. The graceful shape is feminine. The atrium has interstitial sky-gardens that form a continuous green garland spiraling up the interior. A touch of softness. Touch, and how you respond to touch, is the secret weapon in a successful relationship, even with a building. The building showed how accommodation can be made between modern sleek elegance and winding medieval alleys and crooked streets of an ancient city. Unfortunately, other buildings didn't follow its lead."

On the Tube to Kew Gardens, Rosemary explained she was a "draughts," sort of an architectural draughtsman without being an architect. "I examine buildings for their colonial past, class arrogance designed to intimidate, bad taste, parsimonious motives, vulgar sensibilities, and ignoble intent. And, where found, successful humanistic sensibility."

"As a hobby?" Tom ventured.

"I lecture at the University of the Arts London and the University College London's Bartlett School of Architecture on how buildings affect society and the well-being—or not—of individuals."

Hoping to establish a collegial bond, Tom explained he was in London researching his doctoral thesis in Asian Studies. "And the drawing? Are you an artist?"

"Illustrations for my lectures. I re-envision buildings and draw them as a positive force. So many buildings are architectural propaganda. Lies, all lies. False facts stated so boldly, so confidently, with such bravado authority that people accept them as truth. But they are a bad-faith bill of goods meant to create trust: banks are trustworthy, cathedrals are the houses of God, parliaments are fortresses that protect people's rights, homes are snug refuges of comfort and security, monuments are truthful history made solid. No wonder people are so protective of themselves, surrounded by all this deceit."

What the hell was she talking about? For Tom, buildings are what you make them. An old church turned into a disco is a place to dance, no longer a place of prayers. A hovel is a hovel, except if you reappoint it as a home. She sounds like an academic, taking something simple and fussing it up into a paper for publication, necessary for a promotion.

Tom knew that game. He could talk that talk. But he could think of nothing to say. Ask her about the Taj Mahal? Is it a marble heartbeat of love or a tourist attraction? What about the Moscow subway stations with their showy chandeliers? A transit point or a ballroom, if you dance through the rushing crowds?

"Buildings are a good teaching point," Rosemary continued, then stopped. *There's no reason to strew rose petals to lead this guy down a false path. I can barely stand the hypocrisy to tread that path anymore—the respectable critic careful to stay in, and accept, her "safe box," a cardboard fort from which to lob bombasts of opinion. Coward. Waver of false flags, scared shitless to be reckless.*

The rest of the ride was spent in small talk that trailed off into silence. Tom wanted to ask about her empty eye but thought that might be a risky subject. He sneaked sidelong glances at her. She certainly was lovely. Interesting woman. He'd never known a one-eyed woman before.

At the final station, they followed the steady stream of tourists the three blocks to Kew Gardens. And stood in the long line for tickets at Victoria Gate. "Come to Kew to queue," Rosemary quipped.

Tom didn't expect to find a hard clue to Fortune's Brick in Kew Gardens, but perhaps he'd catch a scent of the plant hunter. Robert Fortune had been an employee of The Horticultural Society of London when hired by the East India Company. He probably had known Kew Gardens' botanists. Maybe he didn't send the tea brick directly to Queen Victoria. If he feared interception, prehaps the brick was sent to a trusted colleague. Upon his return from China, Fortune would retrieve the secret packet and present the emperor's tea to the queen. Much more personal glory in that gesture, perhaps a knighthood. Fortune was, by all accounts, an archetypical Victorian, a member of the striving middle class who sought honors and wealth.

Who would he trust with his precious tea brick? Tom wondered. *Where could it be safely hidden until his return? There might be a visual clue in Kew Gardens, something Oriental.*

Once inside the garden complex, Rosemary pointed to a large greenhouse. "That's the Palm House, the most important surviving Victorian glass-and-iron architectural icon. Its construction influenced the design of market halls, exchanges, arcades, and railroad terminals around the world. The St. Pancras and Paddington stations in London are exemplary examples. You'll notice that it looks like the upturned hull of a ship."

In Tom's eyes the building resembled a large rounded glass bread loaf with a bubble on top. As they walked through the arched glass entrance, Rosemary explained Richard Turner, the Irish iron founder and shipbuilder, did the actual construction from the architectural design of Decimus Burton.

The humidity and profusion of warm-climate plants from Africa, Australia, and the Far East gave the enormous greenhouse a tropical rainforest atmosphere. Within minutes Tom felt claustrophobic in the dense foliage of trees and ferns and palms and strange flowering plants.

"There," Rosemary gestured upward, "is one of the most important architectural innovations of the Industrial Age."

Tom followed her finger to a long seam of cast iron. "It's a deck beam, common in shipbuilding," Rosemary lectured. "But when applied to buildings, it was strong enough to span great widths without support. By the mid-1800s, improved manufacturing techniques of rolled iron beams, cast-iron columns, and wrought iron rails, used in conjunction with modular glazing of large sheets of glass, made possible construction kits for pre-fabricated cast-iron structures with glass walls and roofs."

Tom stopped to read an information plaque next to a 70-foot-tall palm with a topknot of fronds: Chusan palm, also known as windmill palm, *Trachycarpus fortunei*, unknown in England until the botanist Robert Fortune sent one from China.

"When was the Palm House built?" he asked.

"Construction took four years, from 1844 to 1848."

The dates fit. The building was completed before Fortune stole China's tea plants and technology. Could the tea brick be buried under *Trachycarpus fortunei*?

They left the Palm House and walked down Pagoda Vista. Tom speculated how to uproot the palm tree in search of Fortune's Brick. A bit improbable, he decided. Besides, the tea search was a lark, an excuse to stay in touch with his grandfather, to learn more before he called his mother. He couldn't simply say, Hey, Mom, guess what? I found your father. He dresses as if he's a Manchu official from two hundred years ago and is obsessed with a mythical brick of tea. Want me to bring him home to dinner?

Tom spotted the top tiers of a pagoda. Something Oriental. Maybe a Fortune connection. "And that?" he pointed.

"The Great Pagoda, a fine example of chinoiserie architecture in English garden design. Would you like to see it?"

They walked down a broad avenue of worn grass between tall London plane trees. Ling followed, using the trees to hide behind.

As they approached the Great Pagoda, Rosemary fell into her professorial mode: "The pagoda is the Chinese version of a stupa. This one, built by Sir William Chambers in 1762, has ten roofed tiers, where an authentic pagoda has odd numbers of floors. The porch with the thin columns was added later. Those fanciful dragons with glided wings are restored versions of the originals."

Could Fortune's Brick be hidden in the Great Pagoda? "Let's go in," Tom said.

Inside, Tom examined the stark red brick walls for a camouflaged brick of tea, or a hidden chamber. He began randomly poking at bricks, as if one might unlatch, like a proverbial bookcase sliding back to reveal a secret room.

"What are you doing," Rosemary asked.

Tom ran a hand along the curved wall, fingertips probing for a mortise lock. "Sleuthing." In all of his research on Chinese culture and business, he had never come across a brick of tea. What does one look like? Is it the size of the bricks in the wall? A thin brick, like a slate? How do you make a brick of tea? He had no idea.

When they emerged, Rosemary said, "Over there is the Imperial Envoy's Gateway. The Victorians were fascinated with all things Oriental. Shall we take a look?"

A man, Chinese by appearance, approached. He bowed to Tom, polite but not deferential.

"The English didn't know how to build a true pagoda, just like they didn't know how to make black tea," the man said in Mandarin. "They create fakes, and then make up stories. That's why people believe Yizhu's tea was stolen by Sing Wa. A story. Not true. Only foolish people chase after such tales. They are so blinded by their own desire that they do not see how dangerous their folly can be."

Ling, watching from behind a tree, thought the man was familiar. The way he moved, the polite bend at the waist while never taking his eyes off Tom. Knees cocked for action. The alertness of a predator. That's how Quiet Killer moved, Ling's rival in Chongqing during their street-gang days. If Quiet Killer was here, then surely Weiwu Long, Mighty Dragon, must be close at hand. Why? To finish the business started in China? To kill Hong Chen? Ling slipped away unseen and hurried to report to Hong Chen.

The man bowed again to Tom and walked off.

"Did you understand him," Rosemary asked Tom.

"A bit." Yizhu was the personal name of Xianfeng, the ninth emperor of the Qing Dynasty. In China, Fortune called himself Sing Wa.

"What did he say?"

Tom was flummoxed what to say. That he and Rosemary were under surveillance. That he had just been warned off Fortune's Brick. Should he tell her anything?

How have I been discovered? Did the warning carry an implied threat?

"Tom, what did he say?"

"He asked about tea, if I knew of a good Chinese teahouse nearby."

"There's a teahouse in Shepherd's Bush. I'll take you there if you wish."

"Yes, that would be very nice. I need to get back to London and do research today. May I call you in the morning?"

Rosemary wrote her phone number on a piece of paper. "I need to see a few more buildings here. Can you find your way back to the underground station?"

As soon as she was out of sight, he called Hong Chen on his cell phone. "How does someone know I'm looking for Fortune's Brick?"

"Come for tea tomorrow afternoon."

CHAPTER 3

DANGER

Tom stood at the curb outside his hotel, waiting for Rosemary to pick him up for their "tea date." After his conversation with Hong Chen the previous day, he felt anxious about being with her.

Hong Chen had sat behind his desk in the sitting room, dressed informally in a black brocade shirt with an intricate pattern and a raised mandarin collar. Tom thought he looked like a stylish Anglican priest.

"Please." Hong Chen motioned to a settee and table across the room. To Tom's surprise, his grandfather slowly pushed himself up from the desk and grasped a walker. Tom realized that during his initial visit Hong Chen had not taken a step.

Hong Chen edged one shuffling step at a time to the table and sat down. The butler/bodyguard wheeled in a tea cart laden with the utensils of a tea ceremony. Hong Chen transferred a small clay teapot from the cart to the table. Tom was enchanted by the pot's graceful

Stephen Foehr

feminine curves that invited a cuddle, and the short spout, cute as a bobbed nose.

"Beautiful, yes?" Hong Chen held the reddish/purple pot up for Tom's admiration. "A monk from the Golden Sand Temple, in the tenth century Song dynasty, made the first Yixing pot. Spiritual awareness even in the simplest tool is a lesson of tea. The Yixing pot is very traditional—and can be very expensive. In 2010, such a pot was auctioned for 12.32 million yuan. That's about 1.8 million dollars. This pot is much more modest."

Hong Chen aligned, with deliberate respectful movements, the tea holder, the tea pitcher, a beautifully carved wooden tea scoop, and two small teacups on the table. A silver water canister with a self-regulating heater remained on the cart.

Tom felt as if at a formal state dinner with too many utensils to choose from. What could they all be used for? A cup, boiling water, and a tea bag were all he ever used. Seep until he liked the color. Add milk or sugar or lemon to taste. Cardamom, cinnamon, or cloves for extra kick.

"Tea is integral to the Chinese spirit. It will always be a Chinese drink," Hong Chen said. "This is as true today as it was when Lu Yu, the Tea Saint, wrote *The Classic of Tea* in the eighth century. The Chinese made tea. It is ours. Tea is part of the Chinese character as blood is part of the body. Tea is fundamental in Chinese art, philosophy, poetry, songs, literature, and spiritual life. The traditional name for the tea ceremony is *he*, which translates as peace; *jing*, which means quiet; *yi* for enjoyment; and *zhen*, truth: *he jing yi zhen*. The tea ceremony blends the philosophies of Confucianism, Taoism, and Buddhism. The tea ceremony is a ritual of respect for nature and the need for peace."

Hong Chen checked the water temperature gauge. ""Tell me about this Chinaman. Tell me his exact words."

Tom repeated the massage. "Why did he tell me not to pursue Fortune's Brick? How did he even know I was interested? Who is he?"

"I don't know," Hong Chen lied; he had a very good idea who was watching his front door. He filled the clay pot with boiling water and let it rest. "I warned you that others seeking Fortune's Brick are in London. Some may be dangerous men. Please be alert."

Tom watched the traffic, trying to anticipate what kind of car Rosemary would drive. Something on the high end of moderate, a sedan, gray or black, suitable for a professor, he guessed. Was he attracting danger, as Mysterious Chinaman implied? Was he putting Rosemary at risk?

He still had time to disappear before she arrived. He'd call her later offer a dinner as an apology. Pursue her at a nice prosaic pace suitable for academics, while tiptoeing after Fortune's Brick clues. He'd do just enough to convince his grandfather he was in the game, but not be so bold as to attract Mysterious Chinaman's attention.

A red Mini Cooper swerved out of traffic and skidded to a stop in front of him. Tom jumped back a step. The car's engine revved. He bent down to look through the passenger window. Rosemary waved.

Tom expected she'd be a cautious driver, given her vision impairment. He had barely latched the safety belt before she bolted into traffic, squeezing between a bus and a taxi. The cabbie honked his irritation. Rosemary paid him no mind. "Hello," Tom managed before catching his breath as she edged out from behind the bus for a peek and hit the gas. The cabbie followed, close on her bumper. "Hello," Rosemary replied, looking for the next opportunity in traffic. "Sleep well?" She pulled ahead of the bus and sprinted into a not apparent, to Tom, opening.

The taxi slipped in front of the bus and pulled alongside. Rosemary glanced over; the cabbie nodded. Rosemary downshifted to be prepared, like a runner cocked in the starting blocks, "Yes," Tom replied, and jammed his foot down on an imaginary brake pedal as Rosemary sped towards the car in front. Her timing was exquisite; to let the taxi take the lead, then, with a flick of her wrist, sideslip lanes to tuck behind the cab, actually nudging its rear bumper. Tom braced himself with both hands on the dash.

"You can always trust a London cabbie," Rosemary said, "to know what he's doing."

They came to a roundabout. "This is always a fun part," Rosemary said. "The trick is to keep your line of attack so the other drivers can make way."

The cabbie merged into the middle lane without slowing, with Rosemary in his draft. They made one complete circuit. Rosemary had a big smile. "He's playing." Tom sat back to show he wasn't a scaredy-cat but gripped the safety belt, white knuckles.

"Here's the challenge," she said. "We need to make the next exit." She flicked the turn signal on, then off. The cabbie bullied his way into the outside lane, giving Rosemary just enough space to spurt ahead and keep her line of trajectory into the exit.

"A classic slingshot," she exclaimed with a laugh. "I love to drive." She glanced at Tom. "You can breathe now."

She slowed on the residential street. "We're going to the Teanamu Chaya teahouse. My friend Sandra Chou owns it." She turned onto the street facing Cathnor Park. Tom saw nothing that looked like a business. "It's a former worker's cottage indistinguishable from the other three homes flanking it. Look for a yellow door and **Teanamu Chaya** carved on a wooden sign. There."

She neatly swerved into a fortuitous parking slot.

Inside, the teahouse atmosphere was more home than shop. A carved wooden antique Chinese table stood in for the family dining table. Leather sofas fronted by low tables, and chairs in private groupings, made for a cozy environment. High shelves along two walls displayed teapots and canisters of loose tea, and some antiques.

A young-looking Chinese woman waved cheerfully to Rosemary, who flashed a smile back. "That's Sandra Chou, the tea master and expert in the gongfu tea ceremony. I recommend you ask her about the pu'er tea."

Rosemary took off her oversized sunglasses. Tom couldn't help but stare at her empty eye socket. The skein of skin in the depression was colorful, as if she had artfully applied makeup—or watercolor—to give the impression of a mini-sun rising inside her skull.

She touched the edge of the eye. "When we know each other better."

When Sandra came to the table, Tom asked about pu'er.

Rosemary sat back to watch Tom's reaction. Sandra's tea tutorial would be a test of Tom's character. If his attention wavered, he was a tea-bag man: take him back to his hotel and wave goodbye, with a smile.

"The pu'er we serve here is *heicha*, authentic Chinese black tea from vintage fermented tea leaf," said Sandra with enthusiasm. "The leaves have been dry roasted in a large wok, which arrests most enzyme activity in the leaf and prevents full oxidation. This is called 'killing the green.' Then the leaves are rolled, rubbed, and shaped into strands to lightly bruise the tea. The bruising is important in helping the minimal oxidation to occur. Green tea is the same leaf as black tea, but is not bruised and is dried with hot air after the pan-frying stage so as to completely kill enzyme activity."

Tom also learned that tea is classified by vintage and grade. The less desirable higher grades are the older or larger, broken or less tender leaves. "We use tea with low numbers and leaves picked only in the spring, when they are the most tender and tasteful," explained Sandra.

Tom, thinking of Fortune's Brick, asked if a 170-year-old tea would be a rare vintage.

"Yes, very rare. A well-aged pu'er gains value over time because it doesn't lose quality with aging, although the flavors can change dramatically. A strong earthy taste, clean and smooth, may emerge, reminiscent of the smell of rich garden soil or an autumn leaf pile. I don't know of any pu'er, or any tea, kept for 170 years."

"Would such a tea be regarded like an Old Master painting, valued because it is one of a kind?"

"That would depend if it were a master to begin with," Sandra replied with a sly smile. "I have a 1960 Tong Xing Hao Ji Yiwu by the tea master Liu Kui if you'd like to taste. Or a Gyokuro from Japan. Or," she said, gaving Rosemary a coy smile, "a Vintage Narcissus Oolong."

Rosemary considered the Vintage Narcissus, a rare tea that cost $6,500 per kg, but decided that would be too much of a shock for Tom. The Gyokuro cost around $80 to $100 for 20 grams. She ordered a pot of Tong Xing as a good middle ground. Tom seemed genuinely interested in tea, so he deserved a decent cup without breaking his bank.

Sandra delivered the tea to the table and carefully poured hot water into pot. "There should be no bubbles," she said, "Bubbles on are not aesthetically pleasing. It's like the tea has shingles."

With her first sip, Rosemary said, "Such a nice tea, with tastes of camphor and ginseng."

Tom had always associated camphor with mothballs and Vicks VapoRub. How could it possibly taste good? He took a cautious sip. "You know a bit about tea?"

"Sandra's my mentor. She's amazingly knowledgeable. And you? Asking about 170-year-old tea. Is there such a thing?"

Tom hesitated, deciding how much to answer. A tidbit for conservation wouldn't hurt. A peek to pique her interest. "Are you a gardener?"

"I've tried a few plants."

"Have you heard of Robert Fortune? He's responsible for many of the plants and flowers found in English gardens. The Winter Flowering Jasmine, Bleeding Heart, blue peonies, azaleas, chrysanthemums, cumquat, White Wisteria, Climbing White Rose, officially known as *R. fortuniana*, were collected by Fortune and shipped to England."

"I had a Climbing White Rose," Rosemary exclaimed. "It died."

"Fortune collected more than flowers."

Tom told her a brief history of Fortune's Brick. "And now there are rumors that the brick of tea actually exists and may be in London. I have no idea if that's true. But as a sideline to my academic research, I'm thinking about doing a little sleuthing to find places associated with Fortune, as an entertaining diversion. That's why I went to Kew Gardens."

Tom hesitated. Tell her that Mysterious Chinaman had hinted at danger? Perhaps there was no danger. Mysterious Chinaman was merely pointing out the folly of wasting time searching for a Fortune's Brick that didn't exist. But Hong Chen had said dangerous men were on the hunt for Fortune's Brick. If he started to explain all that, then she'd ask about Hong Chen, and he'd have to delve into family business. That was private business. Besides, ever since Aimee, complete honesty hadn't been his strong suit.

Aimee was the only serious adventure he had had with a woman. They met at Berkeley when he broke into the dean's office to leave the Quan Yin statue. While Tom rappelled from the roof to the dean's third floor office, jimmied up the sash window, and slid feet first into the room, Aimee was picking the lock on the dean's door. She entered the office as he hit the floor. They looked at each other, startled. He wore black from head to foot with a Lone Ranger mask on his face. She was dressed in knee socks, a short pleated skirt, and a jacket open over a lacy black bra.

She said, "Replace the mask with a cat face."

He said, "Wear smeared mascara and smoke a cigarette."

He set Quan Yin on the dean's desk.

She laid a used condom next to it. "That's him in there. He promised me an A in exchange for a fuck. He didn't deliver. Now I'm delivering a threat to tell his wife what a scumbag she married."

Aimee had white-blonde shoulder-length hair (dyed), a brilliant smile ($10,000 orthodontics' bill), was as buxom proud as a full-figured mermaid prow (all natural), and had the presentation of a beaming ball of innocent sunshine whose God-given purpose was to spread happiness (a malicious persona). Tom fell instantly into testosterone–charged love.

For the remaining three months of their senior year they romped—and Tom learned firsthand the craft of dishonesty by omission. She was sex without love, an artful lie hidden by her hyperbolical declarations of fidelity. Tom took her on face value (she fucked with such sincerity) and she didn't correct his mistake. The day after graduation, he presented her with an engagement ring. He mistook her laughter as a delightful acceptance, until she said, "Silly boy. I was just playing."

Tom was totally knocked off his joy, staggering, gasping for breath. She saw the crushing disappointment and reached out to steady him.

"You deceived me," he wailed into the crook of her neck.

"Sorry you think so. But look at it this way: you had a lot of fun, great sex, learned emotional stuff you never would have realized otherwise, and you're wiser for it. Once you get over yourself, you'll understand."

And in time Tom did come to understand the value of Aimee's stratagem of dishonesty by omission, concealment, and deception.

Dishonesty by omission was his edge of advantage. Keeping back information concealed him. The omissions distorted his intentions so others couldn't draw a bead on him. That was part of the game, the way a pitcher hides his curveball to make the batter strike out. His inner hero needed the chutzpa to try a fastball, spitball, changeup, whatever, to make Tom interesting to himself.

Tom finished his tea, swilling it around in his mouth in search of the camphor and ginseng taste. It wasn't bad tea. A little strange for someone accustomed to Earl Grey, but not bad.

Sandra placed the bill on the table. Tom gallantly reached for it and his wallet at the same time. He did a quick calculation. His eyes bulged in disbelief. Forty-five dollars per cup, without tip.

Rosemary leaned across the table to see the tab. "Sandra gave you a generous discount. An ounce of 1960 Tong Xing Hao Ji Yiwu cost $350, which works out to $60 a cup."

As they left the teahouse, Tom said, "I'd greatly appreciate your advice on which part of London I should look for an apartment. I expect to be here for a few months." He figured the cost of the tea was fair exchange for her guide services.

"Be glad to. I'll pick up you at your hotel in the morning."

Neither noticed the car tailing them as they drove away. Or Ling on motorcycle tailing the car.

CHAPTER 4

CHASE

Rosemary didn't know why she agreed to be the American's tour guide. *An excuse? A folly? Hope for something? He'd been good about not staring at her ugly eye, and he sucked it up and paid for the tea without a whine.*

She washed sleep off her face and scrutinized the empty eye socket in the mirror. "How shall I dress you today, my friend?" she said aloud. "Feel like being a pirate? Or a mysterious movie star? Or an embarrassment trap to catch people staring? Or do you want to remain a smooth and shiny non-eye, like a burn scar?" She put a hand over the missing eye. "Or a memory hidden, out of sight?" She smiled at her pun. Before leaving her flat, she put on oversized sunglasses that hid her face from eyebrows to mid-cheek.

Which me shall I be? She pushed that conundrum aside as she started the Mini. It was a question of loyalty, and she was confused about the answer.

Was Tom an excuse to step out of her normal life? An unknown who might lead her to adventure? He was mildly handsome, she admitted. His light-toasted skin color and tilt of his eyes showed Asian heritage. The widow's peak suggested a dash of daring, or the onset of baldness. The glossy black hair swept straight back said vitality. Evenly spaced black eyes. A straight moderate nose. The mouth was rather small and too tight to stretch into an easy smile. A round normal chin.

The overall impression was of a tidy man, shoulders square but not bulky, chest firm, stomach more flat than domed. Trim hips. She had noticed his small bum sloped down and in, as if being sucked between the thighs. She rarely found the male bum interesting, except that flamenco dancer, and the soccer player—hard to forget those bare-butt gluts.

What the hell; go with the flow, she decided as she pulled to the curb for the waiting Tom. He buckled himself in with a genuine glad-to-see-you smile. A glance in the wing mirror and she pulled back into traffic. "Thought we'd tour parts of London to give you a feel for where you'd like to live."

Light chatter as she thumbsketched Hampstead Heath, Earl's Court, Chelsea, and "possibly Clapham. It's a hot spot for creatives."

After ten minutes, she began to frequently change lanes, glance in the rearview mirror, check the wing mirror, and make sudden turns. Then, "Zuk."

"What's zuk?"

"Cockney slang. What the zuk. A motorcycle has been following us since we left your hotel."

Tom craned around to look.

"On your side. Behind the third car back. Why would someone be following you?"

"Maybe a courier," Tom said. "Or just a guy on a motorcycle." But the motorcyclist made him nervous. First, Mysterious Chinaman with his oblique warning, and now being followed by a man wearing a helmet with dark face mask. *What was the guy going to do, pull a pistol and shoot him through the car window? Not likely.* This was an opportunity to let his hero flash, to impress Rosemary with his man-of-bold-action.

He spoke with calm confidence. "Let him catch up."

Rosemary slowed. The motorcyclist, trapped between two fast moving cars, was forced to keep pace. He moved to squeeze in behind Rosemary. She abruptly slammed on the brakes, causing the car behind to close the gap and nearly rear-end her, cutting off the motorcycle. The driver hit his horn to blare at her stupid driving. The motorcyclist had no choice but to draw alongside.

Tom faced forward, darting glances out the side window at the motorcyclist and back to Rosemary. Her head swiveled between the car in front and Tom. He reached for the door handle, hunching his shoulder into a shove—and held the pose to show strength and discipline, a resolute man.

"Tom?"

He looked at the motorcyclist now directly at the window. The rider didn't acknowledge Tom, his attention on the traffic flow.

"Tom?" Rosemary reached over and tugged his sleeve, as if to pull him away from slamming the door into the motorcyclist.

That's what he wanted, her belief that he was capable.

He shifted a fraction towards her, a gracious gesture for her comfort.

"What was that about?" she asked.

"A precaution." He gave a tight but reassuring smile. "In case he was some idiot, an insane man, a jealous lover after you. Why would anyone in London be after me?"

She had no jealous lover, or lover period. No adventure in her life.

Why was the motorcyclist following them?

A familiar tingle buzzed in her fingertips. Fear started that way for her, a fizz in her hands or a flutter in the stomach. She thought of fear as a boxing opponent who gives her glove a tap at the beginning of the fight and says, Give it your best, you underdog.

She downshifted, a gesture to push risk-taking towards recklessness; she never allowed herself to become reckless. Perhaps, she admitted, that's why her love affairs always remained soft jabs, never body blows. Maybe that's why she never actually blew up an offensive building, content to lay dynamite at the foundation with her criticism.

Fear was managable—if she kept it under control. She disappointed herself that way, keeping control.

She categorized her fears by taste: pudding, sorbet, boiled sweets, and cake. Pudding tasted not too strong, not too bland, was easy to swallow, and in that, easy to master. Driving through London traffic was like scooping her way through a bowl of pudding.

Sorbet had a tangy chill. The light taste encouraged indulgence, which, if she wasn't careful, led to a stomachache of worry.

Boiled sweets began piquant, a comfort, like settling down with a sugar rush. She could roll one around her mouth to feel the flavors smooth on the tongue. The fear would glide along without menace, until that moment it pounced to paralyze her. She never knew when that may happen, when risk become recklessness. But that didn't stop her from being curious.

Cake, a triple-layer German dark chocolate, dense and heavy, weighed her down. She lost all her zest. She cowered, scared to death. The one, maybe two, times she ate fear cake, she gulped it down as fast as possible in order to shit it out. That's the only way she knew to get rid of it.

She watched as the motorcyclist pulled ahead five cars, then edge across into the far lane, then slowly fall back until even with her again, then drift two cars directly behind. She tasted pudding fear. She licked her lips—as if to get the last bit of creamy custard—then punched the gas, nudging the car bumper in front, nudging again. The driver gave her a middle finger. She flashed her lights and bumped again, trying to push the car past the over-the-road lorry next to her. The driver, sensing an emergency—perhaps a pregnant woman making a dash to hospital—slipped into the next lane.

Rosemary charged even with the lorry cab, got next to the front wheel, then, with exquisite timing, squirted in front, the lorry's bumper filling the rear window before she slipped over another lane, allowing the lorry to pull alongside.

Tom, stiff with fear, looked up at the lorry driver, who smiled down and ever so gently began to drift into the Mini. Rosemary tapped the brakes. The lorry cab crossed the lane line and stayed there, forcing Rosemary further back, which was fine with her. The motorcyclist couldn't see her hiding behind the lorry's double rear wheels.

"Shall we take a tea break?" Rosemary asked. "Tea always has a settling effect. That's how we Brits survived the war, drinking tea while the bombs rained down and as terrorists attempt to blow us up."

She abruptly took the next turn, before the motorcyclist could recover his position; spurts of speed and abrupt turns before crossing the Thames on Blackfriars Bridge. She found a parking space within an easy walk of the Tate Modern. "The observation deck on the museum's tenth floor has a panoramic view of the city. You can see hundreds of years of history in one sweeping glance."

Ignoring the floors of art, Rosemary led Tom to the promised view. St. Paul's dome rose directly across the Thames. Rosemary pointed to the Millennium walking bridge connecting the museum to the cathedral's riverside. "An architectural masterpiece of minimalist functionalism at its best. Shakespeare's Globe Theater is a minute walk upriver." She pointed to a cluster of building. "There is the Kitchen Corner. The Gherkin and the Cheese Grater. Construction of the Cucumber in Westminster, where the Parliament sits, has been given the green light. And that"—she pointed to what appeared to Tom as a tapered glass flat smokestack—"is the Shard, the tallest building in London, in Western Europe. It's not as good a neighbor as the Gherkin. It's too aloof from its context, lords over the neighborhood that dates back hundreds of years. The ground-level public piazza has the presence of a showpiece rather than a welcoming place for people to gather. The building is a beautiful object, a bright silver tower of glass that shimmers to iridescent in bright midday hours. It's like watching a flapper perform."

Walking around the observation deck brought into close-up view a gleaming silver building. "I call it the Pregnant Maiden," said Rosemary, "because of the bulge. Officially, it's the OXO Tower. Should be tagged the tic-tac-toe building, don't you think? But the honor of most unfortunate new building in London belongs to"—she gestured to a towering hulk—"the Walkie-Talkie. *Building Design* magazine awarded it the Carbuncle Cup as the worst building of the year. The *Guardian* called it "thuggish comedy" and a "villain of a building." The design creates winds at street level strong enough to blow away food carts and nearly knock people off their feet. The glass façade reflects the sun's heat down so it blisters paint on the shop fronts. It's hot enough to fry an egg on the sidewalk."

She shifted to look directly at Tom. "I'm developing a new lecture series on architecture as the sense of touch. Touch is the sense most closely linked to emotions. If you are having an argument with someone and they touch you on the arm, that touch can be perceived as unwanted, even threatening. But if you are touched in a loving moment that touch is welcomed. Buildings have the same effect by their presence; they can be oppressive or liberating. It's about the intimacy of space and mass."

"A building reaches out and touches you?" Tom had never associated buildings with the sense of touch.

"A building's stance touches us physically and emotionally." Rosemary continued, in full professorial mode. "We associate heaviness—as in massive, solid buildings—with weightiness and seriousness. That's why government buildings, court buildings, and cathedrals are so ponderous and self-important. They are meant to intimidate. They touch our fear. Such buildings bully us. They set a social and emotional tone to our cities that is detrimental to how people feel about the urban space. Is a building in harmony with its context, or imbued with happiness? Or is it a menace to the psychology of the community? Does a building convey class prejudice? Is the edifice a symbol of power and dominance? How does a building display and reinforce political and cultural ideology? Or the architect's ego? Does budget efficiency override aesthetics? The design of some houses encouraged divorce. A building is far more than the physical structure. A building has rational intelligence, and emotional intelligence, just like a person does."

Her favorite-thought game was to analyze a person as if he or she were an architectural construct. In the back of her mind she was assessing, *What kind of building is Tom?*

He wasn't this moment's trend, a hip construct with the latest outrage of colors, a new and daring façade that deconstructs tradition in search of modernism—or some meaning. That was not Tom in his nice but mundane clothes.

Nor was he a monument of self-importance, like the grandstanding Monument Victor Emmanuel II in Rome. He did have a whiff of minimization in his sparseness of self-statement. Nothing about Tom was self-advertising—the perfect cover of deception. He was too polite, like a box of chocolates with the ribbon still on, which meant there was much more to experience; which meant he was concealing. That was part of his intrigue.

She turned and grabbed his bicep so his entire attention swiveled away from the London panorama and back to her. "Buildings, like personal relationships, should be designed using emotional intelligence as a guiding principle. Then we wouldn't have so much ugliness around us."

Tom didn't know how to take Rosemary's little speech. He had never considered intelligence as being emotional. Emotions were flash floods, spikes of fear, balm of satisfaction and gratification, unexplained impulses. But guiding principles? To take action without thinking was not an intelligent act; it was an emotional impulse. That spur pushed him forward to kiss her on the lips—quick in, quick out. "I have an offer."

The kiss confused Rosemary. It wasn't a romantic kiss, so she took no offense. It did surprise her, although she gave no reaction. What deal was being offered? More importantly, would she make a counteroffer? The ambiguity of the kiss—more an opening negotiation move than a personal invitation—tweaked her interest, like a colorful door on an otherwise bland building. What surprises might be behind the gesture? Did she want to risk finding out?

"What's the offer?"

"I want you to help me search for Fortune's Brick. We can make it like a treasure hunt."

Another emotional impulse: ignore the implied danger in Mysterious Chinaman's warning.

To Rosemary, the offer sounded innocuous enough to be safe.

"And why would I want to do that?"

"For fun."

"Crossword puzzles are fun."

"The challenge comes from making the puzzle into a mystery, then solving the mystery."

A banner scrolled through Rosemary's mind: *Thinking can compromise you, make you a coward.* She leaned back, her lips now out of his range. "All right. How do we do that?"

"A puzzle is not having enough information to figure out the solution. Right now, I don't have enough information about Fortune's Brick, but there are clues.

Like that Chinaman at the Great Pagoda." He saw interest flit across her face so quick as not to disturb her cool composure. "A mystery is having too much information. It requires judgments and the assessment of uncertainty. Together we might be able to shake out enough information to solve the mystery."

"What about that Chinese man?"

"There's someone you should meet."

"Who?"

"Another Chinese man. You know how to get to Berkeley Square?"

Ling, who, with daredevil skills, had managed to follow Rosemary to the Tate, waited patiently for her and Tom to return to the Mini. He tailed them across the Westminster Bridge until sure of their destination. Then he took a shortcut to alert Hong Chen that Tom and a woman were on their way.

When Tom and Rosemary arrived, Hong Chen sat behind his desk—the polished surface free of papers, pens, telephone, or computer; a statement of competency and secrecy—and did not stand when they entered. No tea service had been laid out.

Tom led Rosemary to the front of the desk. "This is Hong Chen," he introduced, "an esteemed tea connoisseur, who has asked me to find Fortune's Brick. And this," he said, touching Rosemary's elbow, "is Rosemary, who has graciously agreed to help me in the search."

Rosemary took off her sunglasses. Most people couldn't help but stare at her deformed socket, a mockery of an eye. Hong Chen's glance slipped over the unadorned dent in her skull; his expression said that he had seen worse. Experienced worse. He glared at Tom and spoke rapidly in Mandarin. "No. Only you and me. No outsider. She's not Chinese."

"Neither am I."

"This is too important."

"I agree," Tom replied in English. "That's why she's part of the team. She knows the local territory, which will save a great deal of time. She has contacts to tea insiders."

Rosemary studied the old Chinaman as she would a building. The structure appeared sound. He physically didn't take up much of a footprint, but his presence was that of a throne room—imperial, verging on haughty, demanding obsequiousness. His face was a façade clean of wrinkles with no crumbling at the edges. An interesting building with character.

Hong Chen glanced at her, then back to Tom. "And who might those insider tea contacts be? Earl Grey?" he asked in English.

Immediately Rosemary liked him. The humor, even as a put-down, was a touch of humanity. "Sandra Chou of the Teanamu Chaya teahouse. She's a renowned expert of the gongfu tea ceremony. Perhaps you know of it; literally 'making tea with skill'?"

Tom was pleased with her impertinence. Hong Chen regarded her more carefully, as if he had pricked his finger on an unsuspected sharp knife.

"I've given her"—Tom nodded to Rosemary—"the historical background on Fortune's Brick. Now it's time to bring her up to the present. What have you found out about the Chinaman who approached me?"

"Nothing," Hong Chen replied, in stiff-upper-lip English. He turned slightly to Rosemary. "Do you know of Geoffrey Milner?"

"Yes. He's a well-known collector, a gadfly, regarded as a well-heeled dilettante with a good eye and social ambitions."

"Geoffrey Milner has taken an interest in tea, perhaps because of his family history—his great, great grandfather was a director of the East India Company. That's the foundation of Geoffrey Milner's wealth."

"We should talk to him," Tom said.

Hong Chen held up a cautionary hand. "Know your enemy before you hunt him."

The admonition dinged Tom's attention. Was Milner connected to Mysterious Chinaman?

Rosemary also heard the warning. Was Milner a potential enemy of Tom?

"I know him because Geoffrey collects architectural blueprints of historical buildings, like the schematic of the Parliament building showing the underground chamber where Guy Fawkes set his barrels of gunpowder." She quickly explained her professional interest in architecture. "Geoffrey lives not far from here."

Hong Chen gave an almost imperceptible nod, which Tom took as acceptance of Rosemary.

Back in the car, Rosemary asked, "Who is he?"

Tom stared straight ahead, thought about diverting the conversation back to finding an apartment, decided not to but needed a couple minutes to compose himself. It was crucial to hit just the right tone, the convincing timber in his voice. Otherwise, she might hear the undertone of the bluff and that was, as experience had taught him, a tell of dishonesty by omission. The bluster of trying to convince has a slightly hollow sound, where the missing truth should be. He must infuse his voice with genuine sincerity and full confidence, which required he totally believe what he was saying, or she might detect the liminal between dishonesty and honesty.

"Hong Chen is a family connection, on my mother's side. He's a student of Chinese history and culture. Fortune's Brick is a bit of an obsession with him as a link to the glory of China under the emperors." That sounded good to his ear; he had hit the right notes, and it was true, therefore totally believable.

"Why did he ask about Geoffrey Milner? And the warning about knowing your enemy before you hunt him?"

"It's a clue for me to follow. Milner must be another person pursuing Fortune's Brick. The warning was not to tip my hand that I'm connected to Hong Chen. If Milner is in competition to find that brick of tea, Hong Chen wants to remain invisible."

No need to mention the secret auction. It might be just a rumor. Even Hong Chen didn't know the when or where, so nothing was certain.

"The Chinaman at the Great Pagoda, he's in the hunt, too?" she asked.

"Maybe. We don't know anything about him."

"Is anyone else chasing after Fortune's Brick?"

"Hong Chen thinks there might be others. If so, they haven't surfaced yet."

Rosemary drove aimlessly while mulling over the possibility. "Where are we going?" Tom asked. She glanced around to get her bearings. Regent's Park. Geoffrey Milner lived in Regent's Park. She had been to his house once for a soiree. Somewhere near the zoo. In the Primrose Hill neighborhood.

She stumbled onto St. John's Wood Terrace and recognized the street. "There," she pointed. "Geoffrey Milner's house. Want to see if he's home?"

"No. Not yet. We have to have a story first."

Rosemary drove back to central London without noticing the car following her.

CHAPTER 5

OW

Hong Chen, he's crafty, Rosemary thought as she negotiated traffic. *His throne room contains an oubliette.* She unconsciously licked the air. Hong Chen tasted like sorbet, tart with danger. Hong Chen intrigued her because he was more than he offered; Tom intrigued her because he wasn't what he offered.

Tom saw Rosemary's tongue flick, wetting her lips, perhaps a nervous tick as she calculated speed, distance, and timing to get around the bus in front before the oncoming car closed off the opportunity to slip past. He ignored the potential head-on collision by wondering how to hide information about himself from Geoffrey Milner, yet gain information to help solve the Fortune's Brick mystery.

What might Milner know about the secret auction?

Should he kiss Rosemary again? Yes.

Rosemary caught his glance. What to do if he tried to kiss her again? The gesture of the kiss, rather than the kiss itself, was meant to get her attention. Should she make it personal? Why? She didn't know. Why do you eat one bowl of sorbet too many? To find the line between satisfaction and greed? She didn't know. She'd never thought of herself as greedy.

"What's next?" Tom asked.

"I've got commitments for the next couple days."

"I'll scout for housing."

They rode in silence. Tom asked, "How well do you know Milner?"

"We know each other professionally."

"Can you call him up and make an appointment?"

"When I have a story."

When she dropped him off at his hotel, Tom tried to think of a plausible reason to prolong their time together. It was too early for a drink and he was a bit sick of tea. "Call me when you have a story we can tell Milner."

Two days later, Rosemary called Tom. "We have an appointment with Geoffrey Milner this afternoon."

He told her he'd found a two-room bedsit in Earl's Court and gave her the address.

"I'll pick you up at four."

"You have a story?"

"I have an architecture blueprint to discuss with him. You're a businessman, a facilitator, with an interest in tea. Wear a suit."

Geoffrey Milner had sounded delighted to hear from her, an esteemed scholar he admired. Yes, he assured her, of course, do come. Would love to discuss the possibility of Roman ruins under the Ministry of Defence. Yes, do bring your friend. An American businessman, you say.

Tom wore his best, and only, suit, an all-purpose dark blue. Rosemary dressed professionally in a well-fitted skirt and jacket. She filled her empty eye socket with shimmering silver makeup rimmed with pale blue to give the impression of light beaming out of her head. Milner, when he greeted them at the front door, showed no surprise. He shook Tom's hand and escorted them into the living room.

The room reflected Milner: bit of a shamble, informal in a studied way, books in haphazard piles next to chairs into imply an autodidactic flair, framed art on the walls to show a moneyed-eye for culture. Tom recognized a famous Cubist. Tables were a disarray of knickknacks that could have come from Grecian ruins or Babylonia digs. Milner dressed casually but expensively in black linen slacks and a wrinkled yellow raw-silk shirt, top three buttons undone. A silver ankh glinted in his chest hairs. Tom expected someone older, but Milner appeared to be in his mid-thirties, trim and fit. His black hair with deep purple highlights was artfully cut in a mussed up shag, to appear indifferent to fashion or expense.

Milner offered drinks—A brandy, perhaps? Tom asked for tea. "Of course, only take a moment to brew a pot." While Milner was in the kitchen, Rosemary unrolled a seismographic graph and a street map of

London on the table beneath the windows looking out on a groomed garden. Tom wandered about the large room, examining a collection of ancient coins under glass, shards of clay with what appeared to be hieroglyphic marks, and a display of teaware. He recognized a teapot as Yixing, similar to Hong Chen's but with a deeper, richer patina of age.

Milner returned with a tray bearing a teapot, three cups, and a plate of chocolate digestive biscuits. Setting the tray on the table, he bent to examine the graph.

"We used sound wave technology," Rosemary said, tapping the paper, "to reveal what appears to be the outlines of a possible ruin twenty feet beneath the Ministry of Defence. We think"—she placed a finger on the city map and traced Richmond Terrace to Victoria Embankment bordering the Thames—"that the river's bank was higher up several hundred years ago and that the ruins might have been a warehouse fronting a pier. If so, it could contain evidence of trading during the Roman times and give clues to such a network reaching back to the Levant."

"I don't suppose the Ministry would allow us to dig under its foundations," Milner asked, with amused speculation. "No telling what kind of buried embarrassments might be found."

The timer on the tea tray chimed. "Shall we?" Milner gestured to chairs at a cleared table. "This is a new tea I'm curious about, Silver Tips Imperial from the Makaibari Estate in India, founded by the Banerjee family in 1859. The tea is rather special, handmade in very limited quantities. I was fortunate to secure a few grams. This oolong is known for its anti-aging properties, not that you should have such concerns," he nodded to Rosemary. "Love the eye," he added as he handed her a cup of tea.

Tom accepted his cup, poured from an ordinary porcelain pot. "I noticed the pot there." He nodded toward a tea ware display. "Yixing, isn't it?"

"Yes. I would have used it but I'm not sure this tea deserves the honor. A quality Yixing pot is more porous than porcelain to better preserve the delicate taste, color, and fragrance of the tea. You don't want to preserve the taste of inferior tea, do you? That would ruin the pot." Milner poured himself a cup. "Perhaps you can judge if this tea deserves a Yixing pot."

Tom glanced at Rosemary and followed her lead: hold the cup under the nose, sniff the fragrance, assess, and then, if approved, slurp a mouthful with air to cool the tea. Seemed a bit overdone and déclassé; his mother always reprimanded him for a slurp. But he slurped, and added a satisfied smack.

"Not as earthy as aged Da Hong Pao," he pronounced, "but worthy nevertheless. Do you know if the Banerjee family planted any of the root stock Robert Fortune sent from China?"

Milner raised his cup and held it before his lips, a moment for a decision. "Robert Fortune the botanist?" Milner lowered his cup. "Fortune was the greatest plant collector of his time, perhaps of all times. I have some of his flowers in the garden." He gestured out the window.

"He also collected tea plants." Tom watched Milner's eyes for a side-glance of avoidance, but Milner held a steady stare. "I suppose you know that. Sent the lot from China to India a few years before the Banerjees founded their estate. I wonder if perhaps some of Fortune's plants were the source of this fine tea."

"I wouldn't know. I've always associated him with winter roses and peonies." Milner smiled over his tea-cup, a show of friendly honesty, but Tom saw the faint squint, as if to squeeze down the lie so it didn't show. "What exactly is your business, Tom? You don't mind first names, do you, being an American?"

"No, not at all. I'm a facilitator."

"A fixer?"

"I introduce people to each other for their mutual benefit."

"Can you introduce me to a woman?"

Tom let the implied insult slide, but noted the hostility meant to back him off.

"Depends on your business interests. I know women in the export/import business, banking, finance. Professional women. Some in the tea business. Do you know Sandra Chou, owner of the Teanamu Chaya teahouse in Sheperd's Bush? She has a fine collection of excellent teas. I'll introduce you if you'd like."

"Yes, I'd like that." Milner hoisted his teacup in a salute before turning to Rosemary. "Now, what about this maybe Roman warehouse the Ministry of Defence is squatting on?"

Rosemary and Milner spent nearly an hour discussing how to visually transform the sonic squibs into an architectural rendering of a Roman warehouse. "It would be a first," Rosemary said, "an important technological breakthrough. We could use 3-D CAD/CAM with custom programming based on what we know about Roman storage facilities. If we get a match, then we can make a proposal for a dig. If that's turned down, which is likely, we can at least make a model, perhaps scale it up for a museum piece. That would take some backing. You interested?"

Milner sat back and laughed. "I thought Tom was the facilitator, the fixer of the handshake. You don't need him at all." Milner extended his hand to close the deal.

Ling, sitting on his motorcycle a half block from Milner's house, watched Rosemary and Tom drive away. A black Ford Escort pulled from its parking space and followed Rosemary's car. Ling did a double take as the car passed; Quiet Killer was behind the wheel. Twice now he had spotted Quiet Killer following the American Hong Chen had instructed to keep under surveillance. What was the connection? And who was the woman? Ling gunned the motorcycle in pursuit.

The woman was a snake driver, slithering in and out of traffic, showing fangs of aggression. Quiet Killer didn't seem accustomed to the British rules of the road, more than once getting in the wrong lane and barely avoiding a crash. His clumsiness pleased Ling; Quiet

Killer was on unfamiliar ground and that made him unbalanced. The woman driver, on the other hand, could be dangerous; she was daring and in control. The earlier maneuver with the lorry had given him appreciation of her skill. Maybe together they could cause Quiet Killer to have an accident. Play little games with him.

In the car, Tom asked, "Was that for real? The Roman warehouse under the Ministry of Defence?"

"Close enough. Gives us a reason to keep in touch with him."

That would be like touching slime, in Tom's opinion. He didn't like Milner any more than Milner liked him. The insinuation that Tom was a pimp—the guy deserved a kick in the balls. The insult implied in his noblesse oblige snobbery—give the guy a slap on the head. The smarmy familiarity with Rosemary a bruise on Tom's manhood—smack him where it hurts, in his ego. *Why should I care if "Lord" Milner leers after Rosemary,* Tom wondered, surprised at his own reaction.

"I don't think he would be useful to us." Tom didn't disguise the dismissive sneer in his voice. "If he knows anything about Fortune's Brick, he's not willing to share. He's a waste of time."

"But Hong Chen sent us in his direction. He must have had a reason." Rosemary thought for several moments. "Something underhanded is going on, and we don't have a sense for it. But I know someone who does have a nose for the smelly. We need to talk with him."

Geoffrey Milner opened the hidden safe and drew out the envelope. The black invitation card was there: phase one. Phase two, the details of time and place, were still unknown. But someone from the outside was onto the game and had sent Tom to sniff around. His questions about Robert Fortune were not even subtle. *Typical American—straightforward, arrogant in his right to know, a form of dominance. Well, nobody is better than the English at domination of inferiors, especially someone with my blue-blood ancestry*, Geoffrey thought. *Who linked me to the auction? The association could well put me in danger, if that person planned for me to be their backdoor—or Trojan horse—to acquire Fortune's Brick. What am I going to do about it?*

He tapped the invitation on the palm of his hand. Rosemary had brought Tom to him. She must be part of the whatever. Milner had always fancied her for her beauty and professional achievement, and for the perverse eye. *Roman warehouse under the Ministry of Defence, my foot, or I should say, my eye*, he mused. *Could have well been seismographic squibs from a Norwegian oil field under the North Sea. I'd like to poke her in the eye, literally.*

Rosemary whipped out into traffic.

"Where are we going?"

"Peckham, one of the oldest areas of London—and, according to many, one of the roughest; worse than Tottenham, if you can believe it. Knives and brass knuckles are the weapons of choice in Peckham. My brother Howard lives there. Most people call him Ow, which perfectly describes him. You look at him and think, Ow, no way he could look like that and not be a thug. Best to cross the street before he gives me an owie. Some people like rough. Me, rough didn't look so sexy when I grew up, the whole family doggy paddling like mad to keep our heads about the torrent of crime. I escaped, but Howard likes rough and tumble, so he stayed with his mates. He doesn't appreciate inquiries into what he does for a living, so I don't ask. But he's very protective of his little sis, and he has the skills to get his way. He's actually quite sweet, once you get used to him."

Twenty minutes later, Rosemary said, "Nearly there. One thing you should know about Ow: he's a man of few words and he's smart."

"That's two things."

"While you're keeping a list, add tough, loyal, enjoys a good dustup, and is as strong as he looks."

Tom didn't realize they were in notorious Peckham until Rosemary said, "Look for a parking slot." The streets appeared ordinary, a bit worn—a couple hundred years would do that—not unattractive just well lived in, more working-class than criminal.

"Yeah, all that's true," Rosemary replied to his comments. "So is everything else said about Peckham."

She crawled down small side streets in hopes of finding a parking spot, and looped around. "That's where we're going," she said pointing to the pub Cock & Spur, and suddenly slammed on the brakes. A man stood in the street with his hand up, like a traffic cop out of uniform. A car pulled away from the curb, and the man, with a sweeping bow, motioned Rosemary into the space. "Must be a friend of Ow's."

The Cock & Spur had none of the charm Tom associated with a British pub. The brick façade gave the impression of a fortress wall. Narrow windows were set high on either side of the door. A random pattern of dents—hammer blows?—and a large depression—a body slam?—marked the metal door. "Architectural details of local handicraft," remarked Rosemary, pushing the door open.

A man with dreadlocks stood behind the bar placidly wiping the surface with a cloth. Tables, all empty, filled the center of the room. Booths lined the rear wall. Rosemary moved toward a high-backed booth in the corner. Tom didn't see the hulk until he stopped next to her at the booth.

"Allo, Howard." Rosemary slid into the booth, and Tom followed.

"Rosie." They touched hands briefly.

"This is Tom."

Tom extended a friendly handshake, the automatic reflex of an American.

Ow ignored him. "Could be."

An ox of a man. A mound of muscle hunched in a canvas coat. A child-eater and, by the scowl on Ow's face, the kid hadn't been tasty. Heavy face, clean-shaven but with a dark five-o'clock shadow, thick brows hooding his eyes. Dark hair, black or brown, hard to tell in the low light, bit of a haystack slipping down his forehead.

Ow swung his bulk of shoulders towards Tom, a bull shifting to charge. "You didn't tell me he's septic," he said without looking at Rosemary.

"Didn't want you to prejudge the cod," she replied.

Tom, trying to understand "septic," gave Rosemary an inquiring look. Septic described a wound infected with bacteria. Was the insult intended?

"Septic tank rhymes with Yank," she clarified and nodded to confirm the insult was intended.

Ow stared Tom hard in the eyes. "I don't like Americans. I don't like their fake chumminess. I don't like their false gifts. I don't like their attitude of savior smugness. Why's he here, Rosie?"

"We have a caper you might enjoy. It's about tea."

"I like tea. My favorite beverage."

"Seems to be a mystery around this tea that we don't understand. Might be a rare and expensive tea. People lurking about in shadows. Thought you might have an insight as to how we might find out about the lurkers."

"Did you now."

"No need to tell secrets, Howard"—Rosemary had willfully remained ignorant of the details of Ow's professional life—"but your experience may be useful."

Ow had always respected his sister's escape from their upbringing, so gave her a lie she could believe in. But they both knew he wasn't only the Cock & Spur owner, a modest small-time businessman tucked away in his corner. But she had never brought a Yank around before, an outsider, and he had a visceral mistrust of outsiders. Ow lurched his head forward, a foot from

Tom's face, to intimidate. "You know why Rosie thinks I may have a special 'sense'? Because I'm a crime boss."

The blatant admission, the breach of their etiquette, surprised Rosemary.

"You know why I became a criminal?" Ow leaned closer to Tom, his very-bad- man stare a death threat.

Tom didn't blink. "Because you're a pervert who enjoys beating up people and stealing. Because you don't have what it takes to make it in the real society."

Ow literally snapped at Tom's nose. "I became a criminal because it suits me. I feel real joy as a tough guy, pounding on someone, deserving or not. I *like* seeing pain scrunch some bastard's face when I slam the hammer down on his fingers, one at a time, talking softly to him between each blow, being solicitous—or just talking about our football teams. I like being a hard-arsed crime boss. I relish the thrill of getting away with crime."

Tom forced himself to stay in position, not to tremble. He saw himself swinging through the dean's window in his hero disguise and relived the admiration in Aimee's eyes at his boldness.

Rosemary saw the look Tom couldn't hide on his face—This lout, this bully.

Ow's shoulder twitched, his arm being loaded and cocked. She pushed her face between them. Ow wouldn't punch if she were in the way.

Ow talked over her head. "I don't like an American messing with my sister. Fair warning."

"He's not messing with me, Howard. He invited me on an adventure." She told about the mysterious

Chinaman in Kew Gardens, and Hong Chen, and
Fortune's Brick, and Geoffrey Milner. "Those are the
bits of the puzzle. We don't know how they fit together."

"You in danger, Rosie?"

"Not that I know, but there's a lot I don't know.
That's why I've come to you. You might have a better
feel for this."

"I need more information. My boys and I will keep
a sharp eye. You won't be seeing me until you need to."

She reached out and laid a hand on his forearm.
"Thanks, Howard."

On the drive back to central London, Tom ventured,
"Nice man, your brother."

Rosemary shot him a look. "Don't ever, in any way,
get in Ow's face."

Howard's attitude disturbed her. Something was off,
like he got up on the wrong side of bed, or had a tiff
with the wife. But Howard didn't have a wife, had never
had any thing but fluff on his arm.

Rosemary dropped Tom at his Earl's Court bedsit.
"Let's meet in a day or two to sort this out."

CHAPTER 6

PUZZLE

Quiet Killer slowed to watch Tom enter the bed-sit's front door.

Ling, on his motorcycle, hung back a discreet distance, and followed Quiet Killer to a five-star hotel three blocks away. Quiet Killer found street parking and hurried into the hotel.

This must be Mighty Dragon's lair, thought Ling. *So, the game is on again. But why was Mighty Dragon hunting Hong Chen in London? Why was Quiet Killer following the American and the woman?*

Mighty Dragon opened his hotel suite's door to Quiet Killer's coded knock. He motioned his henchman to enter and locked the door behind him.

"Hong Chen's associate has not taken your warning." Quiet Killer reported following Tom and Rosemary to the Cock & Spur. "A rough place. Perhaps they were meeting friends. Perhaps Hong Chen is arranging a surprise."

"Then we strike first. Take that man away from Hong Chen. Show Hong Chen that he is powerless before me. I want him to be a rabbit trembling in its hole, knowing I will skin him."

Tom spent hours that evening trying to sort out Hong Chen, Fortune's Brick, Milner, Ow, Rosemary—pieces of a jigsaw puzzle that somehow fit together.

Geoffrey Milner: Did he have a connection to Fortune's Brick? He wanted to hook up with Rosemary. Tom took that personally, but wasn't clear why. A male territorial reaction? Two apes beating their chests to possess the female?

Ow: How to keep that brute from sticking his nose under the tent? If there was a Fortune's Brick, and if it was worth a great deal, then Ow would try to steal it. That's what criminals do—take things that don't belong to them.

Hong Chen: What the hell was he up to? He hadn't even inquired if his daughter was healthy or happy. Not one question about Tom's childhood. His fixation was on Fortune's Brick. A mysterious Chinaman had tried to scare Tom off finding Fortune's Brick. Somehow all this was rooted in China. What was Hong Chen's back-story in China?

One thing Tom was certain of: Hong Chen was keeping information back. Time to pay Hong Chen an unannounced visit.

After a breakfast of tea and toast, Tom decided, without checking the weather, that it would be a fine summer day. He dressed as if for a stroll on Santa Monica's beach; the only concessions were to forego shorts and to wear a solid color short-sleeved shirt rather than the Hawaiian color splash job.

As Tom was preparing to walk to Hong Chen's, Quiet Killer, wearing what he considered inconspicuous casual—a track suit and running shoes—was on foot a block from Tom's bedsit. His plan: Knock on Tom's door, burst in, and beat the hell out of him. Not death but serious injury requiring weeks of hospital time. Clear message to Hong Chen: You are defenseless against Mighty Dragon. We will come for you whenever we want. We beat you once and you ran away, you yellow-livered coward. Now you have no place to run. Nothing can save you.

When Tom unexpectedly came out the front door, Quiet Killer spun on his heels and dropped down to pretend to tie a shoelace. Tom paused for a moment on the sidewalk—the summer morning was gray overcast. Certain the clouds would burn off, as they dependably did in California, he walked along Cromwell Road. Quiet Killer followed twenty feet behind. A light drizzle began to fall by the time Tom reached Exhibition Road. He thought about taking refuge in the Victoria & Albert Museum at the corner of Cromwell and Exhibition, but knew there was no such thing as a short visit to that outstanding museum. Besides it wasn't really raining; his shirt was only damp.

He picked up his pace to Kensington High Street. Rain began to trickle down the back of his neck. People waiting to cross at Alexandra Gate to Hyde Park popped open umbrellas. He followed the crowd into Kensington Gardens and turned right towards Hyde Park Corner. The gray rain muted the green park. He broke into a run, cursing that he didn't have an umbrella. How could he be so stupid as to not have an umbrella in England?

Quiet Killer picked up his pace to keep Tom in sight. Tom ducked into the Hyde Park Corner underpass to Piccadilly, and wiped his hair and face with his hands. Quiet Killer ran silently on his toes, planning to bring Tom down with a kick to the knee. Then a stomp on the ribs. Break an arm. Hold his victim's nose shut, heel of hand closing his mouth until the lack of oxygen made the possibility of death a reality. Whisper in his ear, "No more Hong Chen." Spit in his ear to emphasis the insult.

A steady stream of people from the Tube exits swirled around Tom. The crowd would be helpful, Quiet Killer decided, the jostle of people a camouflage for the attack. With his skills, it would appear as a bump-and-tumble, the helpful offender preventing the victim from falling, hauling him aside out of the flow, and leaving behind a limp body.

Quiet Killer pushed into the crowd, got blocked by three chatting young women, slid around them, and nearly knocked over a little girl. The mother caught her off-footed daughter and confronted Quiet Killer with an insult: Bloody foreigner. Get back to your own country and take your disease with you. Before Quiet Killer got within striking range, Tom had climbed the short set of stairs and stepped out of the underpass onto the busy sidewalk. He picked up his pace and briskly passed the Ritz Hotel. At the next corner, Tom crossed the street onto Berkeley Street leading to Berkeley Square, ten minutes from Hong Chen's house. At the Bentley dealership, he paused to admire a truly beautiful silver coupe in the showroom. Quiet Killer picked up his pace. Tom started down Bruton Street toward the passageway that led to Bruton Place. When Tom turned into the passageway, Quiet Killer saw his chance. No one around. No place for Tom to hide. He broke into a full sprint.

Unaware, Tom turned the corner onto Bruton Place and had passed Bellamy's restaurant when Quiet Killer put on a spurt to catch him. A man stepped from the restaurant, pushing a trash bin to the curb. Quiet Killer, in mid-stride, tried to dodge around him, slipped on the wet pavement, spun to regain his balance. The bin man, trying to avoid the rude man, sidestepped, his feet tangling with the rushing idiot, and they both went down. Quiet Killer righted himself in time to see Tom disappear in a recessed doorway halfway down the block.

Tom rang Hong Chen's door buzzer without noticing the kerfuffle behind him. The butler took one look at sopping Tom and confined him to the foot of the stairs.

"Remove your shoes." Tom did. "Wait here."

Tom rung out his socks and put them back on. The butler reappeared and dropped slippers at Tom's feet. "Follow, please."

Hong Chen sat on the settee in the sitting room wearing a round Mandarin hat—alternate red and black panels, with an embroidered black band—resting high on his forehead. The silk Tangzhuang hip-length jacket of deep burgundy with a high collar was derived from the traditional Manchu surcoat. On his right thumb he wore a fergetun, a ring worn to protect the thumbs of Manchu warrior archers. The traditional fergetun was made of reindeer bone; Hong Chen's was of lustrous jade.

"I didn't expect you," he said as Tom entered.

You always sit around dressed for a costume ball? Tom thought, but held his tongue. "Thank you for receiving me without notice."

"Would you like a scotch?" Hong Chen spoke the English in a stilted looking-down-the-nose manner. For a moment Tom thought he heard a twinkle of humor mocking the colonial power that had disrespected China in the Opium Wars.

Hong Chen saw the flash of recognition in Tom's eyes and was pleased. His grandson, despite his American upbringing, had a feel for Old China. Hong Chen's outfit was reference to his hero, Lin Zexu, who, in 1838, was appointed by the emperor as imperial commissioner. His mandate was to stop the British importation of opium that had become a crippling addiction among the people. Lin Zexu ordered the Hongs, business allies of the British, to turn over all the British opium in their warehouses. A token number of cases were given as a face-saver gesture. Lin Zexu was not appeased. He ordered the arrest of a leading British opium dealer, forbid foreigners from leaving the port of Canton, and blockaded their factories. After a month, the British surrendered 2.8 million pounds of opium worth two millions pounds sterling.

Prime Minister Lord Palmerston's response was to start the First Opium War, which ended badly for the Chinese—and for Lin Zexu, who was sacked by the emperor. Nevertheless, Hong Chen deeply admired the man who stood up for the honor of his country.

Tom turned down the offer of scotch. "I'm interested in tea," he replied. Hong Chen reached for the silver bell to summon the butler. "But only Fortune's Brick tea." Hong Chen didn't ring the bell. "I need to know exactly what I'm looking for."

Hong Chen gestured for Tom to sit next to him, which Tom took as a familial offering. How close to sit to his grandfather was a political decision. Thigh-to-thigh would suggest warmth and acceptance. A five-inch separation might be within the family circle, without the eagerness of a lapdog. The politeness of a full body width was a more neutral zone. The furthest distance possible, at the other end of the settee, would imply diplomatic hostility. Tom needed his grandfather's cooperation, so he sat a compromised one cushion away.

Hong Chen noted Tom's choice with the satisfaction of a man who had lured a wary dog into almost-touching distance. He turned his head, not his body, to Tom and spoke Mandarin. "Tea was originally compressed into hard, durable bricks and wrapped in yak skins to protect them from damage when carried on the trade routes, banging along on the backs of camels and mules. A brick of tea weighed twenty-seven kilos, about sixty pounds to you Americans." Hong Chen gestured to the bookshelf with his tea books. "Hand me the large, flat one."

Tom twisted around, pulled the book down, and presented it.

Hong Chen flipped through to the page he sought and laid the open book on the cushion between them. "Today, you can buy a brick of tea the size and shape of a building brick. But Fortune's Brick was ornamental, a ceremonial brick of tea to be presented to the emperor." He pointed to the full-page drawing. "It weighed about a pound and measured eight inches by ten inches by one inch. Decorated tea bricks from that time are very rare and very expensive, if they ever come on the market. A Mi brick dating back to around 1850 is worth $1.5 million, and only two are known to exist, one in a museum.

"Fortune's Brick will have a large bas-relief of a chrysanthemum in the center. That flower was the symbol of Xianfeng, ninth emperor of Qing, who ascended the throne in 1850 after the death of his father. Embossed on the tea brick beneath the chrysanthemum was Xianfeng's title, name, and the year of his crowning." Hong Chen traced the Chinese characters. "In Chinese, chrysanthemum translates literally as 'gold flower.' Fortune's Brick was nestled inside a box made of gold."

"So I'm looking for a golden box full of old tea." Tom took a photo of the drawing with his cell phone.

"The box may be gone. Some ignorant person may have thought the box more valuable than the emperor's tea."

"Why did you send me to Milner?"

"He is a renowned collector with a family connection to the East India Company, Robert Fortune's employer. If the rumor is true that Fortune's Brick has surfaced, and will be sold at a private auction, then Milner was a likely candidate to receive an invitation. A very few select tea connoisseurs would have been on the invite list. I'd hoped that, by talking to him, you might get an impression if he was in the know."

"Why haven't you received an invitation?"

Hong Chen closed the book and held it on his lap, looking straight ahead. "I am not welcomed."

"Do you know any other tea connoisseurs who might be on the invitation list?"

"There is that fellow in Manila who bought the Da Hong Pao sold by the Chinese government for $900,000. There are whispers about a Russian who can't find a football club to buy. And a woman from India whose family owns a tea plantation dating back to the mid-1800s. There are probably others. The world in which some teas are held as valuable as Old Masters is a secretive one. And the trade is equally as cutthroat as the art world."

"What about the Chinese government? Seems they'd have a vested interest."

"I would have heard," Hong Chen replied in a dismissive tone, as if a junior assistant had pointed out an obvious fact in contact negotiations. "There are people in China who consider me an enemy because I want to save China. Fortune's Brick is the key to awaken the Chinese people to their destiny to look after and to protect the world. It symbolizes the victory of good over evil. Whoever possesses that symbol has the power to lead China to the greatness for which it was created. Our leaders today are all about factories and Western suits and market shares of global trade. That false foundation will crumble, which has been the fate of all empires and nations built on material wealth. China has become a cruel country. Crass opportunities corrupt us. Now it's who will win with no regard for who will lose. Man-eat-man. That's China today. We must return to the principles of family honor and national value."

Tom replied, "The Chinese man in Kew Gardens who warned me away, he's an enemy?"

Hong Chen didn't answer.

"I think you're holding out on me. I think you're playing me for a sap. You're being disrespectful to our family. Why won't talk to my mother?"

Such insolence from a grandson to a grandfather was intolerable, a punishable offense. But Hong Chen dipped his head, looking at his hands folded in his lap. "So. . . so how is my daughter?"

The softness in his voice took Tom by surprise. He asked, in Mandarin, "Why did you desert us?"

Hong Chen raised his eyes to Tom, "I'll tell you when you deliver Fortune's Brick."

The rain had stopped before Tom left Hong Chen's. A mist fog hung over Berkeley Square, smudging the buildings and trees into barely seen vague shapes, creating an aura of mystery, which Tom found romantic. How would Rosemary critique this lovely scene? Why do I even wonder the question? Tom asked himself. As he made his way along the edge of the park, he felt unease, as being stalked. He glanced around but nothing moved. He walked along Berkeley Street back towards Piccadilly. Quiet Killer, unseen in the shadows, moved with him.

A taxi came down the street and stopped as Tom waved it down. He settled into the back seat and directed the cabbie to Earl's Court. Should he call Rosemary and invite her to dinner? He had information to share about Fortune's Brick. But his real intent, he knew, was to probe for clues to the Rosemary puzzle.

Tom punched in her number on his cell phone. Each ringtone made him catch his breath in anticipation. He had no way to calculate all the possible outcomes of a relationship with her. The thrill of the uncertainty was irresistible.

That's when he realized Rosemary wasn't the mystery; the mystery was what he intended to do about her.

She hadn't answered by the fifth ring.

Where was she? Did she have a lover? He broke the connection. *Why did he care? A piece of the puzzle.* He didn't care, just wondered, he assured himself.

In the morning, Rosemary answered Tom's call on the third ring, sounding alert, voice clear—no late-night hangover and, Tom noted, no rustling of a man in the background. "I have new information on Fortune's Brick," he announced. "Can we meet for tea this morning?"

"Give me an hour and I'll pick you up."

Tom spent the waiting time pacing from his bed to the table in the next room. He stopped in mid-turn and stood still to fully hear his question: *Are you willing to step—leap—into the uncertainty of a future you have no way of calculating? The pursuit of Fortune's Brick could bring great reward or get you killed. Still time to back out and revert to being a research scholar.*

"Tommy boy," he said aloud, poised with one foot in the air, "that's not the real query. You are at a pivotal moment." He completed the pirouette and planted both feet. *What the hell; why not? Why not give his hero a chance?*

He stood on the curb when Rosemary arrived, right on time.

"Shall we go back to Teanamu Chaya?" she asked. "It seems like the appropriate place to contemplate tea."

Only two other customers were in the teahouse. Sandra Chou gave Rosemary a hug—a friendly nod to Tom—her happiness beaming from her face. "I've got such good news." She led them to a table in a far corner, where they couldn't be overheard. "Wait until I bring you tea."

Tom took the chair with his back to the wall, giving him a clear view of the entrance. Rosemary sat to his right and set her small purse on the table. "So, tell me your news about Fortune's Brick."

Tom related his visit to Hong Chen and showed her the photo on his phone of the ornamental brick of tea. "That's what we're looking for, with a chrysanthemum imprinted in the middle and the emperor's name below." He pointed to the Chinese characters. "We just don't know where to look."

Sandra returned to the table, carrying a tray with a delicate teapot and three cups. Rosemary complimented the teaware. "It's very special," Sandra said, her voice small-room quiet to contain her excitement. "I use it only for occasions of honor and respect. This tea," she said, filling the cups, "is worthy of the pot. That's my good news."

She sat next to Rosemary, shoulder-to-shoulder to create a confidential space. "You'll never guess who came into the shop yesterday." Rosemary nodded her agreement. "A representative of the Makaibari Estate in India. She wants me to carry this tea." Sandra patted the pot. "Rare Silver Tips Imperial." Tom's memory bell gave a tinkle. "That's the most expensive Darjeeling tea in the world. She wants me to be the exclusive retailer in London. Isn't that fantastic!"

Tom sipped the tea, a dusky oolong, hoping the taste would trigger his memory. It reminded him of pu'er. And of Milner's finely crafted Yixing teapot worthy of a tea from the Makaibari Estate. A woman from India might be a player in the Fortune's Brick auction, according to Hong Chen.

"This is excellent tea," Tom said.

"Picked under the full moon."

"Do you have some for sale?"

"She left me samples to test the market. If I find customers, she hinted at a very special edition of tea soon to come on the market. She's looking for select outlets to sell it."

"That's really exciting, Sandra." Rosemary clasped her friend's hand in a two-handed knot. "Do you know why she chose your shop?"

"She spent about a half hour examining my teas and asking questions—very educated questions—about the provenances. A very lovely lady. I made a tea ceremony for her. Then she introduced herself, said I deserved my high reputation, and made the offer. I'm still trembling from good fortune."

"Did she leave a card," asked Tom.

"No. She said she would contact me in a couple days."

"And her name?"

"Rupa. Rupa Banerjee."

Tom's memory bell gonged. The Banerjee family had owned Makaibari Estate since the mid-1800s, when Robert Fortune shipped purloined tea plants from China.

"I'd like to buy all the Rare Silver Tips Imperial," Tom said. "It would be an honor to be your first customer."

"Yes, yes," Sandra exclaimed, turning back to Rosemary, "that would be perfect. I'm so glad I got to share it first with you."

Tom tuned out the chat between Rosemary and Sandra. Is Rupa Banerjee here for the private auction? Is her plan to break up Fortune's Brick and sell ounces through exclusive teashops? He imagined the marketing campaign: "Authentic rare aged Emperor's Tea available for the first time." The backstory about Fortune's Brick, the Chinese emperor, and the British queen would be worth millions in free advertising for Makaibari Estate. Demand for their tea would increase worldwide.

Sandra excused herself, then quickly returned. "Your tea." She bowed while presenting Tom a silk bag puckered by a drawstring. When he accepted, she discreetly slipped the bill in his hand. "Follow me, please, to my office."

Tom looked at the bill and converted pounds into dollars: $800. *Better be damn good tea*, he thought. Sandra ran his credit card. "Friend's price," she said handing him the receipt with a big smile. "If you know someone who would like to buy the tea, please don't tell your price."

"I know someone who would very much appreciate this tea. He might place a large order for the special edition tea. Will you please contact Rosemary when you expect Rupa Banerjee again?"

"Yes, of course. Gong De Tian surely is rubbing her magic pearl for me." Sandra laughed and hugged Rosemary and bowed to Tom and showed them out.

"Who is Gong De Tian?" Rosemary asked after they settled into her Mini.

"Goddess of Good Fortune and Happiness. She rubs her magic pearl to grant wishes." Tom buckled himself in, carefully cradling the world's most expensive Darjeeling tea in his lap.

Rosemary put the car in gear and nosed out into traffic. "Are you going to share the tea with Hong Chen?"

"Maybe on a special occasion." Tom glanced out the window so Rosemary didn't see the satisfied smile on his face. *But,* he thought, *I won't share Rupa Banerjee with Hong Chen.*

CHAPTER 7

MOM

"I need to do some research," Rosemary announced on the drive back to central London. "Want to come along for the ride?"

"Research what?"

"Windows. Beautiful things. Virtue."

She drove with her usual aplomb of good judgment bordering on recklessness; passing a car with inches to spare to avoid an oncoming bus, turning the center stripe into a third lane, weaving between four cars as if on a downhill slalom course. Tom, clutching the coward's strap, involuntarily cried out, "What are you doing?"

"Practicing. See a motorcycle behind us? No. Not any longer."

Rosemary *was* a bit distracted. Milner had called to "follow up on our conversation. Are you free for a simple meal?" She couldn't say no to a potential backer. Besides, she enjoyed Geoffrey; getting to know him better would be a bonus. That's where she had been when Tom called the night before.

The restaurant had been simple and elegant, the signature of expensive Belgravia restaurants. Geoffrey had already ordered the wine when she arrived. The first glasses were consumed with bonhomie, social skills Geoffrey was born into and Rosemary had mastered. Geoffrey inquired about her work, probed if she was entangled with a partner or a serious interest. "I toast your chutzpa and humor," he said, raising his wineglass in admiration for the soft pastels of dawn that she had applied to her blank eye socket.

Rosemary raised her glass. "Beauty shines from the inside."

When the entrée arrived, he steered the conversation into the sincere. "I want to be seen as authentic," he confided. "Not as a dilettante, a rich man playing. But here's my problem: I've been cursed with being an autodidact with enough money to indulge myself. There are so many fascinating things to discover and learn about that I'm a bit of a butterfly that way. I've become addicted to seriously amusing myself."

He reached across the candlelit table to hold her hand, sincerity giving his eyes a moist, almost weepy, sheen. Rosemary kept a fork in one hand, knife in the other.

"I want to leave my mark with a real contribution." Geoffrey sat back and spoke so softly Rosemary had to lean forward to hear. "Perhaps finance a medical expedition to Africa. The chief cause of blindness in Africa is glaucoma, and dirty water is a big culprit. A clean water effort would be a tremendous benefit."

This wasn't the first caring-heart flirt Rosemary had experienced. She opened her clutch, took out her eyeliner pencil, and unerringly drew a black tear streak from her missing eye down her cheek.

"Yes, I know, it's so sad, the suffering." Geoffrey—oblivious of the parody—slumped, head bowed, as if weighted down by respect for the unfortunate. "We could join together to start a project to save people's eyesight." He leaned forward with enthusiasm. "We'd make a good team with your personal experience and my empathy and money." He reached for her hand. "What do you say; a deal?"

She leaned forward with a coy smile. "Write a check to The Water Project. Do it now. Right here. They do wonderful clean water projects in Africa."

Geoffrey's smile didn't falter, but the light in his eyes dimmed as in that moment when a guy hears the rejection but hasn't formulated a response. He sat back a couple of inches to pat his breast pocket. "I haven't a check with me. Would you like dessert? They specialize in wonderful crème brûlée here."

Rosemary declined.

"A coffee, then? Geoffrey paused while the waiter poured the two cups. "Tell me more about Tom. What's his con? That man is fishing with a bare hook." Geoffrey said it with a laugh, as if a genteel poke at an aspirant without proper means. "But, one should never underestimate an American, don't you think? They can be marvelously inventive. Perhaps we should take him up on the invitation to tea. He seemed to have curiosity along those lines. And Robert Fortune, the plant collector. We might find a common interest. Shall we meet again soon to explore possibilities?"

"Yes, we should. Maybe he would join you in your clean water for healthy eyes project. Americans are very 'can do,' aren't they?"

Replaying the conversation, Rosemary wondered what to share with Tom. That Geoffrey had made a pass at her? That he had hinted at knowing about Fortune and the tea connection? But he really hadn't said anything, had he? Hadn't made any offer.

She cut through traffic up Oxford Street with the authority of an ambulance on an emergency run, took a sharp right on Duke Street, barely slowed before crossing busy Wigmore, and swung onto the one-way around Manchester Square, a green oval hedged by trees. "Ask that Goddess of Good Fortune to rub her magic pearl for us; we need a parking space," she told Tom. And, magically, a slot appeared.

"This is an oasis of classical Georgian architecture," Rosemary said as she opened the car door. "But it's been blemished by educated ignorance."

Tom stood waiting on the sidewalk. "Notice," she said as they walked along the northwest side of the square, "the window frames." Tom duly noted the frames of four-inch steel I-beams painted white. Rosemary didn't say another word until they reached the southeast side of the square. "Look at these window frames." A narrow white strip inset flush with the brick wall.

So, Tom shrugged. In truth, he wasn't interested in Rosemary's buildings and their sociological accusations.

"The architects, when they redid the office block over there"—she gestured across the square—"wanted to harmonize with this side. So they framed the windows in white. But they also wanted a modern mark on the classical façade, thus the intrusive four-inch I-beam frames. The result destroyed the square's quiet elegance by overweighting the balance."

She took his arm and pulled him to a stop. Tom shuffled awkwardly, not sure if he should face her or glance around at window frames.

"This is"—she spoke to his chest, then glanced to his eyes—"a visual representation of unhappiness." Then she lost her nerve. "The architects' emotional ignorance"—she turned to face the square—"infects the atmosphere of this space. The relationship between the two sides is askew, one side trying to dominate the other side." She turned back to Tom, took a deep breath, and looked to his face. "And that robs people of experiencing the gentle touch of harmony and subtle beauty." Then she covered herself in a safe tutorial summary. "We, as a city, are poorer for it. Good intention poorly executed, the bane of most relationships."

Good god, you're hopeless, she muttered to herself. Her tongue probed her mouth for a taste of fear, something she could savor rather than the distasteful ambiguity of herself. She didn't fear Tom: he was an opportunity. Did she fear herself? That thought had never occurred. Her tongue tapped the roof of her mouth for a taint of fear. Nothing. Perhaps that was the trouble.

When they returned to the car, Rosemary said, "I live not far from here. Shall we drop in for tea?"

As she drove past a horizontal arch of classical buildings, Rosemary, on impulse, stopped. "I don't live here but I want to show you something. Park Crescent. Come take a look."

They stood side by side on the sidewalk facing the gentle arc of buildings. "If these residencies had been built in a straight line, they'd be just another row of terraced houses," Rosemary pointed out. "John Nash, the architect, used great skill and design discipline to maintain the harmony of the order in relationship to the disruptive curve. The curve is a reminder that we don't have to live within rigidity and regulation. When I look at the balance Nash achieve—" She heard her lecture voice and stopped.

She cleared her throat to start again. "Every morning when I look into the mirror"—she spoke down the front of her body so Tom couldn't read her expression—"I see the imbalance on my face and try to find a way to bring the empty socket into harmony with me. That sets the tone of my day. Some days are better than others."

She ducked back into the car, as if nervous about being in the open. Tom got in the car as she engaged the gears. "My place is on Park Crescent Mews, a street over."

The mews was a cobbled alleyway converted into a coveted dead end. The ground-level garages once housed carriages and horses, with living quarters above for hired help. "Hope you don't mind going in through the garage," she said as the door lifted up. "We're not allowed to park outside. Not enough room for cars to maneuver."

The living room was Danish minimalist designed to capture light, the floor honey oak and the walls eggshell white. Three large abstract paintings pulsed vibrant colors. The black leather and silver steel sofa, and the three chairs—straight-edged, sharp lines—were unobtrusive. The stark simplicity was impersonal, yet the warm glow from the floor and the cozy grouping of the chairs and sofa gave the subtle sense of a hearth.

"I'll put the kettle on. Make yourself at home."

Minutes later she set the tea tray on the low glass-topped table before the sofa, where Tom sat. "Home. Such a simple word." She poured the tea. "The psychological space of home is easy to abuse. A home determines what we are able to believe in. What we identify as "home" is a vision of our self, in terms of beauty and security, as a place of refuge where we seek solace for our vulnerabilities. Don't you find it so?"

Without waiting for a reply, she continued, "My mentor Alain de Botton, the philosopher and author, very astutely observed that bad architecture is as much a failure of psychology as of design. The failure to create congenial environments contributes to our unhappiness in other areas of our lives. To take away beauty is to diminish our ability to understand who we are. Ow is a living example."

Ow's unhappiness was a much safer topic than her own dissatisfaction. "You need to understand where Ow comes from if we're going to work with him. The neighborhood where he and I grew up was haphazard in every way. The streets were willy-nilly. The buildings a jumble of indifference, cheapness, and lack of imagination. The physical presence of the place beat you down; it was a continuous gray day. An out-of-sorts place that made the people cross with themselves and their neighbors. Many, like my brother, harbored a deep jealousy towards those who lived in orderly and optimistic places.

"Ow and his mates took out their rage in physical violence on people, and places, that represented beauty. That neighborhood ruined my sweet brother and made him into a brutish person. I hoped that my study of architecture would give me insight into how I might help him find his way back to his essential nature, to that kind and caring boy I grew up with."

Rosemary set her cup on the glass-top table and turned shoulders and knees to Tom, as if to say, Now about me. "You know why the window frames at Manchester Square make a difference? Those window frames distort beauty. Stendhal wrote, 'Beauty is nothing other than the promise of happiness.' We miss an opportunity for happiness whenever we don't actively engage in creating beauty in everything we do, in every gesture and word."

Tom set his cup on the table and leaned towards her.

"I had dinner with Geoffrey last night," she said to block whatever advance Tom might be planning. "He's curious about you. He raised the possibility of having tea and talking about Robert Fortune. Geoff is an interesting man."

Tom, much to his surprise, flushed hot at the mention of Milner's name. "Do you think he might be in on the hunt for Fortune's Brick?"

The phone rang. Rosemary took the call in the kitchen, out of range of Tom's hearing. "That was Ow," she said, returning. "He wants us to go to the zoo, get out and do things like that."

"What?"

"Said we should go out and about in public places, see a bit of London for a couple days while he checks things out. Then he'll call a meeting." Rosemary thought Ow's request strange, but he was never one for idle play so he must have a reason. "We could visit the wax museum. There are royal jewels in the Tower Bridge. And the parking lot where they found the remains of Richard the Third."

Tom wanted to ask what she found so interesting about Geoffrey Milner.

"I'll make a list of attractions." She gathered the tea things and took them to the kitchen.

Dropping Tom off at his bedsit, she asked, "You like fish? We can do the Sea Life Centre. I've wanted to experience the Shark Walk, an underwater tunnel, since the place was renovated in 2009. A friend, Derek Elliott, oversaw the project."

Late that night Tom called his mother to reach her during California daylight hours. "Yes, yes, I'm settled in London. No, the weather's not too bad. Have been rained on only once so far."

How was he to tell her? Just blurt it out. "I've met your father."

The silence on the other end of the line was so long he thought the connection had been broken. "Mom? Mom, you still there?"

"Tell me." Her voice was barely above a whisper. "Is he well?"

"Yes, he seems to be. He has a house with a butler." Tom decided not to mention Hong Chen's offer to make Tom his heir; he didn't understand Fortune's Brick enough to explain. "He uses a walker. Do you know anything about his health, or is he just getting old?"

"I haven't"—his mother's voice had the whispered awe of seeing a ghost—"I haven't seen him or heard anything from him for more than thirty years. I don't know how to feel about this. The walker? He's been crippled since the beating he survived as a boy."

Tom listened intently as his mother told the family history he'd never known:

"My mother died when I was fifteen. This absolutely devastated my father. For weeks he didn't speak. I had to practically hand-feed him. She was his trusted confidante, the only person who knew the horror he had lived through, a nightmare he battled against every day.

Her presence, her smile and kindness, were the only reasons he tried to be happy. I remember Father as a caring man who could be playful. After months of grieving, he pulled himself up to where he could at least peek over the rim of depression. That's when he decided to share his earlier life with me, because it was important in our family history and to who he was as a man. I became his lifeline to the memory of my mother.

"As a young boy, Dad lived through the Cultural Revolution. His father was a university professor, his mother a devoted wife, and his elder brother his best friend. They had a happy and comfortable life. Then Mao set loose the Red Guard. One night a squad of the Red Guard, eight boys, banged into the house while everyone was sleeping. They pulled them from their beds and herded them into the living room. My father told me he remembered how sorry he felt for his mother, embarrassed in her sleeping shirt.

"At first the threat wasn't taken seriously because the leader was a boy about my father's age. But he had the meanness of a very angry adult. Dad vividly remembered that. He had never seen a boy, or anyone, in such a rage. The leader—his name was Weiwu Long—accused the professor of being an enemy of the people, a parasite who produced nothing, a Big Head who puts false thoughts into the minds of his students. Dad remembered the veins pulsing in his neck as he screamed that they were traitors. He swept the books off the shelves and smashed the chairs, ranting that such Western things were proof of the family's betrayal of the Chinese spirit."

She paused, and then continued with a soft chuckle. "Dad told me that his father had shouted back, called the boss-boy a baby having a temper tantrum." Her voice caught. "He told me, Dad told me, that he knew from firsthand experience that his father was a proud man who did not take kindly to disrespectful children. Dad said that he expected his father to slap the shit out of that kid. Instead, the gang clubbed him to the floor."

"Mom, I had no idea . . . ." Tom began, then stopped, afraid of diverting her narrative.

She rushed on, perhaps afraid that if she stopped she wouldn't have the fortitude to dredge up the painful past.

"All the years later Dad remembered the bloody details of how the Red Guard gang viciously beat and kicked his father. His mother fell on top of her husband to protect him. A blow crushed her cheekbone. Dad told me that every day since he's heard that crunch of bone, her sharp cry. He sees the image of her eye hanging down her cheek, a ball on a string dangling from the optic nerve."

Her voice shuttered. Tom heard her gulp, and then her soft voice again. "The attackers beat Dad's mother and father as if trying to kill rabid dogs. The beloved older brother leaped into the melee and grabbed the club of an attacker. Three boys set on him, jabbed with the butts of their clubs on his kidneys, his neck, the side of his head. They smashed his nose flat. One boy stood on his neck while another broke his leg.

"Dad was crying as he recounted how the grunting boys pounded on his family, the thwacks against the bodies, wet sounding, laundry being beaten on rocks. He turned to run. A blow across his back knocked him off his feet. He couldn't breathe through the pain, couldn't move his legs. Dad's family died in front of his eyes.

"A neighbor found him after the killers left, his spine broken. The brave man took him home and secretly nursed him for months. His spine healed, but imperfectly. Dad couldn't walk properly. He learned to hold himself stiff and walk with a shuffle. He went onto the streets to find the Red Guard gang leader, Weiwu Long. He lived by his wits, sleeping rough, sometimes begging, seeking a way to revenge the death of his family. He stopped living like that when he met my mother."

Tom's mom broke into open, gulping sobs. "I'm sorry, son." Deep breath. Slow expulsion. Deep breath. A long wheezing sigh of sorrow. "I haven't allowed myself to think of my father for many years."

Tom gave her a moment to recover. He tried to find the broken boy in his stern, imperial grandfather. Very difficult to imagine. His mom's tears helped him to at least seek sympathy, if not empathy, with Hong Chen. But the man was deceiving him, Tom was sure. In that—deception—he shared a common ground with his grandfather. However, that encouraged distrust, not bonding.

Tom's mom regained control. "This is important to understanding my dad," she said. "He learned an important lesson while living on the street: Poor people are powerless. He dedicated himself to becoming rich.

And he never stopped searching for Weiwu Long. Dad became a clever man at business, at taking advantage. I don't understand exactly what he did, but it involved buying real estate and companies. And making enemies of people. Sometimes such people would come to the house and beg him not to ruin them. Or they'd threaten him, even shoot at him.

"After Mother's death, he became even more cunning, secretive, cruel, an evil to live with. I was dying in that house with him. I met your father when I saw him studying at the university, where he was an exchange student. It was love at first sight—still is. I don't know how he saw through my misery, but thank God he did.

"When his year of study was up, he asked me to marry him and go to the States. I said yes. Father was very angry but I didn't back down. He turned stone cold. I left his house that night."

Her tears were silent now, but Tom heard her grief. "Mom?"

"Will you see him again?"

"Yes."

"Tommy," she managed, "be kind to him. Tell him I love him. I want to talk with him."

CHAPTER 8

HERO

For three days Tom and Rosemary played tourists: they went to Sea Life Centre, and rode the nearby London Eye. At Leicester Square, they spent hours sitting on a smooth stone ledge watching the gallimaufry of entertaining fashions parade past; cleavage, Tom noticed, was the flavor of the summer. Four bare-chested young men—black, white, and tan—entertained a large crowd with hip-hop songs, dancing, acrobatics, and fast patter. At a nearby table, two bearded Muslim men offered explanations of the Koran, occasionally wandering through the crowd with a platter of dates; they had few takers. Two young Japanese guys sat on a blanket and cheerfully enticed passersby to stop to have their names written in calligraphy—for a donation. They were so positive and friendly they had many takers.

The sheer continuing mass of humanity was nearly overwhelming. *Here*, Tom thought, *is a walking, talking common people's UN. This is why the world will continue, despite the odds.*

At Trafalgar Square, Rosemary directed his attention to the four plinths at each corner of the plaza. "That one," she pointed to the left rear corner, "as never had a permanent occupant. Some wanted a statue of Winston Churchill, but there are those who have never forgiven him for being Churchill."

She led him between the two large, clover-shaped fountains to the base of the thirteen-foot high block of stone. A very colorful representation of an ancient Mesopotamia god crouched on top. "That's a lamassu, a winged bull with a human head and coifed beard, a protective deity, according to mythology. The artist Michael Rakowitz used empty Iraqi date syrup cans and other Middle Eastern foo packaging to create it. It evokes Iraq's destroyed economy."

She turned in a full circle to survey the square with the 143-foot stone column crowned by Lord Horatio Nelson, a memorial to British imperialism. "He died in the Battle of Trafalgar, 1805, defeating a combined Spanish and French fleet, the battle confirmed Britain's navel supremacy, for which our national honor, and business interests, were eternally grateful," she added, dryly. "Now, who will be our hero in the Battle of Brexit. Let's go eat."

She treated him to an expensive lunch at the Portrait Restaurant on the top floor of the National Portrait Gallery, behind The National Museum overlooking Trafalgar Square. "One of the best views in London," she said, as they sat by the window lining the restaurant, "and perhaps the only view of Lord Nelson's backside. Worth the cost of the overpriced food."

Tom agreed, about the view and the food. The sweeping view took in Big Ben, the spires of the Parliament building, the domes of government buildings adjacent to St. James's Park, and the arc of the London Eye.

On Sunday, Rosemary took him to the Brick Lane street market, a tourist attraction as much as a livelihood for colorful characters. "Here you'll find lots of appealing oddities you may want but don't need, and some very good treasures. Plus, the street food is terrific."

Four blocks of the street, in the Indian/Pakistan neighborhood, were jammed with gawkers and street stalls selling vintage clothes, antique compasses and cameras, nicely made leather goods, vinyl records, military uniforms, appealing fresh vegetables, assorted baubles, fridge magnets, and, on the side streets, a mash-up of junk from attics. An enclosed area under roof featured finely done art, jewelry, cashmere sweaters, shiny brass water bottles with burn in designs, one-off clothes sold by the designers, fashions for dogs, and Himalayan salt body scrub.

Tom spotted the London Tea Exchange, the elegant façade reminiscent of posh London. "We can't pass this up," he told Rosemary. The interior, three walls lined with tins and jars of teas and coffees from around the world, had the solemnity of a library. The helpful manager told them the London Tea Exchange provided product to twenty-four royal houses, including the Queen's.

"We have four types of luxury teas—green, black, white, and oolong—from five countries," the manager said. "Would you like some?"

"Have you ever heard of Fortune's Brick?" Tom asked.

"A brick?" queried the manager.

"Of tea."

"We don't carry tea in bricks, or tea in bags."

Late morning on the third day, after meeting for a formal English breakfast at the Savoy, Tom and Rosemary walked along Victoria Embankment, between the hotel and the Thames. They circled Cleopatra's Needle—Had nothing to do with Cleopatra, commented Rosemary. Further on they stood before heroic Robert Burns on his pedestal, enfolded in cast iron, staring poetically into the distance.

"This one is particularly pathetic," Rosemary said as she pulled Tom to a stop before a plinth with a bust on top. "Sir Arthur Sullivan, a profoundly disappointed man. He and his collaborator, W.S. Gilbert, were adored for their light operas. But Sullivan wanted to be recognized as a serious composer of highbrow music. However, he could never escape his stage fame. This crushed fan," she said, reaching out to pat the slim iron figure clinging to the plinth, "is Muse of Music, weeping inconsolably, her clothes falling off, presumably in disarray of grief."

Rosemary's cell phone rang. She looked at the number. "Allo." Listened. "Right." And rang off. "Ow wants to meet tomorrow morning. He says we are to split up and disappear until then. So, you go that way." She pointed upriver. "And I'll go that way." She pointed downriver. "Don't linger. I'll pick you at ten in the morning." She quickly strode off.

Tom didn't share Rosemary's sense of urgency to disappear. He wandered away from the river, towards Covent Gardens with its shops, and fell into musing about his Hero. Dashing, of course. Bold and strong. Romantic. He hadn't felt that attitude since he had swung through the dean's office window, rope in one hand and the Quan Yin figurine tucked in his waistband—and saw Aimee, hip-cocked in a come-fuck-me stance. Play time.

Why not play, Tom thought, *with this cast of character— a delusional Manchu emperor, a crime boss thug, a mysterious Chinese slipping him threats, a beautiful woman with a beguiling deformity, and an English lord poof. I'll be Hero; always wanted to be a hero. If I'm going to be a hero I want to be seen, and that requires a costume.*

Near Covent Gardens he paused to look in the Paul Allen front window, but thought the clothes too trendy. He wanted to be a hero that didn't go out of style. At a leather shop he considered a Hells Angels menace look, black leather jacket with silver buckles and chains. No, something more James Bondish. He saw a black, tailored three-quarter-length coat of soft Moroccan leather and went in to try it on. The salesman also tried to convince him to add a pair of Doc Martens with steel-toe caps.

"A strong foundation, don't you think, sir? In case you need to lash out."

Tom rejected the suggestion, but he did need shoes to match his new coat, shoes that said less junior executive and more man with expensive taste. He had heard that Bond Street was good for shoes, but, after a quick survey, he was appalled at the prices. He found the right shoes at a shop on a small street running parallel to Oxford Street—Italian black leather running shoes with waffle soles. Style that could be put to work if he had to run for his life.

In the morning, as he waited for Rosemary to pick him up, Tom admired his reflection in a shop's window: black T-shirt under the black leather coat; black, sleek shoes; black opaque wraparound sunglasses; his hair mussed for that just-out-of-bed-but-ready-for-action look. The scrim of whiskers gave him the urban dash of a men's fashion magazine model. Suave, but not afraid to get sweaty.

He heard a car squeal to a stop behind him. "My, my," said Rosemary through the open passenger window.

"Beauty is the promise of happiness," he paraphrased, as he ducked into the car.

She laughed good-naturedly. "Won't you be a surprise."

"Are you surprised?"

"Ow will be surprised." Rosemary revved the engine, waited for a break in traffic, and then peeled out in front of a bus.

Tom closed his eyes to the distractions of her driving, then remembered he needed to practice hero attitude.

He opened his eyes, swelled his chest with a big breath, and slouched to appear casual. "What the news?"

"That's what we're going to find out. Ow's boys have been following us the past days."

Ow received them in his usual back booth. "What the 'k are you dressed up as?"

The slap down made Tom self-conscious of his hero's costume, more a cologne ad than a brass-knuckles statement. He dialed up a Mafia tough guy, the only persona he knew to chest-butt a criminal: "You got something worth saying, say it. Don't waste my time."

"Tuck it in and zip it up, both of you." Rosemary didn't understand why Ow was being so prickly. Maybe this was the real Howard capable of inflicting pain, a man so insensitive he could reduce another to a howling, sobbing, bloodied lump. Not another human, just a lump.

Still, she chose to believe her brother wore the costume of a criminal to hide the knight in shining armor. He once told her, without being specific: "I'm the finger up the nose of those who put a heel on the necks of poor sods. Remember the poster I made as a kid, the one taped above my bed? The Avengers, the team of superheroes from Marvel Comics—Giant Man, Hulk, Iron Man, Thor, Wasp, and Captain America. I gave each one my face. I changed Captain America's outfit to the Union Jack flag. That was the first thing I saw the first thing every morning and the last thing I saw at night. I still have that poster."

Rosemary thrust herself as negotiator between her scowling brother and glowering Tom. "So, tell us, Howard."

"Two Asians followed wherever you went. First a car. Second, a motorcycle, always hanging back. They didn't seem to be together. The car has a room at The Kensington, bit of a fancy hotel. The motorcycle parks in the garage behind a place on Bruton Place."

That surprised Tom. The mysterious Chinaman might be the car. But the motorcycle? Hong Chen lives on Bruton Place. Hong Chen was having him followed? Might have been following him all his life. Hong Chen knew about the Quan Yin stunt. He knew when Tom had arrived in London. Now the long-distance surveillance was up close. Face-to-face. Tom's earlier confidence that he'd outfox his grandfather as revenge for his mother's hurt began to pale.

"What do you think?" Rosemary asked Ow.

"Nothing to think about. Just something to watch. Not at all sure this is worth the risk to you, Rosie. Too many unknowns. Him, for instance," Ow jabbed a finger at Tom.

Tom tried on Clint Eastwood's *Dirty Harry* make-my-day stare.

Ow laughed. "I've seen that movie, too. You imagine the gun, but can't picture the bullets, can you?"

Ow turned a shoulder to Tom, an eraser removing a smudge. "I think you should cut your losses, Rosie. I don't see profit in this giggle."

"It's just a bit of adventure; no harm done." She nudged Tom with her hip to get him moving out of the booth.

"Don't throw a wobbly, Rosie." Ow tried to draw her back with big brother concern. "We need to have butchers at what's swirling around to see who needs to be sorted. That's all I'm saying."

Ever since she was twelve she had hidden her love/hate for Ow. They were kids sword fighting with sharp sticks. The moment his stick pierced her eye, the blinding darkness fundamentally cleaved her: one half in a panic away from the out-of-control rage of her brother; the other lingering with that brother, titillated by the freedom of his fierce disregard.

She had hated Ow for his carelessness. She didn't want to hate Ow, so she convinced herself that the missing eye was her talisman. She gave it magical powers by making it fanciful, like a unicorn. She sprinkled the hollow eye with fairy dust to enchant—and to mask the desire to avenge her destroyed eye.

As she walked out of the Cock & Spur, she linked arms with Tom, hoping Ow would see. She wanted to hurt Ow. The taste of satisfaction in the back of her mouth appalled her. How could love allow such a thought?

Tom asked, "What's a butchers?"

The Cockney slang was so familiar Rosemary didn't realize what he was asking.

"Why does Ow need a butchers?"

"Butchers hook means to take a look." Rosemary jerked open the Mini's door and started the car before Tom managed to completely jump in. He buckled up as she pulled into traffic without checking for oncoming cars. "Hardly anyone, even Londoners, understand

Cockney slang anymore. Ow's saying he doesn't understand what's going on around Fortune's Brick, and doesn't think it's worth his time. He wants me to stand aside."

Rosemary vented her frustration by attacking traffic. "This whole thing is loony, like we're in an Agatha Christie parlor game." She crowded the car in front, then, her impatience fuelled by fury, rammed the car. The driver 's head snapped back, then whipped around. He threw a hand up in disgust and motioned her to follow him to the side of the road to assess the damage. She slammed down the accelerator and surged past.

The sudden speed jerked Tom's head back. "Why do we need Ow?"

"Because he's more ruthless than either of us. Because he knows how to deal with dodgy. And there's definitely something dodgy about Fortune's Brick."

Yeah, but . . . Tom reflexively stiffened his legs to brace him into the seat, shock absorbers in case she hit another car. Ow was a danger to him. Had no respect for him. If push came to shove, Ow would push *and* shove him under the bus. How to neutralize the threat? How to make Ow indebted to him?

By saving Rosemary's life.

By being a hero.

Tom relaxed in his seat, pleased with his half-baked idea.

"We go on the offensive."

Rosemary glanced at him. "What?"

"We capture and interrogate Mysterious Chinaman."

Rosemary's silence of incredulousness prompted Tom: "He's the only person besides Hong Chen who has spoken to me about Fortune's Brick. He must know something. We need to get lead him into a trap."

"Like in a men's room? Then you'll what? Tie him up with toilet paper?"

Tom was thinking so hard he missed the putdown. He didn't know any likely places in London, except . . . . He reached for the straw. "In the morning, we go to Kew Gardens. Mysterious Chinaman will follow us down a path to an isolated place,"—he was making it up, a hero's movie—"we grab him and pin him down. Ow will still be shadowing you, right? He wants a 'butchers,' right? I'll show him who's a threat to you."

"Blindingly brilliant." The satire missed its mark with Tom. Would Ow be protecting her? "And how exactly are we to do this?"

"What any good hunter does. We bait the trap."

He outlined an impromptu plan: first thought, best thought; action for action's sake.

"There's no real danger," he assured her. "Ow and his men will be nearby, lurking in the trees. They'll be Johnny-on-the-spot once I get the Chinaman on the ground."

"That's insane." Insane to believe that Ow would be there for her? Insane to risk the proof that he loved her?

"You have a better idea?" Tom asked.

In the morning, on the way to Kew Gardens, Rosemary drove with her usual verve and skill, while Tom snuck backward glances to spot a tailing car. "Lots of cars," he periodically reported. In the town of Kew, knowing street parking would be impossible, she drove to Kew Retail Parking, next to the National Archives, and found a spot. "It's a ten minute walk back to the Victoria Gate," she told Tom. "Keep an eye out for a Chinaman keeping an eye out for us."

Halfway to the Victoria Gate entrance, Tom knelt to tie a shoelace, while surreptitiously looking under his arm for the Chinaman. Another time he abruptly spun, but no one ducked to avoid being seen. They were first in the ticket line, with ten others behind. None of them was Chinese.

Inside Kew, Tom steered Rosemary to the left, away from the popular destination of the Palm House. The night before he had studied the Kew Gardens map picked up from the previous visit. He pulled the map out. "We'll follow this path." His finger traced the yellow line running along the perimeter of the landscaping. "Most people will follow the path when it juts up to the Temperate House. We'll go straight, through the Ruined Arch. That stretch between where the path drops down from The Pavilion café appears to be less used. Maybe we'll find an ambush place there."

"Ambush?" exclaimed Rosemary. "Who are we going to ambush? Or are we going to be ambushed by?"

Tom tugged her by the elbow along the path. "Don't hurry. Give everyone time to get in place."

They strolled down the path through the well-kept lawn, the trees and bushes too far off the path for an effective hiding place. Rosemary asked, "Are we alone?"

Tom glanced around, as if admiring a flowering bush. "As far as I can tell."

But somewhere nearby the Chinaman must be stalking them, he hoped, and Ow stealthily following the Chinaman.

"So what's your plan?" Rosemary asked.

"You're the bait goat."

"Bait goat!"

They left the paved way and followed a dirt path, where the foliage crowded close to the edges. At the Ruined Gate, a crumbling block of craved stone with an arched passage, Tom stopped. "Maybe here. I can hide behind the gate. You stay here and pretend you're taking a stone out of your shoe or something. When you hear Chinaman coming, start walking. When he follows you, I'll leap out and grab him."

"Tom . . . ."

He held a finger to his lips to hush her doubt. "Have faith." After he tackled the Chinaman and started yelling, Ow's cavalry would rush to the rescue, he was certain.

He concealed himself. Rosemary waited nervously on the path. Minutes passed.

"I hear someone coming," whispered Rosemary.

"Start walking."

She disappeared down the path.

Okay, Hero, show your stuff. Tom took long slow breaths to pump up his courage. Forget mild Tom and transform into BRUTE, THE ACTION MAN. Tom wished he had played football so he'd know the mechanics of tackling. How hard can it be? Throw yourself at the knees and hang on. Or jump on his back and ride Mysterious Chinaman down. That's how football players do it on TV.

He waited as long as his nerves allowed—perhaps two minutes—and edged forward for a look.

An arm hooked around his neck and jerked him back.

"What are you playing at? Indian in the woods?"

Tom tried to twist out of Ow's grasp, but the big man held him firm.

Someone was on the path. "Let me go. He's coming," Tom hissed, "the man who's after your sister."

Rosemary appeared, accompanied by two of Ow's men. "No sign, Boss," one of the men said.

Tom freed himself. "You scared him off," he accused. "Now we've lost our chance to get information."

"Leaving my sister alone like that." Ow chest-butted Tom, driving him back a couple steps. "Leaving her unprotected while you hide." Ow grabbed Tom by an ear and twisted. The indignation, more than the pain, caused Tom to backhand Ow across the chin. Ow put Tom in a headlock and cocked his fist.

"Stop!" Rosemary cried out. "I was never in danger."

Ow pushed Tom away and jabbed him in the chest. "You never freelance with my sister's life again."

Ow and his men stalked off.

Rosemary and Tom walked back to the car without speaking; Tom humiliated, Rosemary feeling prized by Ow. She noticed scratches on the Mini's hood. Tom recognized the Chinese characters keyed into the paint. "Mysterious Chinaman was here," he said.

"What does it say?"

"Last warning."

Tom also noticed a dark smear on the hood.

Quiet Killer had followed Tom and Rosemary. Ling had followed Quiet Killer. Quiet Killer was bent over scratching the warning into the hood's paint when a blow smashed his face into the metal. A jab in the kidney pinned him with pain. "Stink bug, you only brave enough for vandalism now?" Ling sneered. He banged Quiet Killer's face on the hood, causing a nosebleed.

Quiet Killer, on the strength of pride, tried to twist free. "Ling, you coward, sneak attack from behind without warning. You have no honor, never did."

Ling, forearm on the back of Quiet Killer's neck, bore down with his full weight. "What do you want? Why are you here?"

"I'm here to cut your balls off and have them for breakfast," Quiet Killer managed to croak.

Ling laughed, grabbed Quiet Killer's belt, and yanked hard, giving him a painful wedgy.

"You all right there?" called a man from across the car park.

Ling stood Quiet Killer upright but kept two fingers pressed into the nerve behind his ear, a paralyzing pressure point. "Wave to the helpful man," he instructed. Quiet Killer waved.

"Your Big Man in town, too? Yes. Can't have a dog without the master holding his leash."

The good Samaritan strode purposefully towards them. Ling let go of Quiet Killer and wiped the blood from his face. "All fine. Friend fainted and hit nose. All fine now." Ling cleaned his hand on Quiet Killer's jacket. "We fine now. Thank you very much." He spotted the black Ford and walked Quiet Killer to it. "Tell Mighty Dragon he should go home now."

Rosemary, tracing the scratches on the hood with a finger, asked, "Last warning for what?"

"We need to talk to Hong Chen."

"Why?"

"He's tied into this."

"Who is he, then?"

"My grandfather." Incredulity popped Rosemary's eyebrows high.

"I didn't think it was important to mention earlier." Tom had the good grace to be ashamed, but not to the point of apology. "We're not close. I met him for the first time here in London, when he asked me to help him find Fortune's Brick."

The same butler/bouncer opened the door. "Please tell my grandfather we are here on urgent business." The man didn't move aside. Tom repeated himself in Mandarin. The man replied in kind, Wait, and shut the door, leaving them outside.

The man gestured them to enter. Tom took the stairs two at a time, Rosemary on his heels, hurried to the library, and barged in without knocking. Heavy drapes pulled across the windows gave the room a solemn cast. Hong Chen stood at his desk, the desk lamplight highlighting the silver blade of the samurai sword in his hand.

"Ling was nearly killed," Hong Chen shouted and swung the sword as if to behead an invisible enemy. "A car knocked him off his motorcycle. Then backed up and ran over him. Only his helmet saved him from death."

"When did this happen?"

"An hour ago."

"Where?"

"Near Kew Gardens."

Rosemary thinking, Ow.

Tom thinking, Mysterious Chinaman.

"Where's Ling now?"

"In hospital. The police have asked questions about the mangled motorcycle and the tire tracks across his back. He called me. I told the police I was sending my lawyer to assist them and my employee with this matter. Certainly a traffic accident."

Hong Chen whacked the flat of the blade on the desk, furious. "This was no accident. We've been attacked."

Hong Chen hadn't expected the warning to be so brutal, but brutality was Mighty Dragon's hallmark. Each crippled step reminded Hong Chen of the night his family had been beaten to death by Mighty Dragon and his Red Guard gang. He had spent years in China trying, by stealth and cunning, to destroy Mighty Dragon. But his nemesis always had the upper hand with more money and powerful political connections. And the ultimate weapon—a bigger and better armed gang. After one spectacularly blazing battle, Hong Chen fled for his life and went underground in London, rarely leaving his fortified house.

Hong Chen's vehement flare-up startled—and thrilled—Rosemary. This old guy who could barely walk, trembled with fervor.

"We received a threat." Tom repeated the words scratched on Rosemary's car. "I suspect the Chinaman. How is he connected to this?"

Hong Chen's plan depended on Mighty Dragon coming to snatch Fortune's Brick from under his nose, the ultimate insult. The attack on Ling was a message not to interfere, a power play meant to humiliate.

"What was meant by 'last warning'?" Rosemary asked.

"Scratching on paint. How dangerous is that? It's an empty threat." The warning was clear to Hong Chen: Your people will die if you try to take Fortune's Brick.

Hong Chen knew that Mighty Dragon never made empty threats. But he'd turn that puswad's arrogance into a weapon against him, gut him, send dogs to gorge on his offal. Mighty Dragon was on his territory now, and walking right into his trap. No harm would come to Tom. Hong Chen was confident he was too clever to let Mighty Dragon have that satisfaction. When he had vanquished Mighty Dragon, his daughter and grandson would honor him in his victory, love him for his devotion to the righteousness of his cause.

Everything depended on Tom delivering Fortune's Brick.

"The message is to scare you away. That is all." Hong Chen raised the sword, a general saluting his troop, and flashed a smile. "No worries. No fears," he said, with forced joviality. "I'm here."

When a monkey bares its teeth, beware: it's a toothy warning. Tom took the smile for the signal it was—a false flag.

CHAPTER 9

FORBIDDEN

Ow was furious at Tom for foolishly risking Rosemary and leaving her exposed. But then, he had been pissed off all his life. Rosie had told him that, as a boy, he'd been sweet and kind, with a high giggly laugh. He couldn't remember such a time. He still had a giggly laugh, which embarrassed him. He sounded like a castrated bear, so he seldom laughed, or even smiled.

Everything in the world had disappointed him from childhood. The teachers who condemned him as "thick." The dreck life of poverty. The blank space where his father had been. The sickly mother, God rest her soul. She tried her best but was shown no mercy by the arsehole landlord. Land lord. Lord of the land, the overlord, the privileged rich who lorded over with their power and wealth. God, how he hated them.

He remembered Da's funeral, the weight of it, Mum and Rosie sitting on his shoulders, the "little man of the house" now. Wasn't much of a house—small, dark, creaky, never smelled good. He spent as little time as possible there, preferred to roam the streets, find mates, find bread to bring home, find trouble.

He had done juvenile crimes since age twelve—shoplifting, mugging younger kids for their lunch money, purse snatching. He wore steel-toed boots and would kick the shit out of anyone. Big for his age. Raging with aggro. He and his mate Jimmy were a team, and Ow the natural leader. He wasn't career minded—what twelve-year-old is—but gained confidence and a liking for what he was good at, like a footballer developing skills. It was fun to turn a punch into profit, to empty the pockets of those he crumpled. He enjoyed physical crime.

Ow had saved Jimmy's skin more than once, being bigger and more wrathful and willing to inflict pain, and eager to put his fist on the nose of authority. The first time he saved Jimmy from a beating happened when they jumped a kid outside the candy store, and failed to notice the dad trailing along. The enraged parent had Jimmy by the scruff of his neck, shaking him like a whelp, when Ow jumped on the man's back and bit his ear. Jimmy got away and so did Ow, but with a good kicking from the father, who booted him along for a full block before running out of breath.

Ow learned a useful lesson that he applied for the rest of his life: Be vigilant.

He also learned that a leader earns respect and loyalty by putting himself on the line.

By the time he was twenty, Ow had assembled a gang of five, with Jimmy as his right-hand man. He ventured into car theft, selling the cars to a hack shop or to a ring that drove the hot items up to Scotland for resale. Ow's network expanded and his reputation grew. He established a territory that rippled out for several square miles from the center, his headquarters at the Cock & Spur.

But he had to walk a fine line between his double life as a good son and brother, and that of a criminal. His mother, who passed when Ow was twenty-two, was a Christian lady. She would have been mortified and ashamed to learn where the money came from for the washer and dryer, the telly, the new front room furniture. Ow told her he was part owner of a pub, where he spent his time. How did that happen? she asked. Where did you learn anything about running a business or keeping accounts? He explained that the elderly gentleman who owned the pub had taken a shining to him. They were both Spurs fans; that's how they met, at the pitch. The old man was teaching him the ropes.

He was equally discreet with Rosemary, but knew she wouldn't buy the good benefactor story. So mostly he stayed opaque until she took the hint that it might be best not to know. Besides, by the time their mother died, she was working on her own plan to escape the bitterness of their neighborhood. She became educated.

Crime, like capitalism, is an opportunistic business; when you get a better offer, take it. Jimmy had been grateful and repaid Ow with loyalty—until he didn't.

Ow didn't take it as umbrage when Jimmy deserted to join Bogside John's gang, with the signing bonus of a new Mercedes. The rival stealing Jimmy away was meant as an insult, but Ow knew Jimmy had made a business decision; he accepted coins in exchange for his soul. He had given Jimmy a call to offer condolence. "You're an ant now, a BJ tool," Ow said, his voice sincere with sympathy. "With me, you were a friend."

To replace Jimmy, he promoted Bess, who had earned her stripes as his most productive debt collector. He became convinced of her mettle when she accosted a debt dodger in a bar. The man protested he didn't have the money on him to pay up. She commanded him to strip and took all his clothes, leaving him butt naked. "Harsh," was the verdict. Ow liked harsh people.

Bess fit in with the gang. She was more handsome than female attractive, with a square, strong chin and jaw. She wore her dark hair in a buzz, so it couldn't be grabbed in a fight. Her eyes were chestnut brown soft; she couldn't intimidate with a hard stare. But she used that to her advantage. Her lovely eyes disarmed men, so they'd drop their guard. Then, if necessary, she'd double them over with a gut punch powered by shoulders and biceps given heft with weight workouts. Her voice was her best intimidator—low octave deep in the throat so it came out as a growl. She called it her tiger voice. She backed up the voice threat with her attitude—rude, crude, straight-arm to the Adam's apple, and other masculine fruits.

"Digestive Acid" Bogside John had always been a pain in Ow's gut. Bogside John, the Pretender, boasting about pulling off richer heists than Ow engineered. Having the bigger and better armed gang. Being strong enough to drive Ow out of his territory. "I'll shunt him off to Coventry or Cambridge, down to the minor leagues where he belongs," was a brag that came back to Ow.

Ow knew that would never happen. His gang of mates, his place at the Cock & Spur, that's where he belonged. Felt accepted. His mates liked him. He provided a livelihood, an identity for them, and they stuck by him. The economy didn't offer any attractive place for a school dropout like him. His Peckham Empire was his stake in the ground that he'd defend to his dying breath.

Still, he needed to knock some sense into that arsehole Bogside John. He'd get around to it—sometime. That attitude, which had been sapping him since Gilly, that indifference of will, could get him killed. He disappointed himself; he'd never admit to it, any more than admit the depression. He wasn't a touchy-feely crime boss, like Tony Soprano. No lying on the couch weeping to a therapist. He couldn't even let Rosemary into that private torture chamber of his life, so why crack open the door to a stranger?

Every morning he had to struggle up from the depth, swimming toward the surface like mad before he ran out of breath and sank, pulled down by the anchor around his ankle. Every morning was a panic attack. Some mornings—and afternoons and nights—he tried to surrender, give up, drift into oblivion, into the sweet bliss of nothingness.

But his stubborn spirit refused to acquiesce, and that caused more disappointment. He couldn't even quit. And that spurred anger. Not the anger felt when someone cut him off in traffic, or when his beloved Tottenham Hotspurs lost to those toffs Chelsea or to Manchester United, cocky SOBs. That was a sharp, competitive anger. His anger wanted to smash the offenders in the gob. Put a limp in their victory dance with a stomp on the instep.

Ow was in a mood, a funk, when Rosemary stormed into the Cock & Spur.

"I want to thank you," she said, confronting him at his back booth "office." But she didn't sound, or look, very thankful, her eye flashing anger, her shoulders tense, ready for a fight.

"Go back and come in again, Rosie. Bring a smile with you this time."

"I want to thank you for disappointing me at Kew Gardens."

"What are you talking about, girl? I had you under my eye. I was there to save you."

"No, you were there to claim me." She slid into the booth opposite him. "Howard, this thing with Tom, I'm trying to be reckless, to get out of my safe box. It may seem pathetic to you, but I'm venturing into unknown territory. I asked you for protection, little sis to big brother." She leaned forward on her elbows. "Look at me, Howard. I was asking you to let me into your world. I had hoped you would welcome me without reservation.

But you said I wasn't worth it. 'I don't see profit in this giggle.' That's what you said. You rejected me."

Ow started to protest, but she cut him short. "When I asked for your help, I"—she faltered with fear or embarrassment, she didn't know which—"I …. I was asking for your love. I was asking my big brother, my only family, to be loyal because I was his sister. I didn't want your bodyguards; I wanted your unqualified acceptance and support. You disappointed me, Howard, by treating me like a client."

Ow opened his mouth to deny her accusations but stopped the kneejerk reflex. Disappointment. The charge resonated deep in his chest. Disappointment had hollowed him out. If Rosemary knew, she'd lose faith in him. To acknowledge disappointment with himself would be to show weakness. If Bogside John knew, he'd find ways to stuff him in a hole and jump on his head.

Ow looked at his dear sister—her head bowed, perhaps to hide tears, perhaps to hide her humiliation, perhaps not to let him see her scorn—and felt fright like he had never felt in his life. She was the exception to his disappointment, his one hope that goodness and beauty were innate in human nature. She lifted the burden off his spirit. She never accepted pity for her disfigurement, never took advantage of his guilt. And now he was on the verge of losing her.

He hunched forward, hands on the table not actually reaching for Rosemary but not keeping his distance, either. "Rosemary, do you ever feel lonely?"

The question startled her, coming from Howard.

"Yes, Howard, I feel lonely every day. I feel loneliness as a disconnect from the people around me, even when shoulder-to-shoulder in the Tube. I feel this city as a lonely place, despite millions of people crowded in. The architecture creates and fosters this loneliness. Buildings can create a lonely feeling because they're not designed to be in service of community. Such monstrosities surround us. They literally block our sight so we can't visualize being together. No wonder we rush past each other with eyes down and adverted. The place doesn't make us feel safe, so our automatic response is not an open face and smile, but being protective of ourselves."

That was her professional answer, her lecture hall I-share-your-pain to win over the crowd. That was her safe box. She saw Howard sag away from her. She had taken wind out of his sail by not opening her heart. She reached across the table and took his hand to pull him back.

"I'm sorry, Howard. That was disrespectful. But yes, I'm very lonely. I am lonely in the gilded cage I've built for myself. My whole professional life has been a fight against the loneliness growing up in that neighborhood that was a crime against aesthetics. That soul-deadening place that sucked all joy out of our childhood. But here's the real truth, Howard. I'm lonely because I'm dishonest with myself."

Ow kept his face turned away in the childish belief that if he couldn't see her, she couldn't see him. He needed that protection in order to say, "Disappointment makes me pucker up inside. The heart goes all crinkly and closes up on itself." To make eye contact would invite her to ask the obvious question.

She waited patiently.

He began to "uh" and "ah" his way into his admission. If he looked up and saw anything but accepting love in Rosemary's eye, he'd lose his nerve. So he talked to the tabletop, beginning with the destruction in the hothouse and working his way backwards into the love affair, and finally uttering Gilly's name.

Gilly wasn't from the neighborhood. Ow met him at the annual Chelsea Flower Show while admiring a bush of Moutan peonies—red, lush, fluffy balls, just gorgeous—when a tall willowy fellow stopped just off his shoulder. "Makes you want to dive right in, doesn't it?" He had a proper accent, not the chunky slurry Ow grew up with.

Ow turned to the stranger. The man, older than Ow, had a patrician face, the kind that comes from blue-blood breeding—slim, straight nose; high forehead; honey-blond hair slicked back, as if he were facing a gale and standing his ground. Sleek. As were his clothes, the light wool jacket draped like flowing water. His type was Ow's favorite target, when they stumbled drunk and satisfied out of their private gambling clubs, and he violently mugged them.

The man smiled as if they were best of friends. His blue eyes were lively with humor, so sincere in their welcome. He asked, "Have you seen the roses? They are a particularly rich display this year." He touched Ow's elbow, a suggestion that they walk along together.

Ow stepped away from the man's warmth. Kill him on the spot, his matador shouted. Kiss him on the spot, his longing countered. He settled for prudence, and fell in step to the roses, careful to keep their bodies from touching.

Afterward, they went to an ordinary pub, not the posh places Gillian took Ow a month later. Gilly kept the banter light to draw out reticent Ow. Talked about flowers, almost swooning when Ow admitted to growing African violets. "They require such a delicate touch, don't they? You must have a gift." Ow agreed patience was as important as water to coax a violet along. He relaxed talking about his flowers, the only creatures he dared to touch with tenderness, to croon over. When he told Gilly that he actually sang Frank Sinatra to his violets, Gilly clasped his hands in exclamation. "Good for you, old mate. Violets are a heart flower. They need love." Ow ducked his head, uncertain he trusted enough to show his smile.

"Let's meet again, shall we?" encouraged Gilly. "I'll show you my hothouse."

A week later, Ow told himself that he was just going to see flowers, but he wore a new musk cologne. Gilly greeted him at the door of his better-than-good address wearing a satin smoking jacket. "So good of you to come," he said, patting Ow on the upper arm. "Would you like a drink before the tour?" Gilly's sitting room was dusky in an Old World way: dark wood, a real fire in the hearth, English landscapes in heavy frames. The aged Guillon Painturaud cognac, smooth and oaky, was complex in Ow's mouth. He was as nervous as a thirty-year-old virgin, which he was.

The hothouse, the length of the back garden, was indeed hot. Gilly nonchalantly pointed to the varieties of orchids, the lilies—"Flowers of death and resurrection, if you believe the Christian imagery. These you'll enjoy," he said, flamboyantly gesturing to the peony bushes.

Gilly removed his jacket and draped it over his arm. His silk shirt, top three buttons open, transparent with perspiration, clung to his hairless chest. "Aren't you warm, dear boy?"

Ow stiffened when Gilly ran his hands over his chest. "You are such a solid boy, aren't you? Bit of a bear. I like bears, dancing bears."

When Gilly kissed him, tongue in mouth, Ow didn't know how to respond. "First time, is it then?" Gilly patted him on the cheek. "Lucky me."

When Gilly caressed Ow's hard cock through his pants, Ow flinched. "Just relax," Gilly soothed. "Let me give you a newbie's welcome." He kissed Ow passionately, while unzipping his pants.

Over the coming months, Ow did relax. He let Gilly dress him in bespoke suits. Gilly gave him a sweater of the finest cashmere. The sweater represented all the loveliness denied him. He didn't have to be a rough boy, a boss of rough boys. Gilly was a guilty pleasure. A breath exhaled.

With Gilly, Ow accepted his secret of wanting to be lovely. Isn't that what love did, transport you into a dream?

He couldn't run the risk of acknowledging Gilly lest he be judged a sellout, a traitor to his class. He left the posh clothes in Gilly's closet, and went to Gilly's private parties, and met his louche friends with their languid boys. Gilly was solicitous, jovially affectionate, referring to him as "Bear." Ow later learned that, in gay slang, bear meant big and hairy, otter was the middle ground, and a twink was slim and effeminate.

But Ow always felt awkward. He never mastered the knack of insouciance, which seemed to be the shibboleth into the tribe.

He began to hear the condescending undertone to Gilly's quips. His "suggestions" on how Ow could "improve" himself were instructions in a velvet glove. He endured the demeaning attitude because he loved Gilly. He tried to adapt. But increasingly, when with Gilly's crowd, he felt himself a fictive character. He was being made over, made up, made fun of, as if he was a badly written buffoon in a bedroom farce.

He became grouchy. Rosemary had noticed and commented: "I'd think you were in a love affair gone bad if I didn't know better." His mates treated him like a lion with a thorn in his paw. Gilly began to complain, to needle him, the barbs more and more astringent. Ow, having no experience with love, was confused. How could this man who had pursued and won his heart be so cruel? Why was he treating him so badly?

The final straw was at a party when Gilly offered Ow to another man. "Take him, take him," Gilly shouted. "He still squirms like a virgin." Ow fled to the hothouse in mortification. If it had been anyone but Gilly, he would have put a heavy heel on his neck. Ow's tears enraged him. The crime boss, the hardarse who liked to hurt people, came sputtering to the surface. He was ashamed and humiliated. He ran amok, uprooting flowers, tearing down the air orchids, grinding delicate colors underfoot, heaving peony bushes through the glass walls.

Gilly and his gang came rushing in, shouting, waving arms, not at all foppish but a pack defending their territory, viciously pummeling the intruder, the clown who dared take offense. They overwhelmed him, at least twenty piling on to bury him, kicked and pounded him helpless. Then, with Gilly holding the front door open, they unceremoniously threw him onto the street.

"Oh, Howard, dear love." Rosemary came from her side of the booth to sit next to him, put her arm around his shoulder, and pulled herself tight to him. "Howard, sweet boy." He leaned into her, heads touching; Rosemary stroked his cheek in comforting acceptance.

"I don't know what to do, Rosie." He stopped before the words began a sob. "It's so new. At first I wanted to wail on someone, beat the shit out of anybody, didn't matter, in blind fury. Your American was a soft target."

Ow shifted a couple inches to create space between them. "You're right, Rosie, I didn't want you in my world, where it's necessary to degrade other humans.

The other day I had to do some business. I started to hum with each blow, as if a man in his woodwork shop perfecting a cabinet. I may not mind being dehumanized. I'm more efficient that way."

"You're bullshitting me now. That's not the brother I know."

He turned so she could better see his face. "I've taught myself to be that way."

CHAPTER 10

MURDER

Rosemary, home after her heart-meet with Ow, sat on her sofa, feet tucked up, cup of tea warm in her hands, to plot against her brother's abuser. Gilly was a Mies van der Rohe building: Bauhaus sleek, cool, seemingly transparent, reflective façade concealing the interior of despicable, lowdown, diabolical, contemptible rooms where Gilly had shamed Ow. How to shatter such a person? How to wrap his intestines around his heart in a tight double knot and yank; give him a heart attack untreatable by doctors?

How to make him howl in remorse?

How to throw big chunky bricks to put holes in the Gilly building? She didn't know how to throw big chunky revenge, didn't know how to heft it against someone's head, or ribs, or drop it to break a fragile foot. She hadn't gotten that far into Ow's world. She wished she had. Could she be brutal, a moral criminal for a good cause?

Maybe, if she had a partner in the deed.

Tom had the sneakiness to do such a deed.

He was holding back something about Fortune's Brick. He had kept his relationship to Hong Chen hidden. That's what had bothered her about him from the very beginning, what he had been trying to hide—a dishonesty of character. That's what made him interesting.

To include Tom in a triangle of love and loyalty with Ow was intriguing. They'd be collaborators to help her to explore the netherworld where everyone—without exception—is mad, furious, in a homicidal rage; where morality is a sharp knife to skin others before they hack you to pieces; where a show of kindness is a sure sign of deceit; where after you steal someone's shoes, be sure to cut off their feet; a place where the operating creed is: Power is an aphrodisiac, and I'm going to fuck you blind.

Ow's world.

Be careful what you wish for.

The BBC six o'clock news, unobtrusive in the background, caught her attention—violence in Regent's Park. The esteemed collector and scion of a prominent family, Geoffrey Milner, had been found dead in his home. She spilt the tea in her dash to turn up the volume. An apparent burglary, although "the police have found mysterious circumstances," according to the newsreader. She called up the BBC news page on her laptop, hit BREAKING NEWS, and read more details: broken window set off the alarm connected directly to the local police station. Officers found Geoffrey dead of a gunshot to the head. The house had been ransacked.

She phoned Tom. "Have you heard the news? Geoffrey Milner has been killed, shot in the head."

Tom's first reaction was disbelief. "Was it a possible accident?"

"Police think it might be a burglary gone bad. Someone broke in through a window."

Tom was thinking that must be the explanation. No connection to his and Rosemary's visit, no linkage to Hong Chen and Fortune's Brick.

"Maybe the alarm frightened the burglar off."

"Silent alarm. When I attended a soiree at his house, Geoffrey bragged about his state-of-the-art security system."

Tom didn't respond so long Rosemary asked, "Tom? Tom, are you there?" His palms were sweaty. "Yes." A cough to cover his stuttered breathing. "Just a bit shocked. Look, Rosemary, give me a moment. I'll call you right back."

He phoned Hong Chen: "Geoffrey Milner is dead."

Hong Chen didn't respond.

"Was he in the chase for Fortune's Brick?"

Hong Chen hesitated, then decided to tell the truth. "Geoffrey Milner was a likely candidate. He might have been organizing the auction."

"Why do you think that?"

"Milner was known as a facilitator for antiquities without papers."

"His house was ransacked. Someone was looking hard for something, like Fortune's Brick. If there was a Fortune's Brick, perhaps the killer has it."

Hong Chen paused before answering. "No, I don't think so. Milner would have never keep it at his house. Too dangerous."

"And now, after my visit, he's dead. Shot in the head. You don't seem surprised."

"It's not totally surprising that someone would kill him sooner or later."

"The other people looking for Fortune's Brick, could they have killed Milner?"

"I don't know. I have no idea who they might be."

Tom didn't believe him. Hong Chen was a dishonest man. Tom could smell the aura of deception, a stink of unscrupulousness that hovered around him, faint as last winter's mothballs—but just as distinct. And as familiar, Tom recognized, as his own stink. It wasn't duplicitousness exactly, but rather a whiff of decay that comes from not sharply defining morality, in order to keep your options open. Hong Chen operated with the mindset that utility was a fundamentally amoral concept: any tool is a good tool as long as it gets the job done. That's how he had survived.

Tom punched in Rosemary's number on his cell. "I need to talk to you. I'm coming over."

His first words, when he sat in her living room: "Milner may have been murdered in connection to Fortune's Brick."

"Murdered?"

The very thought stunned Rosemary. Geoffrey's death caused her sorrow, but the possibility of murder—the desecration of his humanity—plunged her into grief. She had seen the brutality of murder. When she was fifteen, walking home in the dim of her wretched neighborhood, she came upon four boys beating on a body in the center of their circle. She screamed. The boys with silver fingers spun towards her, blood dripping from their knives. One started towards her, but his mate pulled him back and they ran, exposing the small, thin boy curled on the ground, ribboned in blood, his face and chest cut open. He looked like a butchered dog.

"Why do you think he was murdered?"

Tom told her about the rumored secret auction and Hong Chen's warning that dangerous people were after Fortune's Brick.

That was the first Rosemary had heard about a secret auction, another deliberate omission by Tom.

"I asked Hong Chen if Milner was involved in the auction. He thought it possible. I don't know if that's true. I don't know if any of this is true, but, as you said, there's definitely something dodgy around Fortune's Brick. Ow might be right; there are too many unknowns for you to be safe."

A visceral rill surged through her; she had fallen into a gang—Tom, Ow, Hong Chen—of reprehensible miscreants. Would she metaphorically cut her palm to share bonding blood with them?

"You should tell the police," she urged Tom.

"The police are already on the case."

"But perhaps not looking in the right direction."

"We don't know if Fortune's Brick even exists. So why send the police on a false trail and waste their time and resources."

Rosemary ran her tongue around her mouth, scooping up the taste of fear. Tamarind, she decided. Tamarind was used for pickling. She could be pickled in her own fear, shriveled up. But tamarind was also tangy, a zesty condiment when combined with sugar to make a sweet-and-sour chutney. The Ow/Rosie/Tom chutney.

The ringing phone brought her back into the room. She answered. When Tom heard Sandra's name, he stood next to Rosemary to overhear the conservation. Rupa Banerjee was expected at Teanamu Chaya within the hour.

"Tell her we'll be there," he whispered. "Ask her to introduce us to Banerjee as tea connoisseurs." After all, he had bought all of her Rare Silver Tips Imperial. And, if Milner's murder was connected to Fortune's Brick, then she should be warned, or at least looked after.

"We need costumes," he told Rosemary when she hung up. "Something that says Euro-trash hip backed by serious money. Dallas goes to Paris."

"What?"

"The confidence of insouciance to mask the arrogance of entitlement."

"Sandra knows who I am," Rosemary protested. "I can't ask her to lie."

"But she doesn't know who I am, really. Whatever you wear to give a lecture, put it on. Then we'll swing by my place for my Euro-trash look."

Forty minutes later, Rosemary, wearing a dark tailored business suit, a white satin eye patch, and a trailing Hermès scarf over her shoulder, followed Tom into Teanamu Chaya teahouse. He wore his expensive Canali white shirt—open at the collar—rumpled jeans, the Italian running shoes, the Moroccan leather coat, his hair artfully tousled. The scruff of beard said, I couldn't bother. The place was half full with the late afternoon tea crowd. Tom strolled around the edge of the room, pretending to examine teaware displayed on the shelves, while looking for an Indian woman. One particular item caught his attention—an antique tea press, the kind for making tea bricks. The lid of the press was the imprint of a chrysanthemum. The flower, Tom recognized, as the symbol of Xianfeng, ninth emperor of the Qing dynasty.

Rosemary nudged him as Sandra and a woman wearing a sari emerged from the back office. Sandra spotted her friend and came over, her usual effusive self. "Rosemary, dear Rosemary," she said, embracing her, "may I introduce Rupa Banerjee. This is my old friend Rosemary Hocks, a very knowledgeable lover of tea."

The two women gently shook hands, Rupa politely not staring at Rosemary's eye patch. "Sandra has told us about your extraordinary tea. My associate"—Rosemary stepped aside to bring Tom into the circle—"was so impressed with your Rare Silver Tips Imperial, he bought the whole lot."

Tom, all open-American friendly, extended his hand. "A pleasure and honor to meet you."

Rupa gave him a firm handshake. "I hope you enjoyed my tea."

"Yes, but I'd love your advice on how best to prepare it. Rare teas are often idiosyncratic, don't you find?"

"Shall we have a tasting?" Sandra suggested, steering her guests to the small outdoor patio.

Tom sat next to Rupa and chatted about roil, not broil; seeping times ("Is Rare Silver Tips Imperial more robust by brewing slightly over three minutes, or does that submerge the more delicate undertones?"); and best roasting temperatures for black teas, Tom speed-thinking the arcane details of Hong Chen's tutorials. Rupa seemed impressed and utterly charmed.

"I've always wanted to visit Darjeeling," he confided. "I understand it's devastatingly beautiful and the climate delightful, especially for tea bushes."

"You must, as my guest." Rupa relaxed, friendly to the point that Tom felt he had established his credentials as a tea maven.

"That region is where the indigenous tea trees first took root, isn't that right? My wish list includes visiting the remaining King Trees."

"Those trees are in Yunnan, across the Chinese border from Darjeeling. I've toured the King Tree sites. It is a pilgrimage to the cultural sages of China's history. People, especially Western people, don't appreciate what an enormous civilizing affect tea has had on the world."

"I couldn't agree more." Tom was so bold as to pat Rupa's hand. When she didn't object, he knew he had been accepted as a compatriot. He spoke fluently, if glibly, about the quality of teas from Fujian province and segued into tea from northern India. "The quality of the tea on the original British plantations in Darjeeling was, excuse my French, terrible. Only by the daring efforts of Robert Fortune was Indian tea able to take the market from the Chinese. I wonder, did the Makaibari stock come from the plants Fortune slipped out of China?"

Sandra interrupted with the tea service. She set a plate of small golden cakes, about the size of a silver dollar, in the center of the table.

"You may recognize these, Rupa."

"Flowers honey," Rupa exclaimed. "How did you find these?"

"My friend Piano has one of the best tea shops in Kunming. When I order his honey teas, he always includes these cakes. Do you know why he calls his tea Honey Tea?" she asked, and without waiting for an answer, "Because he's from the Hani tribe. He thought honey would be more familiar to the Western market than Hani. Clever, isn't he?"

"You must try one," Rupa urged Tom. "It's a very fine bean curd with honey infused with rose essence." She was so enthusiastic Tom thought she was going to hand-feed him.

Sandra said, while pouring four cups, "This tea is also very special."

"About Fortune's . . ." Tom hesitated for a moment. ". . . Fortune's tea."

Rupa spoke around the crumbs of cake on her lips. "My family's public legend does not credit Fortune with our fine tea. But, at the dining table," she added with a wink, "we know about Robert Fortune."

"There seems to be a renewed interest in Fortune and his tea," Tom said quietly, as if a confidence between trusted friends.

"Yes," Rupa agreed, and took a sip of her tea.

"What do you think?" asked Sandra. "Of the tea?"

Tom also took a sip and savored it long enough for Rupa to comment. "Very good. Is it from Piano?"

Sandra triumphantly set a tea box on the table. "It's grown here in England. Down in Cornwall."

"Tea grown in England?" Rosemary asked. "I didn't think it possible."

"Yes," Sandra said, delighted by the success of her surprise. "On the Tregothnan Estate, established by the Boscawen family in 1334. There's also some tea grown up in Scotland, but that really doesn't count."

"The ornamental gardens?" queried Rosemary.

"They've been growing tea since 2001. Amazing, isn't it?"

Tom picked up the box to look closely at the logo— a chrysanthemum blossom. The symbol of Emperor Xianfeng. On an impulsive hunch, he leaned to Rupa with the logo deliberately held in her sight. "I understand there's to be a black," a slight emphasis on *black*, "tie"—slurred to be mistaken as tea—"event to be held at Tregothnan. Invitation only." He spoke quietly, so only Rupa could hear.

Rupa nodded. "Yes. The details arrived today. But I have no idea where Tregothnan is. Do you?"

Tom glanced at Rosemary. "My assistant is native born. She knows the country well." He turned to Rosemary. "Do you where the Tregothnan Estate is located?"

"Near Truro."

Tom returned to Rupa with a warm smile. "We will gladly offer you a ride."

"Much appreciated," Rupa said with evident relief. "I do feel so exposed on my own."

"Where shall we pick you up?"

Rupa told him her hotel.

Tom leaned to Rosemary and asked, "How long does it take to drive to Truro?"

"About seven hours."

Tom turned back to Rupa. "What time will be convenient to pick you up?"

"If we are to arrive by eight o'clock, we should leave by one, don't you think? Perhaps a bit before. I'd like time to look around those famous gardens."

"We'll call for you at one P.M. at your hotel. Tomorrow then."

"No," Rupa corrected, "The *event* is not until Wednesday."

"Yes, of course, my confusion."

As they drove away from the teahouse, Rosemary asked, "Why are we going to Truro?"

"To steal Fortune's Brick, in two days."

"You know where Fortune's Brick is?"

"No."

"Then?"

"We need to do three things, fast. You borrow that old tea press that Sandra has on her shelf. And we'll need a couple pounds of loose tea leaves also. I'll talk to Hong Chen. And together, we'll make a plan with Ow."

"Why the tea press?"

"It's part of the plan with Hong Chen."

"Ow's not convinced Fortune's Brick exists, and if it does that it's worth the effort."

"But now we have a place, time, and date. When I tell him the value of Fortune's Brick, he'll want in."

The next afternoon Rosemary returned to Teanamu Chaya. Sandra rushed her into the office and shut the door. "The deal is on." Sandra grasped both of Rosemary's hands, her voice earnest, her eyes delighted. "You can't say anything to anybody, you promise? Not for a few more days."

"What deal?"

"Rupa is going to make me her exclusive agent in England for a new line of tea she's bringing to market. Isn't that exciting!" Sandra hugged Rosemary, then stepped away. "I'm so glad she liked you and Tom. We'll have our own tea club, just the four of us."

"Yes, that will be wonderful. And speaking of tea, I have a favor to ask. Yesterday I noticed the old tea press you have on display. I'd like to borrow it for a couple days."

"Of course."

"Tell me, how did you get it?"

"By rooting through a garbage tip," Sandra replied with a laugh, and told Rosemary the story.

When Tregothnan Estate started producing tea, the owner, a friend, asked Sandra to consult on the quality of the tea. "To tell the truth, it was abysmal," Sandra said in a low voice, as if they could be overheard in the small office. The biggest problem was England, although the Cornwall climate is not vastly different than the famous tea region of Darjeeling. But no one had grown tea in England before, and for good reason. Tea plants thrive best in wet climates at the altitude of around 7000 feet. They like sunny days and the coolness of mountains. "Tea is much like coffee that way," Sandra said. "Shall we sit? The story goes on for a while."

Sandra and Rosemary settled on the couch in the office. "Tregothnan Estate is only thirty-one feet above sea level. The owner thought that England's cool and wet climate would compensate for the lack of altitude. He tore up twenty acres of potatoes, peas, and carrots and converted the patch into a tea experiment. Over the years, the quality of tea did improve. Even Tom and Rupa thought is was passable, right? They sell it now at Fortnum & Mason on Piccadilly for one hundred fifty pounds for a pound."

Rosemary quickly did the conversion: Two hundred dollars. Tom would be impressed.

"The press?"

"One day at Tregothnan, I was poking through the tip of discarded old garden equipment looking for oddities to display here. I found the press in bits but thought it could be put back together. The owner was glad to be rid of it. Said he didn't even know how it got there. This was about the same time that the new chrysanthemum label appeared on their tea boxes," Sandra said. "I thought that a good marketing move. Gave the brand distinction. Come on, I'll find a box for the press."

"I need a couple pounds of loose tea leaves, also."

Sandra gave her a quizzical look. "A cooking experiment," Rosemary explained, all she could think of on the spur of the moment.

While Rosemary was securing the tea press, Tom conferred with Hong Chen. Hong Chen sat behind his desk, making Tom stand before him, a lieutenant reporting to his commander.

"How certain are you that a genuine Fortune's Brick exists?" Tom asked.

"I believe," Hong Chen replied in Mandarin.

"But is there any real evidence?"

"There are historical accounts that a ceremonial brick of tea was made for the coronation of the emperor. I showed you the sketch of the actual brick. We know that the brick never arrived at the palace. We know that Robert Fortune was marauding in China tea territory at that time."

"But that's conjecture, not proof."

"Same as for God, but people believe. Is God a scam?"

"I could make a case," replied Tom.

"And I can make a case that Fortune's Brick deserves the same belief as the pope puts in Christ."

Fortune's Brick was, for Hong Chen, a vehicle that carried cultural wisdom dating back to the Han Dynasty, the golden age. The spiritual learning, the poetry and art, the sensibilities that molded the Chinese people culminated in the Han Dynasty, in his view. Tea was the bond, in reality as well as symbolically, present in every level of Chinese society. Tea kept the body healthy; the tea ceremony soothed the spirit; the craft of teaware put the example of simple elegance in everyone's hands regardless of wealth or status or power.

The Cultural Revolution had debased the sustaining values of order, of learned wisdom, of the grace of living in harmony. Mao made everyone a brutal peasant, in Hong Chen's experience. The fractured China reknitted itself as a moneygrubbing, materialistic, capitalistic ass-kisser leading to inevitable perdition, in Hong Chen's opinion. His belief transformed the myth of Fortune's Brick into a legend impregnated with emotional fervor of redemption.

Tom had a more pragmatic viewpoint: Someone at Tregothnan Estate started the rumor that Fortune's Brick existed and was for sale. That person was in position to plant the rumor in the small circle of collectors who valued rare teas. The possibility, no matter how improbable, was the bait to lure carefully selected connoisseurs to a private auction.

The Fortune's Brick would have to be a masterful fake, an exact replica of the real thing as in the sketch Hong Chen had shown Tom. Which required a tea press to duplicate the design on the original tea brick.

On the other hand, if Fortune's Brick was authentic, how did it get to Tregothnan?

That mystery wasn't Tom's concern; he had to solve the puzzle of how to steal the tea at the auction.

"I have reason to believe the auction will be held on Wednesday."

Hong Chen kept surprise off his face. He pressed his hands flat on the desk's surface to stop the trembling. "You know about the auction? Where? What time?"

"I won't tell you. Not until I know for certain." Then Tom played his hunch. "I can get to the door, but I need an invitation for entry." Hong Chen must have anticipated that crucial point, Tom reasoned, and had a plan. Perhaps he knew how to open the door, but didn't know how to find the door.

Hong Chen took a three-by-five card of heavy stock from a desk drawer and laid it on the desk. "This is the invitation to the auction, without the date, time, or place." Tom bent over the shiny black card, which appeared blank. Hong Chen tilted the card slightly towards the desk lamp. "Look close." Tom saw faint ridges and swirls that become petals. "A chrysanthemum, the emperor's symbol."

"It was sent to you?"

"No. My friends in China procured it. It will get you past the first line of security. A second card with the auction's details was sent separately. A security double check, like an air lock, so verification can be authenticated. I had hoped you might find a second card at

Milner's. How you actually gain access to the auction now depends on your ingenuity."

That night, after Tom briefed Rosemary, they met with Ow at the Cock & Spur.

"Fortune's Brick is worth millions," Tom assured. "I now have a good idea where to find the tea and when to snatch it." He explained his plan for breaking and entering, threatening rich people, stealing what they coveted, and escaping. "I can tell you the place, date, and time. It's up to you to figure out the how."

"Is he telling porkies?" Ow asked Rosemary.

"Pork pies rhymes with lies," she explained for Tom's benefit. "We'll see you right, Howard." She laid a placating hand on his arm. "I guarantee it."

Ow didn't need Rosemary's assurance—once he had Fortune's Brick, he'd have the advantage. He could eat the pie and not share. He didn't need Tom. He had an ace up his sleeve—Rosemary. At least he thought he did.

CHAPTER 11

AUCTION

At his bedsit, after the meeting with Ow, Tom's mind raced around the circuit of disasters that could befall him: betrayal, lack of courage, distrust, false bravado resulting in violent death, and the sheer stupidity of believing he could pull off the tea heist. He was going to outsmart Hong Chen? He could pull a fast one on Ow? What made him think he could trust Rosemary? Or even depend on his Hero?

He walked to Rosemary's in the gray morning light, pulling in fresh air to pump energizing oxygen into his hero. *Come on, pal, wake up.* He swung his arms to expand his chest, lifted his knees higher with each step. *You can do this.* He pounded on his chest—pretend calisthenics—as he crossed Hyde Park. *Be brave. Believe in the bluff.*

Rosemary opened the door, fetchingly mussed, the tangle of hair a flirt, her shirt carelessly buttoned to reveal the swell of breasts. "Shall we have tea? I've laid out scones with Devon cream and jam. Have you had Devon cream and jam on scones before? It's a very British tradition."

She set a laden tray on the glass coffee table before the sofa. "This will be fun, won't it? Our bit of adventure, a gamble really, isn't it?"

They sat side by side as she poured cups of tea.

"I'm happy in this room because it's full of possibility," Rosemary said to cover her nervousness. "It's without obstacles, like an ottoman to trip over or self-important club chairs to detour around. The openness implies freedom to dance flamboyantly, to spin in sudden directions. Yet, it's cozy, don't you think?" Rosemary felt silly being a chatty hostess.

Tom glanced around the long rectangular room, the dining table at the far end, where the short arm of the L became the kitchen. "This room is optimistic the way a horizon is optimistic." He sounded pompously pedantic, he knew, because there was nothing else to hide behind. He quickly added, to ameliorate the attitude, "This space"—he spread his arms as if opening a curtain—"invites you to invent, the way a horizon invites you to imagine the promise of a new beginning."

Perhaps it was the expansive gesture that caused Tom inexplicably to feel a flush of confidence. He stood and, much to his—and Rosemary's—astonishment, raised his arms above his head, as if a swan presenting. He imagined himself a graceful bird and began to swoop about the room. He felt ridiculous and knew he looked silly. He wanted to give Rosemary a moment of unguarded silliness, on the premise that such generosity would spur happiness.

His spontaneous foolishness fractured the moment and gave Rosemary a glimpse of a possible future. If she let go, would she find the courage to free-fall? Into what? Ow's world? An existence without the safety nets she had so arduously constructed for herself? The unknown of Tom? Embrace her desperation and cast off certainty? Maybe she shouldn't care to have an answer. This was a now-or-never moment.

She jumped from the sofa and became a bumblebee swirling in circles, arms furiously flapping, buzzing as if singing a hymn. No thought. No judgment from the rational mind. No emotional intelligence's feeling. Close the eyes, open the heart, and launch. She spun down the room to the dining table, pivoted, paused, waiting for mindlessness to compel her into action.

She tipped forward on her toes, facing Tom, marveling at his awkward attempt of a grand jeté. But she couldn't get off the stillpoint of balance, the cautious adjustment between rational mind and emotional intelligence. *Now. Now. Don't give a damn. No thought.* She leaned to tip herself forward. *Just run for the hell of it, for the fun of it, and throw yourself into an impulse.*

She ran at him and launched herself in the air.

Tom saw her hurling at him, knees high, elbows pumping, neck stretched towards a finish line. He barely had time to brace himself before she hit him full body, a slam hug. He grabbed her hard, chest high, absorbing the impact. His pelvic thrust could be interpreted as an obscene intent, but he was just trying to keep his balance. The impact felt like morning sex, an awakening without the preamble of dinner and wine, the unexpected promise of a grand day.

Breathing deeply, laughing, Tom knew "the glow of love" was not a metaphor but an actual physical description.

Rosemary saw the deer-in-the-headlights look on his face. "Are you all right?" she asked. She unlocked her legs from around his waist and slid to her feet.

He heard a jumble of silent words: Are you willing to take the risk of love? Are you willing to expose yourself to the recriminations and guilt and sorrow and debasement that come with failure of love? Can you believe, despite the possibility—even probability—that your happiness will be reduced to tatters and tears?

Can I as Hero fall in love?

The allure was to make him interesting to himself in ways he had yet to imagine. Courage defines a hero. Spontaneous courage, acting before thinking of the risks or the consequences, the unselfish impulse to do good—whether to save another's life or by simply telling the truth—was the mark of a hero. That's what gets written on a hero's tombstone: Here lies a man brave enough to be honest and to act on it.

For him to fall in love so purely would require the triumph of hope over self-knowledge.

Rosemary stepped back, a bit unsure, a little flustered. "I'm nervous about this auction." Not the auction itself actually, but the possible follow-up devastation of flinging herself into a void.

Tom reached to pull her to him, but turned the gesture into a wave, a nonchalant assurance to a comrade before jumping out of a plane into battle. "We'll be fine." And then to clarify, "Nobody is going to shoot us. At worst, it will be an embarrassment."

Rosemary turned away. "I should change. What about my eye? What look should I give it?"

Tom tilted forward, as if to kiss her empty eye, then caught himself. "Make it a starburst, then cover it with a patch. If we need a distraction, whip off the patch and, in that split second when our attackers hesitate, we'll run for our lives."

She laughed and patted him on the chest. "I'll be right back. Have a scone, with Devon cream and jam."

He was licking jam from his fingers when she reappeared as a glamorous, but serious, executive in a midnight-blue silk suit and a single strand of pearls. A black satin patch covered her empty eye. Tom leaned forward to better see the small white imprint in the center of the patch: the Jolly Roger.

"It's my sigil," she said. "Jolly Roger will put a hex on my enemies and allow me to escape their clutches."

"Very appropriate, considering the battle we're sailing into."

Tom had decided to go with the louche rock-star look: hair gelled into a drunken brawl, the leather coat over his favorite relaxation shirt—a replica of Tom Brady's white Super Bowl jersey with authentic grass stains—his stonewashed jeans wrinkled with induced wear stress, the Italian running shoes purposely scuffed.

Rupa greeted them in her hotel lobby wearing a dazzling blue and silver sari. Her sleek black hair with streaks of gray was bundled in a tidy bun. A vermillion mark in the parting of the hair just above her forehead aligned with the red bindi dot centered above her brows. On her right arm she wore six sterling silver bracelets, divided evenly by a band of brilliant diamonds. Six gold bracelets, divided evenly by a band of sparkling rubies, decorated her left arm.

"You look absolutely stunning," gushed Rosemary.

"Thank you," acknowledged Rupa. "You have the look of a wealthy professional. And you," nodding to Tom, "need an advisor."

Rosemary eased through traffic so as not to startle Rupa. Tom sneaked glances behind for a tailing car, or a motorcycle. No suspicious car. No motorcycle. Perhaps Ling wasn't out of the hospital after the traffic crash, or assault.

Lively conversation and hearty laughter made the long drive to Truro a pleasure. By the time they reached the old market town at the mouth of River Fal, guided in by the cathedral's steeple, Tom felt Rupa a true ally. The early evening light was strong enough for Rosemary to give a running commentary, as she drove through the town center, on the differences in the Georgian, Regency, and Victorian architecture of the buildings.

She followed the Google map up the River Fal three miles to the entrance to Tregothnan. The bucolic countryside gave Tom hope that the auction would be a genteel, refined confab of peers with casual security. Before they reached the main house, two well-groomed men wearing suits stepped from the side of the road and waved them to a stop. They approached, one on either side of the car. Both men carried walkie-talkies. The man on the driver's side politely bid Rosemary good evening and asked her business. "Special tea," she replied. "Your names, please," the polite man said, holding up a clipboard.

Rupa gave her name from the back seat.

The man checked his name list. "Your card, please."

Rupa handed over the black invitation card.

The second guard came around the car and took the card. He ran it under a handheld device to reveal the chrysanthemum hologram. Rupa's name was checked off and the invitation returned.

Tom gave his name.

The man checked the list. "Sorry, sir. But I don't have you down."

"I, and my assistant, represent Geoffrey Milner. He was unable to attend because of his recent unfortunate demise. His estate assigned us as his representatives." Tom handed over the black card Hong Chen had given him.

"I need some identification also."

Tom presented a letter authorizing him as the agent of the Milner estate.

The letter was carefully read; the card scanned.

"One moment, sir." The guard walked away and spoke on his walkie-talkie.

Tom sat back in a slouch. Rosemary, nervous about the forged letter he had shown her earlier, impatiently tapped the steering wheel, as if affronted by the delay.

The guard returned and bent to talk through the open driver's window. "There seems to be confusion, sir. We were not informed of your arrangement with the Milner estate."

"Not my problem." Tom, adopting the pose of a put-on prince, spoke to the windshield rather than to the man. "We are here. We have presented the proper security card. Now let us pass."

The man stepped away and again spoke into his walkie-talkie. Tom and Rosemary studiously held their sangfroid tightly to prevent telltale fidget.

The guard approached. "Sorry for the inconvenience. Follow the road and you will be directed around the main house." The second guard gestured to a lane partially hidden by trees. Rosemary, with a sigh of relief, drove forward. Tom remained haughty to reassure Rupa.

The road wound through an avenue of oaks, which fanned out into woodland. They caught glimpses of the Truro River in the narrow valley below as Rosemary drove through a grove of conifers, which devolved into mature rhododendrons in full bloom. The road dead-ended at a rustic faux-Tudor house fronted by a small lawn.

"Isn't this a marvelous place," enthused Rupa, leaning forward between Rosemary and Tom for the better view out the windshield. "I hope we have time to walk about."

Tom counted on such a walk to assess the lay of the land, in case they needed to make a fast exit.

A man standing by the front door stepped forward and directed Rosemary to a graveled parking space.

Before they could get out of the car, another man appeared. "Found the place all right then," he said to Rosemary. "If you don't mind, I need to check your invitation cards; security, you know."

Rupa handed over her second card, confirming her invitation. Tom didn't have a second card. "This letter is meant to be authentication." He handed his forgery to the guard.

This was the moment when he would be caught, or he'd get away with the bluff. If Milner's relatives, or his attorney, were contacted, the fake letter would be revealed.

The man checked the guest list. He did a second run-through, looking for a Tom Edelson.

"Sorry, sir . . ."

Rosemary discreetly slipped the gearshift into reverse. She and Tom had agreed that if the game were up, they'd make a run for it.

Rupa leaned forward. "I assure you that my good friends are legitimate. Now don't be rude."

"Excuse me one moment," the man replied and stepped away to talk into his walkie-talkie.

A second guard came to stand directly behind the Mini. Tom gave Rosemary a nudge and eased open his door. She read the alert in his eyes and unlatched her door. If challenged, they'd bolt into the surrounding woods.

The man clicked off his walkie-talkie and opened the driver's door. "Welcome," he said with a slight bow. "Mr. Olson is waiting inside."

"Thank you, Rupa," Tom said. "Very honorable of you, seeing that we are competitors."

"Not really. Whoever has the most money wins. Nothing personal."

Mr. Olson, a portly man dressed in a formal morning coat, heartily shook their hands. "So glad you could come. A pleasure to have you, Honorable Banerjee." To Tom, "Sorry to hear of Mr. Milner's misfortune." He looked Rosemary full in the face without any indication that anything was amiss. "So lovely for you to attend."

He ushered them into the main room. "This was the guest house but is now used for special private events." The room was modest in size, with a fireplace and a sideboard with bottles of drinks and plates of finger food. Heavy drapes blocked the windows. Eight plush chairs formed a semicircle around a plinth. An overhead spotlight shone down on the column.

"Let me explain the protocol," Mr. Olson said. "I am the auctioneer. Fortune's Brick will be placed here." He gestured to the plinth. "During the auction two men will guard the exterior entrance and two men will be stationed at the interior door. Two additional armed men will flank the plinth. Each participant, individually, will be allowed three minutes to look closely at the brick of tea in a bulletproof glass box. When the bidding is over, I will accompany the winner to the back office"—he pointed to a side door—"to make final arrangements. The seating is on first-come basis. As you are the first here, you have your choice."

"Do we have time to look at the gardens?" inquired Rupa.

"Yes, certainly, but only those close to this house. One of the gentlemen outside will escort you, as a guide and for your security."

Tom was surprised the atmosphere wasn't more cloak-and-dagger. He'd always assumed nefarious connections around Fortune's Brick, but the auction appeared to be what it seemed, a private sale for a very select group of wealthy people.

Outside, a guard escorted Rupa, Tom, and Rosemary down the walk around the side of the house to a circular flowerbed featuring the sculpture of a magisterial falcon on a stone pedestal.

"Do you garden?" Rupa asked Rosemary.

Rosemary shook her head. Ow had the green thumb and tenderly nurtured impressive African violets. "I once had a climbing rose, but it fell down. Then I tried a geranium in a tub by my front door, but the poor thing didn't flourish."

Tom, his head swiveling as if to admire the landscaping, looked for escape routes: If his plan went sideways, he and Rosemary would run for it. Ow and his boys could take care of themselves, presuming Ow found the auction site. And if he did, how would he get through the security? And overcome the armed guards? And then escape with Fortune's Brick? The previous night's worries banged on his nerves. *Breathe, Hero, breathe in confidence.*

The guard escorted them down an avenue of palms. "This leads to Snowdrop Hill," he said, "with more ornamental plantings."

"There are palms along the coast of Scotland, where the warm waters of the Gulf Stream touch the land," said Rosemary. "But I didn't expect palms in Cornwall."

Tom looked closely at the palms. "Kew Gardens. We saw the same kind in Kew Gardens. If in London, why not Cornwall?"

"Because in Kew Gardens they were raised in a greenhouse. Here they are in the wild, so to speak. It can get quite cold in Cornwall."

Chusan palms in the Palm House, Tom remembered. Also called *Trachycarpus fortunei* in honor of Robert Fortune, who sent the first palms from China to England.

The guard led them to a locked shed on top of Snowdrop Hill, a modest rise. "I'm a bit of a greenhouse man myself," he admitted, as he unlocked the door. "Built one in my back garden. When we were doing security sweep, we checked all the buildings. I found quite a surprise in this one."

Inside, the guard led them to a large box-like object draped with heavy canvas hidden behind a hodgepodge of gardening equipment. "A bit of history here. The head gardener told me it's the only original one still in existence." He pulled off the covering to reveal a mini-greenhouse, and stood back proudly as if he had personally built it. "It's a Wardian Case, invented by Nathaniel Ward. On long voyages by sailing ships, plants would often die from exposure to violent weather and lack of fresh water. That nearly wrecked Britain's budding tea industry, when tea bushes shipped from China to India didn't fare well. The Wardian Case not only protected the plants on deck from the elements but also provided condensation that watered the plants."

The guard pointed to faint writing on the side of the wooden frame. "Addressed to Evelyn Boscawen, the sixth Viscount Falmouth. He was a friend with Henry Grey, the third Earl Grey, who, at the time, in 1850, was the Secretary of State for War and the Colonies. The current Viscount Falmouth is the owner of Tregothnan. I told the head gardener this Wardian Case belongs in a museum."

Tom stared in astonishment. A direct link to Fortune's tea plants? Perhaps it was not far-fetched that the real Fortune's Brick ended up at Tregothnan.

The guard glanced at his wristwatch. "We should be getting back."

Two cars were parked next to Rosemary's Mini. Inside the auction room, an Asian man and woman stood talking to Mr. Olson. A large Caucasian stood at the sideboard, pouring himself a scotch. "Ah, you're back," exclaimed Mr. Olson. "Did you enjoy the gardens? May I present Mr. and Mrs. Ocampo. Rupa Banerjee."

Rupa bowed her head. "I'm so pleased to finally meet you in person."

Mr. Ocampo held out his hand. "Ah, the woman behind the Makaibari Estate. The honor is mine."

"And this," Mr. Olson said turning to the man approaching with his glass of scotch, "is Mr. Sergi Agapov." The Russian nodded but did not extend his hand.

Before Mr. Olson could introduce Tom and Rosemary, the door opened and two Chinese men entered. Tom did a double take. One of the men was the mysterious Chinaman who had warned Tom not to pursue Fortune's Brick. The other man resembled a toad balanced on short legs. He looked ill fitted, despite the expertise of the tailored Bond Street suit; the jacket slipped down his narrow, sloped shoulders and his pregnant paunch destroyed the suit's drape line.

"Weiwu Long." Mr. Olson stepped forward and bowed to the newcomer. "We are honored you could join us in person." Weiwu Long gave a short, stiff bow to Mr. Olson, and flicked a glance at Tom.

Weiwu Long. The Mighty Dragon Tom's mother had told him about, the killer of his grandfather's family, Hong Chen's hated enemy.

"Now that we're all here, shall we begin?" Mr. Olson stood next to the plinth as everyone took a seat. The lights dimmed, except for the overhead spotlight. A man came from the office carrying a rectangular box covered with a black cloth, which he set on the column.

Mr. Olson lifted the cloth to reveal an ornate brick of tea inside the glass box. "Fortune's Brick. Each of you may examine the object, starting with those sitting on the right side. Shall we?"

Mr. Ocampo rose and stepped forward, putting his nose practically on the glass, as if trying to smell the tea. The Russian made a cursory walk around, without seeming interested in the details imprinted on the tea. Weiwu Long carefully examined the inscription of the emperor's name across the bottom of the brick. Rupa took her full three minutes to study the brick from all sides. Tom checked the embossed chrysanthemum and the emperor's name.

"Is this being sold by the Viscount?" he asked. "The provenance and legal rights are important."

"I assure you all is in order," Mr. Olson replied, without answering the question. "Shall we? Bidding begins at one million US dollars."

Mr. Ocampo gave a slight nod.

"One million to the gentleman from Manila. One point three?"

The Russian lifted a shoulder.

The bidding increased at a steady pace on Rupa's raised eyebrow, a counter by Mr. Ocampo, a pause until Tom boosted the bidding to two million. Weiwu Long immediately raised the forefinger resting on his knee and splayed five fingers.

"Two million five to Weiwu Long," intoned Mr. Olson.

Tom flashed three fingers without moving his hand. "Three million five to the gentleman."

The Russian crossed his arms, holding each elbow tightly, then tapped twice with his forefinger. "Four million five."

Weiwu Long impatiently held up two fingers.

"Five five to Weiwu Long."

No movement for another bid.

Mr. Olson paused for the count of ten. "Going once."

Tom pushed the price to five million eight hundred thousand.

Weiwu Long held up six fingers.

"Six million . . ."

A knock on the door. Mr. Olson ignored it, waiting for a counterbid. A second knock, firmer. Mr. Olson held up his hand to stop the auction and sotto voce told the guard next to him to answer the door. The man cautiously cracked open the door, and immediately stumbled back, forced by the two guards outside the door who, hands tied behind their backs, were pushed forward by four men.

The masked intruders raised pump shotguns before the guard next to Mr. Olson could draw his weapon."Don't be foolish," commanded the burly man in charge. "Hands on heads now, all of you." The guards were herded to the front of the room. Mr. Olson launched an indignant protest, and was quickly gagged with a sock in mouth. Inelegant but effective. The guards were relieved of the automatics in their shoulder holsters, told to lay on the floor, along with Mr. Olson, hands and feet bound with police-grade plastic cuffs, duct tape wrapped twice around heads as a gag.

The leader came along the chairs holding an open Selfridges plastic bag. "Phones, please." Mysterious Chinaman put up a fight to protect Mighty Dragon, and was clubbed to the floor with the butt of the leader's shotgun. Mrs. Ocampo began to weep; her husband put a protective arm around her shoulders. Tom studiously didn't recognize Ow.

"Right now, you lot. Stay in your seats while we tie you up. Good behavior and you won't be harmed."

Tom glanced at Rosemary. She stared straight ahead, the perfect frightened victim. When everyone was tightly secured, each chair was picked up by two of the robbers and moved yards from the others, then gently tipped on its back.

"Comfy?" asked Ow. He picked up Fortune's Brick in its protective container. "Bye."

CHAPTER 12

HEIST

An hour later the outside guards became uneasy. The auction should be over. One guard stepped inside to check. The guards on the interior door were gone. The man tapped on the door. He heard muffled sounds and peeked in through a cautious crack. The room appeared empty. Then he saw on the floor Mr. Ocampo bound to his chair. He shouted to the other guard and stepped into the room, gun drawn.

A flurry as people were untied, duct tape unceremoniously ripped off, walkie-talkie chatter to the front gate, orders given to search the property. The Russian gruffly announced he was leaving immediately. Mysterious Chinaman, a patch of blood over his right eye where he had been clubbed, listened intently to Mighty Dragon. He informed Mr. Olson they were never at the auction, and followed the Russian out. Mr. Ocampo made it clear that any publicity would be a threat to his security. Rupa seemed more amused than upset: "Perhaps foul, but no harm. Nothing lost."

"Why aren't you notifying the police?" Tom demanded of Mr. Olson.

"Why?" Mr. Olson asked, a bit huffily. "Was anything stolen from you? Were you assaulted? Tregothnan Estate will not appreciate the bad publicity. It would affect the other businesses, which depend on visitors and a sterling reputation. The news of thugs running around in the woods would not be helpful. The estate rented the house, and provided my service to a third party. That party provided the security. If the security failed, that's their problem. The decision to pursue the matter is up to them."

"Who is that?"

"I'm not at liberty to say."

Tom huffed and puffed a bit more for the record that, as an innocent, he wanted the police called in; then, with a show of reluctance, followed Rosemary and Rupa to the Mini.

"Should we stay overnight in Truro, in case there are developments?" Rupa asked.

Tom was anxious to return to London. Rosemary agreed to the long night drive. "If you don't mind?" she asked Rupa. "I'd feel much safer."

Pre-dawn lit St. Paul's dome as they drove Rupa to her hotel. "Sorry that was such a dog's breakfast," Tom said, as he helped her out of the car. "Will we see you again?"

Rupa, groggy from her restless sleep in the back seat, said, yes, perhaps. Her plans were a bit in the air now. But she would contact Sandra before she left the city.

Alone in the car with Rosemary, Tom said, "That went well, wouldn't you agree?"

"Now what?"

"Tomorrow we go to Hong Chen. Right now, a few hours sleep, then meet with your brother."

"The meeting is set for seven tonight."

"How reasonable will Ow be?"

"Not very. But we're family. Still, you'll have to make him an offer."

Ow, feeling very satisfied, even festive, enjoyed his morning cup of coffee in his secret office. The heist had gone dazzlingly well, a profitable bit of fun, worth three million at least on the black market, if the bidding was a good indication. Given a proper rest time, he'd find a way to let word leak out in his community. That would stop Bogside John and his boastful mouth.

A discreet knock on the door brought disturbing news. "Aliens have been spotted on our corners," reported one of Ow's men.

"What are they doing?"

"Seems like the drug trade."

Ow barred drugs and prostitution from his territory. Not only did they degrade people—he felt protective of the people in his fiefdom—they invited the wrong kind of criminal and too-intense police attention.

"Know who they are?"

"Bogside John's boys, I'd think, given the street rumors."

"Tonight then. Have a squad ready." Ow returned to his coffee and checked the sports results on his computer.

Tom and Rosemary, refreshed with sleep, arrived at the Cock & Spur on time. Ow sat alone in a back booth. "Glad you're safe," Rosemary said, with a big smile.

"Masterful, wasn't it. One of my best pieces." Not a boast, no high five or grin of accomplishment. Just a statement of fact, a job well done by a pro.

"How did you do it? Suddenly there; suddenly gone."

"You want to know?"

Rosemary had always studiously ignored Ow's business, but she heard his need for praise, an acknowledgment of his skill in planning and execution. "Yes, of course, Howard. That was the best live theater I've ever seen."

Ow leaned back in the booth and allowed a smile. "The best theater is life. More authentic and convincing that way." His smile widened into a grin. "We had a good time staging it."

"Don't leave out any details, Howard." Rosemary reached across the table and took his hand. "This time I want to be completely with you."

"A round of pints." Ow signaled the barkeep.

With the full glasses on the table, Ow said, "Full confidence, right? Not a word outside of class." He gave Tom a hard stare, then told the story of the tea heist.

"The day before, me and the crew looked at the maps and saw the possibility. We loaded up the big van and enjoyed the ride, like taking a holiday trip, you know. High spirits, rowdy football songs, bad jokes, big plans for the money we'd earn. Be like taking candy from a baby. Laughing all the way to the bank.

"Me and Mike took the garden tour, seeing how I like plants. They've got some great stuff there, things I'd never seen. Tempting to go back one day and collect rare plantings for my patch—under the light of the moon, you understand."

Ow gave his sister an Evil Villain leer and wagged his eyebrows. She laughed, happy her brother was having a good time. Rosemary felt a surge of love for him that brought a tear to her eye.

"Two mates went on a wander to find a way through the woods to the river. They're the ones who found the guesthouse. Saw guys unloading a case of booze and piling in fancy chairs. 'Having a party, then?' they asked. 'Somewhere, but not here,' one of the blokes told them. 'This is for some business meeting tomorrow.'

"So I'm thinking, there are two possibilities. That great stone lump of the main house, or the secluded little place tucked away. The owner's family lives in that fake palace. Must be a bitch to heat. Imagine what it takes just to dust the place down. A staff of hundreds. So probably people at all times, doing the upstairs/downstairs, secret passages so the lords and ladies won't see the minions, maids and butlers popping up in the most unexpected places.

"On the other hand, if you want some privacy, if you're doing dodgy and need to control the scene, the little house in the woods was perfect."

"How did you avoid the security?" Tom grudgingly admired how Ow had pulled off the heist. Might be tricky wrestling the tea back from such a pro. He was trained as an academic; Ow was self-taught to break bones and laws. No way he could outmuscle Ow. He could, however, outthink him.

"Know one's onions," Ow replied.

Rosemary answered Tom's silent query of a knitted brow. "To be well versed. Know what you're doing."

Ow took a long pull of beer to build the drama and keep Tom waiting. "We got there before the toy soldiers. This was a military operation. People could be shooting at us, trying to kill us. And more of them than us. So we had to be smart." Ow tapped his temple with a thick forefinger. "Think like guerrilla fighters, use the land and time and the assumptions of the enemy."

"We did that as kids, didn't we, Howard, with our Robin Hood and Sheriff of Nottingham games, sword fighting and chasing about?" Rosemary laughed at the memories of her and Howard, a gang of two against the rich and powerful. "We were taking revenge on injustice."

"Still are, luv." Ow winked at her.

She put thumb and forefinger next to her empty eye socket and made little pinching moves, a finger-puppet wink. "No regrets, ever."

Tom saw a ripple of tenderness tidal across Rosemary's face. He envied Ow.

Ow cleared his throat. "So me and the boys left Tregothnan before closing time and drove down to a quiet spot on River Fal that we'd sussed out before, close but not too close to Truro. Big bushes to hide the van away from prying eyes. We gobbled sandwiches, changed clothes, loaded up our gear in backpacks—the guns and more food, water bottles and piss bottles, and put the scull in the river."

"The scull?" asked Tom, puzzled.

"Howard and his mates are a competitive rowing team," explained Rosemary. "Champions, isn't that right, Howard? Even beat the university boats, right, my dear?"

"Robin Hoods of the River stealing the pride and prizes from the rich."

"What did you do with a scull?" asked Tom.

"Took it for a row, of course. Up River Fal to where the Truro River joined in, then a quick left up that little stream to where we spotted the tree my boys had marked on their exploration earlier in the afternoon. We hauled the scull out and hid it in the bushes, then hiked through the woods following the markers the boys had tied to trees up to Tregothnan. We waited until dark, then broke into the little house, discreet like so no one would notice. The place had already been swept for security. We settled into the upstairs room and waited for nearly twenty hours. Takes discipline to be still and do nothing for twenty hours. Me and my mates meditate daily as part of our training to be successful crooks. A calm mind is more important than a loaded gun."

"I told you Howard was smart," Rosemary reminded Tom. "He could be a legit businessman, or a bishop, if he had the mind to."

"Thank you, luv." Ow bowed his head to his sister. "I appreciate your confidence."

"You mean you were in the house before we arrived?"

"Rested and ready," Ow confirmed. "We listened through the ceiling with a stethoscope to you lot playing Bidder's War. At five million, I'd heard enough. Time for me and the crew to sneak down the stairs, surprise the two guards outside the auction room door, and you know the rest."

"But where did you go with Fortune's Brick?"

"Back the way we came. Out the window, through the trees, taking the markers with us, to the scull. A fast row to the van, load up, and away before you were discovered resting in your chair, as it were. No trace, no tire tracks, no description for the police to stop at a roadblock."

"And you have Fortune's Brick with you?"

Ow looked offended at Tom's doubt of his trustworthiness. Rosemary jumped to smooth the waters before Ow took real offense. "Of course he does. He gave his word."

"And you," Ow turned to Tom. "Are you a man of your word?"

"I'll bring sugar in exchange for your tea, as agreed."

"The bidding was headed for six million before my intervention. How much sugar?"

"A fair share when the deal is done."

"Bit like promising fair weather when the clouds clear. Weather is never reliable."

"I am," Tom said, with a fierce stare of conviction at Ow.

"We'll do you right; you know that, Howard," Rosemary assured.

"When?"

"In a couple days at the latest," Tom promised. "But I need Fortune's Brick to make the deal work." He held his breath in anticipation. What guarantee would Ow demand? What guarantee could Tom promise?

Ow held Tom in a long assessment. "Your word, Rosie?"

"Absolutely." She had no idea of Tom's intention, but in for a penny, in for a pound.

Ow reached for the box at his feet and set Fortune's Brick in its protective glass cube on the table. "On your word. Honor among thieves. Or," he leaned across the table to Tom, "I'll cut your focking throat." The threat was all the more menacing because Ow spoke as dispassionately as if ordering another pint.

After Tom and Rosemary left, Ow called his gang together for an intelligence briefing. He laid out a detailed map of Peckham and they gathered around. "Here, here, here," Ow pointed as he scanned the street map to work out his tactics. "What time do Bogside John's men set up shop?"

"They wait until dark. I imagine business is going now."

"Right, then. We'll give them a message—no business allowed here." Ow looked to his street leaders. "All in on this one. Here's what we do."

For the next twenty minutes Ow drew lines and arrows on the map, giving assignments. "No one escapes without a sound thrashing," he instructed. "But no killing. I want them to limp back to BJ beaten and bloody."

Ow and his squad took the most public corner, where he'd be seen driving out the filth. Four men took up their positions to block escape routes at either end of the street. Ow sat in a car watching the two interlopers, one taking orders and the other slipping away to fetch the product. He got out of the car. Halfway across the street he sprinted, catching BJ's boys' attention. A moment's hesitation before the two realized the threat, then they ran in opposite directions. Ow whacked the closest one on the knee with his sap fitted with a flex handle, to give maximum damage. The man went down with a howl. Ow's men, running up the street, swarmed over the other man, ants on a breadcrumb. The beatings were methodical, a public performance meant to be witnessed and clearly understood: You do business with these types, and you'll get some of the same.

Ow stood in the middle of the street to be seen by passersby. Most ducked their heads and hurried on, a tribute to his authority.

CHAPTER 13

DOUBLE-CROSS

B ack at Rosemary's place, Tom searched the Internet for how to make a brick of tea.

Rosemary rummaged around the kitchen for a big pot. "Do we use tea bags or the tea leaves I purchased from Sandra?"

Tom scanned the instructions. "Either powdered tea or tea leaves have been used since the Ming Dynasty, according to this article. How do we get powdered tea?"

"Cut open tea bags."

"Use the leaves. Seems more authentic. Says to steam the tea leaves. We'll need a binding agent." He read aloud, "'Traditionally, manure or blood was used to give the brick stiffness and durability for transportation on camels or horses.'"

"You could open a vein."

"Or we could use eggs."

Tom propped Fortune's Brick up on the kitchen table—solid and hard as a dark slab of stone—to better see the details. He compared the embossed chrysanthemum to the photo of the sketch he had taken from Hong Chen's book. The Chinese characters of the emperor's name matched. Across the top were the same five stars. "Looks like the real thing."

If it were genuine—worth at least six million, maybe more if the bidding had continued—somebody would certainly want it back. Who was behind the auction of Fortune's Brick? That mystery made the unknown person all the more dangerous. Tom wouldn't know where to look to see the threat coming.

He set the tea press Rosemary had borrowed from Sandra next to Fortune's Brick. The images on the lid appeared to match perfectly the embossed tea brick. Had this Fortune's Brick been manufactured at Tregothnan? Or had the real brick of tea been transported in the press accompanying the Wardian Case?

Rosemary set a rice steamer on the kitchen counter. "How much tea should we use?"

"I have no idea. Better too much than too little."

Tom kept reading the instructions. "'Wring water out of the tea before putting it in the press.' Like what? Use a rolling pin?"

"A towel," replied Rosemary, filling the steamer with water. "Twist the tea tight in a towel."

"Says sixty pounds of pressure will be needed to compress the tea into form. How do we do that?" The tea press had no screw mechanism to force the lid down on the tea. "Weights?" Tom continued reading. "'Newly formed tea bricks were then left to cure, dry, and age prior to being sold or traded.'" He paused at the new problem. "We have to present the brick to Hong Chen tomorrow, if we're going to satisfy Ow."

"Overnight in the oven at low temperature," said Rosemary.

"Low and slow, like barbeque. Easy peasy."

Then the awkward question of "overnight." The memory of the impromptu living room dance was the elephant in the room. An "opportunity for happiness" pinballed around Tom's mind, hitting all the flashing lights and ringing bells of testosterone whoops. This was the natural moment, right? They had an attraction to each other. They had had full-frontal contact—that slam hug.

Rosemary was also aware of the opportunity—the giveaway in the sway of her shoulders as she half turned away, half presented her breasts to him. She touched her hair.

He smiled a reassuring smile, not a leer, but he didn't step forward to offer an embrace. He sensed somewhere deep in his emotional knowing that he'd be crossing a line—a flash of Aimee. What would his Hero do? Tom shuffled his feet, not moving forward or backward.

Rosemary thought, Why not? She remembered her run down the living room at Tom and the launch into the air with no thought about the landing, a test run, a lick on a boiled sweet of fear. She rocked forward on the balls of her feet and then rocked back on her heels. Tom had always hid information and intent. She'd wait for his reveal.

She suggested they check on the tea in the oven throughout the night, so it didn't burn. They'd take four-hour shifts. Tom could do his watch from the sofa. She'd bring him pillows and blankets.

Tom nodded his agreement—relieved and irritated at himself. What the hell? A hero would have taken bold action. Made the move. But a move to what?

Once during the night Tom thought about easing into Rosemary's room. He sensed she had tightrope-walked the line. Perhaps it wouldn't take much for her to fall onto his side. A little charm, a soft touch. A push of arrogance to overcome her reluctance. The risk was too great. Either way he'd lose by taking such a cheap shot.

In the morning they met over orange juice and toast. The baked tea brick looked passable.

Rosemary sniffed. "Smells like roasted tea."

"Feels solid." Tom hefted it from hand to hand.

He phoned Hong Chen. "Tonight, *grandfather*. We'll be there at eight for the tea ceremony."

When Tom and Rosemary arrived, Hong Chen, dressed in court robes of a high Manchu official, received them in the sitting room. The samurai sword, bare blade, lay on the desk. Tom set the bulletproof glass box from the auction on the desk and removed the top. Very carefully, he lifted out Fortune's Brick.

Hong Chen bowed from the waist, hands clasped before his heart. "I honor the emperor's seal of authority." He bent lower over the brick, nose nearly to the surface.

A knock came on the door. Hong Chen called out in Mandarin "Come in." Mighty Dragon and his bodyguard, with a square of gauze taped over his right eye, entered. Quiet Killer and Ling, out of the hospital, acknowledged each other with a murderous stare.

"Ah, Weiwu Long, honored guest." Hong Chen didn't take his eyes off Fortune's Brick. "I expected you."

Mighty Dragon strode to the desk as if he owned the room. Hong Chen knew Mighty Dragon would make the connection at the auction of Tom to him—and walk into his trap.

Rosemary, totally surprised to see the Chinese men from the auction, threw Tom a look of confusion. He blinked away his befuddlement: What the hell was Mighty Dragon doing here?

Mighty Dragon spoke rapid guttural Han. "I knew you'd have it—"

Hong Chen interrupted. "Han is so ugly, a peasant's language. Here we speak only English or Mandarin, a language beyond your class." He knew Mighty Dragon spoke English, learned as a business necessity, but was uncomfortable in the language so avoided using it. To force Mighty Dragon to think in English would hinder him, giving Hong Chen an advantage.

Mighty Dragon replied, in surprisingly fluent English, although with a thick accent, "I drove you out of China and now I will destroy your delusion of grandeur about 'restoring' China. You arranged for the emperor's tea to be stolen at the auction. You want to hoard it for yourself. China's sacred values, the precious traditions, all that is a smoke screen."

"You are a FUCKER of China," Hong Chen roared at Mighty Dragon. "You and your kind have made a tart of our beloved. You sell her soul for fancy buildings that have not one brick of Chinese tradition to honor our ancestors. You create traffic jams of shiny objects and ignore the rituals of the temples." He literally shook with rage as he held up Fortune's Brick, as if Moses raising the Ten Commandments on high. "This is our scepter, the symbol of authority of the righteous China, the China far more powerful and worthy than your wealth and political connections. We, the True China party, will prevail."

"Emperors—and empresses—ruled by the bloody sword or the poisoned cup," Mighty Dragon sneered. "They had court musicians play over the screams of their victims, the thousands who died in poverty and wars. Don't give me your sanctimonious cant about Old China glory days. You want the emperor's tea for your own glory. I will expose you as a man without honor. All those who believe in you will spit on your name."

Tom thought the two old men shouting at each other over a brick of tea was risible, until Mighty Dragon pulled a gun. Hong Chen, still holding Fortune's Brick high, snatched the sword from the desk with his free hand. Ling and Quiet Killer lunged to defend their bosses. Tom grabbed Fortune's Brick from Hong Chen's upraised hand.

Hong Chen swung the sword at Mighty Dragon's head. Mighty Dragon ducked, causing his gunshot to go wide. Tom smashed Fortune's Brick on the desk, shattering it into bits. Everyone froze. Quiet Killer pulled his boss away from the danger. Ling gently, but firmly, took the sword from Hong Chen.

Rosemary looked at Tom in horror. Now they couldn't exchange the fake brick for cash to pay off Ow.

Tom appeared completely startled with himself. His first thought, I've fucked up big time.

"Now there's nothing to fight over," he said. And wished that were true. Ow loved a bit of violence.

Hong Chen looked at the destroyed Fortune's Brick in utter dismay. His face crumpled in sorrow, as if his most beloved had died before his eyes. He bent to the desk, weeping, holding a handful of the tea to his face.

Mighty Dragon said dismissively, "Now it's just old, stale tea, like you, Hong Chen." He and Quiet Killer walked out of the room.

Hong Chen kept his face pressed into the tea until Mighty Dragon was gone. Then he raised his face to Tom. "Where is it?"

Tom feigned ignorance. "What?"

"The real Fortune's Brick."

Tom gestured to the desk, a wordless, *There, in your hands.*

Hong Chen stood straight. "You tried to cheat me. An authentic old brick of tea was made from powdered tea to better carve out details of the emperor's name. This—" Hong Chen flung a handful of tea at Tom—"is made from pressed leaves. You stole Fortune's Brick and made a fake. Where is the real emperor's tea?"

"I'm not going to tell you," Tom calmly replied.

"You'll not betray me." Hong Chen crabbed around the desk on his crippled legs to grab Tom.

Tom watched his grandfather coming closer with slow painful steps, then took three steps back so Hong Chen nearly fell the final step to reach Tom. Tom instinctively grabbed him by the elbows so he wouldn't hit the floor. Tom bent as if to kiss Hong Chen on the cheek and whispered in his ear, "Call your daughter and apologize to her. Ask for her forgiveness and seek reconciliation."

To Rosemary, it looked like grandson and grandfather had reached a tender rapprochement; she couldn't feel Hong Chen's nails digging into Tom's arms, or hear Tom hiss, "If you don't, old man, you'll never see Fortune's Brick."

Hong Chen bowed his head and said something.

Tom didn't understand him. "What?"

"I can't."

"What do you mean?"

Rosemary saw the two men touch cheek to cheek. She remembered Tom doing his awkward swan dance in her living room, and thought, *He might be worth being reckless for.* She moved to envelop them in a hug, when Hong Chen straightened and pushed Tom back.

"I can't talk with her until I've killed Mighty Dragon. Then I'll be worthy of Huihuáng di liming. That's your mother's Chinese name—Brilliant Dawn. To be worthy of her I have to first regain the family honor by taking revenge on Weiwu Long. But I've failed. That's why I don't know how to talk to my daughter."

Tom knew the powerful tug of revenge—that's why he had agreed to search for Fortune's Brick, to get close enough to his grandfather to stab him in the back. To bring him to his knees. To make him beg his daughter for forgiveness.

"The whole idea of revenge and punishment is a childish daydream." Tom had read the quote from George Orwell after Aimee had gutted him. He had thought, *I don't give a fuck. Call me childish.* Now, seeing the sorrow in his grandfather's face, Tom realized that revenge was an act of impotency, a weapon of the powerless. An act sourced by bitter desire, a crude retaliation, a false crown of justice. Lovemaking to cause injury.

Tom turned and walked out of the room. Rosemary saw Hong Chen sag. Ling stepped forward to catch the old man. Rosemary followed Tom out to the car. They sat without speaking, Tom slumped in the passenger seat, Rosemary with hands on the steering wheel.

"What a cock-up," she said, not as an accusation but as a statement of fact. "Now what do we do?"

Tom shrugged, a man standing in the rubble of his house with no idea how to find shelter. "I don't know. Your thug brother expects us to pay him a goodly sum for his assistance. My grandfather will try to kill Mighty Dragon, and soon, before he leaves London. He has no choice if he's ever to see his daughter again. And we have Fortune's Brick hidden in your linen closet."

"Simple," she replied. "Go back to Hong Chen with the real Fortune's Brick. Exchange it for a chunk of money, as planned, to pay off Ow. Not our business if Hong Chen and Mighty Dragon kill each other."

She reached to touch him. He looked out the side window, either not noticing or ignoring her gesture of caring. She took her hand back and waited for him to say something.

That sounded like a reasonable solution, Tom agreed to himself. He'd have his grandfather's blessing and inherit his money. If Hong Chen needed to go to war with Mighty Dragon, that was his decision, a obstacle between himself and his daughter.

But Tom knew he wouldn't be reasonable. He wanted to feast on the bitter desire of revenge. He wanted to deny his grandfather to avenge his mother. His seeming collaboration to get Fortune's Brick had always carried the addendum of collusion, the intent to deceive and cheat Hong Chen. He could still outfox Hong Chen, and outthink Ow.

Tom turned to Rosemary. "You know what mystery and magic have in common? Both show what is not. Mystery conceals what is really happening. Magic doesn't reveal the reality of the trick. They both create illusions."

Rosemary didn't know where Tom was leading, so she waited patiently.

Tom didn't follow up.

"You know any magic tricks?" she asked.

"As a kid I could do the three cups and a bean trick. You know, put the bean under a cup, move the cups around, tell the mark to guess which cup hides the bean. Then reveal that the bean was under no cup. It had disappeared."

If that was Tom's only plan, an amateur trick, Rosemary knew they'd need more to appease Ow. She turned on the car's Bluetooth and hit speed dial. Ow answered on the third buzz. "Howard, we need to talk— now." She listened. "Right, the Cock & Spur. On our way." She put the car in gear and charged down the street. "You be on your best behavior with Howard. He has no tolerance for mystery and no belief in magic."

How do I turn Fortune's Brick into a disappearing bean? Tom thought.

CHAPTER 14

TRAP

The Cock & Spur appeared closed—no lights, no business—when they arrived. As Rosemary slowed to find a parking space, a man stepped from the shadows and motioned her into the alley behind the pub. Another man guided her to a spot. "Evening, ma'am. Ow's waiting for you." He escorted Rosemary and Tom through the rear entrance normally used for beer delivery and down a corridor to a closed door. Three knocks. Pause. Two knocks. The man smiled— "I do that just for effect"—and opened the door.

The secret office was surprisingly well appointed, with a deep burgundy leather tufted sofa fronted by two club chairs and hunting prints on the wall. Ow sat across the room at a large desk, working on a computer with a seventeen-inch screen. "One moment, luv. Checking on the British economic catastrophe and America's dive into one-man rule. Volatile markets always present opportunities."

Rosemary glanced around the room. "Hunting prints, Howard?"

"A reminder of whom I'm after, and it's not the fox."

Tom was impressed not so much with the hidden office but with Ow's dishonesty by omission; the thug had given no hint of being a competent businessman.

Rosemary walked over to a four-by-five-foot table of violets along one wall. "I always thought you kept a pot or two but never imagined anything this ambitious."

"It's an easel," Ow replied.

"Looks like a flower bed to me."

"You're not looking at it correctly. Stand back about five feet."

Rosemary took two steps back without taking her eyes off the flowers. The seemingly random jumble of lavenders, blues, pinks, reds, and whites became patterns. "Is that a lightning bolt?"

"No, it's David Bowie's face, at least part of it."

Rosemary looked more intently at the patterns of dots, each a violet. She saw the eye, then the eye socket intersected by the jagged blue-red-lavender bolt. She automatically put a finger to her empty eye socket.

"The full face is a wall mural in Brixton. Jimmy C did it as a shrine to Bowie."

"I want one." Rosemary's fingers tapped from the middle of her forehead across the eye socket to mid-cheek, as if to imprint memory. "Brilliant, just brilliant, Howard."

Ow came to stand next to her. "I studied the French Impressionists and pointillism to see how they broke the spectrum of light into dots of colors. The subtle color gradations in flowers lend themselves very well to the technique."

Rosemary heard an Ow she never suspected. Gone was the Cockney cheek. This uneducated street boy knew big words. He had a real understanding and appreciation of art.

"I experimented with Cubism," Ow continued, "but found the disjointed sharp edges the antithesis of flowers, the exception being Georges Braque. The harmony and balance of his compositions easily translate to floral arrangement. I tried Picasso, but who wants a woman in pieces—nose jutting in one direction, breasts mere objects in space."

Rosemary regarded her brother in wonderment. "You clever boy." *And here*, she thought, *I viewed myself as superior with my education, my sensibilities of beauty. And this Ow was standing there all the time, waiting to be seen.*

Ow, warming to his subject, launched into a tutorial on how violets don't like bright direct sunlight, but without enough light they won't bloom. "So fluorescent tubes must be twelve and eighteen inches above the plants." Ow motioned to the light rack. "And proper feeding is very important, equal amounts of nitrogen, phosphorus, and potassium. Must take care not to overwater. The soil should be thirty to fifty percent coarse vermiculite and/or perlite."

Too much information, Tom thought as he joined them. *Like Hong Chen and his tea. Or Rosemary and her buildings.* Then his own lightning bolt: Ow was a cultivator of African violets as Hong Chen was a lover of tea. What did that tell him about Ow's character? Obsessive perhaps, and obsession can be a weakness as well as a strength. It gives a focal point, the discipline of strength—and it can narrow vision so one won't see the blindsided shot coming.

"I'm particularly proud of the frame," Ow said, pointing to the edging. "The Delft, with its wavy-edged blooms of blue-lavender above dark slightly furry leaves, is my favorite."

"And those?" asked Tom, gesturing to potted flowers with reddish/purple bell shaped blossoms.

"*Sinningia specioso*, more commonly known as gloxinia, reputed to be the plant of love at first sight. Best close your eyes. The person you first see after looking at the gloxinia is the person you'll fall in love with. Close your eyes, seriously." Tom closed his eyes to humor Ow. "Now, Rosie and I will stand one on your right and the other on your left. You choose which direction to look."

There is always a third choice. That was one of Tom's maxims. The dictate of right or wrong can be muted, or defied by redefinition, a shading of understanding, the skill of obstructionism, the wit of being obstinate. He spun rapidly—right foot rooted, left propelling—until he was so dizzy he staggered. Then he opened his eyes.

"Everything is moving," he said, "like a herd of zebras. I don't know which one to shoot." Steadying himself, he stood perfectly still and looked at Ow on his right. "What do you think," he asked, turning to Rosemary, "about how to make a good choice?"

Rosemary knew that Ow's intent was to take the mickey out on Tom. Tom's cheeky response ran the risk of affronting her brother. *That could get him a poke in the eye*, she thought, then excused herself for making the pun. She took the question personally: How do I make a good choice for myself? Was that what Tom was asking of himself?

Before Ow could take umbrage, Rosemary quickly moved to a large flowering bush. "And this?"

"*Paeonia suffruticosa*, the Moutan peony, first imported from China," Ow answered.

Ow was cultivating a Chinese plant perhaps introduced to England by Robert Fortune! Tom could hardly believe what he had heard. This had to be a ley line of karma, a sign of good fortune for his enterprise. "The Moutan peony was very important in Chinese politics and culture," Ow continued. "It was named the national flower during the Qing Dynasty. It's related to the chrysanthemum."

The chrysanthemum was the Qing emperors' symbol. Robert Fortune stole a Qing emperor's tea. "Can you make tea from the flower?" Tom asked. "The Chinese use chrysanthemum tea to prevent sore throats and reduce fever."

"I don't know about tea, but the skin of the *Paeonia suffruticosa* root is used in Chinese medicine." Ow cupped a hand around the ball blossom. "The Moutan peony can be quite a challenge to cultivate. It takes patience and very focused love," he said, as if to himself. "It's slow to grow and is very fragile. Nearly every type of weather is a threat to its survival." Ow caressed the broad petals, more like a rose than a chrysanthemum. "The flower, when it blooms, lasts only a short time."

Rosemary sensed melancholy in Ow she had never suspected, except when he had told her about Gilly.

"You are a clever sod, dear brother," said Rosemary as she settled on the sofa. "But I always knew that."

Ow nodded to her acknowledgment and walked to the liquor cabinet. "Drink? Got a recent shipment of excellent scotch."

Tom and Rosemary declined, but Ow poured one and joined them on the sofa. "You got something for me?"

"We got a wrinkle." Rosemary explained that a bidder from the auction had unexpectedly shown up as the deal was going down.

"Which one?" asked Ow.

"The Chinaman. Somehow he got onto the game. He and his bodyguard barged into our meeting with the mark. He and our man got in a pissing match over the tea and tried to kill each other. We grabbed the tea and ran." Rosemary was surprised how glibly she lied to her brother, but felt satisfied—for the first time since she joined the Fortune's Brick folly, for the first time since Howard disfigured her, she felt the power to stake her own claim.

"Who were you selling to?"

"Privileged information," Tom injected.

"Not between partners." Ow sounded so reasonable that Tom almost believed his magnanimity of equal partners.

"Personal privileged information."

Ow looked at his sister. "This is on the up and up? Your assurance. Word given."

Rosemary held his challenging look, steady and calm as she had always been—then glanced down before Ow could doubt her. She had never lied to him before. Maybe she did it to assure him that Fortune's Brick was safe in her possession, therefore within his reach. Yes, she decided, I'll believe that, for now.

"We need to wait a couple days, a cooling down period. Then we'll complete the deal. Family honor." Rosemary laid her hand over her heart.

Ow nodded. "Two days. I'll put champagne on ice for the celebration."

"Nice catch," Tom told Rosemary as they drove back to central London. "About Fortune's Brick."

Why had she lied to Ow? Not exactly lied. Told the bones of truth, but omitted pesky details.

Tom knew from personal experience never to trust a liar; he didn't trust himself. Her lie raised the conundrum: What was she omitting from her presentation of herself to him? And the equally unavoidable discomfort: What was he not revealing? *This is not the time to delve into that mystery.* The immediate question was, What to do with Fortune's Brick?

"We have to get rid of Fortune's Brick," he announced.

No we don't. The thought surprised Rosemary. Fortune's Brick was like an outsized window in an otherwise orderly progression of windows. It disrupted the order of her order. Disruption of order introduces instability. Her entire life was built of shielding herself from instability. Her respected, and financially secure, professional life protected her from the poverty. Embracing her empty eye protected her from the stigma of being defective. Fortune's Brick was an opportunity, although she admitted, as she eased to a traffic stop, she didn't know what it was an opportunity for.

She felt oddly calm, with her toes curled over the edge of a chasm she'd ordinarily back away from in fear.

"Fortune's Brick is dangerous for us," Tom explained. "Ow wants it as his pot of gold. Hong Chen wants it as a magic wand to unlock a fantasy of being a national savior for a China that doesn't exist. Whoever set up the auction wants that tea back to recoup the millions lost with the theft. If they have to trample over us, kill us, then that's part of doing business."

"Howard wouldn't do that," Rosemary protested.

"It's his business model."

"Would your grandfather kill you over some tea?"

"He approached me on false pretense. He needs Fortune's Brick in order to show he is still a player. My safety is not his concern."

Hong Chen used me in his elaborate scheme to lure Mighty Dragon out of China. But that didn't feel right. Unnecessarily complicated.

So who was the most dangerous? Ow was essentially a businessman; businessmen did deals. Hong Chen was a bitter old man bent on revenge; rage blinded his rationality. The person behind the auction had the most to lose.

"Let's go to your place," Tom said.

Rosemary didn't ask, What for? She didn't want a definitive answer that might limit possibility. She turned her chin so Tom wouldn't see her sly smile: *What the hell are you about, girl? Don't answer that, not now.*

When they arrived, Tom hurried past her to fetch Fortune's Brick from its linen closet hiding place.

"If anyone comes looking for this, let them search. You don't know where the tea is. Never did. No one can prove otherwise."

"Except Howard."

"Yes, but he's our partner—and your brother. No reason for you to fear him, right?"

Rosemary agreed with a silent nod. "What are you going to do with it?"

"I never had Fortune's Brick, either. Don't know where it is, never did."

"Hong Chen doesn't believe that."

"No, but what's he going to do about it?"

Tom left the apartment on foot with Fortune's Brick tucked in his waistband out of sight. He didn't think Rosemary's place was under observation by Ow or Hong Chen or an unknown. Nevertheless, why take the chance; he could avoid detection, and drop a tail, by flitting from shadow to shadow, taking shortcuts where a car couldn't go. He wouldn't go back to his bedsit, not until after he got rid of Fortune's Brick in the morning.

Rosemary's place was not under surveillance because Ling had followed Tom and her only to the Cock & Spur. When he phoned Hong Chen to report, Hong Chen ordered him to return. *Why had Tom and Rosemary twice visited that pub? Is that where Tom had hidden the real Fortune's Brick? We'll look later,* Hong Chen decided, *but right now I need to find—and kill—Mighty Dragon before he leaves London.*

Hong Chen had the butler bring him his finest tea leaves—those reserved to induce a deep state of calm spirit and a lively mind—and the pot made by a monk in 1850 for the emperor's coronation. *What was the one thing his nemesis couldn't resist?* Hong Chen took a sip of the earthy tea and let the taste linger in his mouth. He never fully understood the mystical effect tea induced in him. Spiritual atavism, a connection to an ancestor—possibly a Manchu emperor? Is that where his vision of return to a glorious China, a pure China, came from? Hong Chen thought that most likely.

What was Mighty Dragon's weak spot? His ego. What appeals to his ego? Humiliating me.

Hong Chen refreshed his tea as he assessed the situation. Mighty Dragon came to London to seize Fortune's Brick. Depriving me of the emblem of China's soul would vanquish me once and for all. Mighty Dragon had Geoffrey Milner murdered to show how weak I was even on my home turf. He had failed in obtaining Fortune's Brick so he doesn't have that bragging right. But he had escaped from my trap. I need for him to come back into my lair. For that he must believe that I have Fortune's Brick. Two things must be done: Spread the word in China that Might Dragon has been tricked, and I still have Fortune's Brick; and get the prize from my grandson.

When Ling checked in, Hong Chen invited him to share a cup. "We stand at the crossroads of my destiny." Hong Chen poured the tea in a delicate arc from pot to cups, the gesture of inclusiveness meant to put Ling at ease. "And you, loyal Ling, will share the glory of that fate."

Ling accepted the offered cup as if acquiescing to his execution. Great risks would be demanded for the reward of being brought into his boss's confidence. He had been at Hong Chen's side following the near-fatal gun battle with Mighty Dragon's gang that drove Hong Chen into exile. A showdown in London would be to the death.

"Have you kept up your skills?" Hong Chen asked.

"I am a regular at the firing range."

"We must be more clever than a dumb bullet." Hong Chen set down his teacup, as did Ling in prelude to receiving his marching orders. "Fortune's Brick will be our bullet."

"But," Ling ventured, "Mighty Dragon thinks Fortune's Brick has been destroyed. He saw it shattered on your desk with his own eyes."

"He will realize that he fell into my trap. He will strike back. And then you can have your revenge on Quiet Killer—as I will have mine on Mighty Dragon."

Ling bowed his head in acceptance of his reward. As young men, Ling and Quiet Killer were street toughs in

Chongqing, a city notorious for its organized crime and corruption, reputed—with cause—as China's most dangerous city. As ambitious rivals, they competed as "comers" in the gang world.

When Ling added marital arts to his skill set, Quiet Killer also became a black belt. Quiet Killer's choice of weapon was the knife, an intimate, up close way of killing. Ling became competent with a stiletto. They never directly confronted each other, until Ling joined Hong Chen's organization and Mighty Dragon recruited Quiet Killer.

Chongqing was Hong Chen and Mighty Dragon's battleground; Ling and Quiet Killer were their street generals.

Mighty Dragon had become wealthy and powerfully connected through his corporation, which rigged contracts during the construction of the Three Gorges Dam. Hong Chen founded, or bought up, construction companies in direct competition with Mighty Dragon. The rivalry heated up to sabotage of equipment, arson of warehouses, and assaults on employees. Corporate gun battles were disguised as street-gang warfare. Mighty Dragon had had enough when his headquarters was firebombed.

Ling heard through the grapevine that Mighty Dragon had ordered Hong Chen's execution.

"Have you read *The Art of War*," Hong Chen asked when Ling told of the assassination plan. "The great General Sun Tzu's axioms is to make the enemy believe you are weak. Lure him into false confidence and his troops into an ambush and crush them. Let Mighty

Dragon believe we are running and hiding in fear. We will retreat to the hunting lodge."

The lodge, a log structure twenty miles from the city, with only one road access through the dense woods, would appear unprotected. Vulnerable to attack. Ling designed the ambush. Let Mighty Dragon's forces come down the road. Then open fire from within the hunting lodge. Mighty Dragon's men, led by Quiet Killer, would scramble off the road into the woods, where Ling's forces waited.

The strategy might have worked, but Mighty Dragon came with a superior force armed with battlefield-grade machine guns, grenade launchers, night-vision goggles, and flamethrowers. The battle was a total rout—grenades and flamethrowers the deciding factors. Ling and Hong Chen escaped from the burning lodge by waeving through the dense forest on a motorcycle.

Back in Chongqing, Ling, deeply ashamed, offered to kill himself for having failed his master. Hong Chen told him not to be such a coward. They must prepare for the next battle, but first they had to save their skins. That night Hong Chen and Ling flew, without luggage, from Chongqing to Hong Kong, and on to London.

Now, years later, the final battle was on. Hong Chen poured the last of the tea. "Let your heart inspire you." He lifted his cup to Ling in a toast. "Now rest. We have a busy time ahead."

Alone after Ling left the library, Hong Chen called his informant in China. "Any whispers about Fortune's Brick?"

"Qiangjie zhe."

That made sense. "The Looter" was capable of having Fortune's Brick, or hosting an elaborate scam to sell a fake. He was the notorious head of a syndicate that specialized in stolen archeological treasures obtained by looting imperial tombs. But to stage the Fortune's Brick auction in China would be too risky. Besides, holding the auction outside of China would attract rich non-Chinese bidders to drive up the price. Tregothnan was a perfect front for him. Veneer of British upper class to set the tone, but plebian enough to rent out rooms. Isolated so he could provide security using local talent.

Hong Chen was relieved to hear the name. He didn't know The Looter, but he knew how to deal with criminal businessmen. He'd been doing so all his life.

"What's the whisper?"

"The man wants his tea or his money. Word is he has a contract with London connections to solve his problem."

"And Mighty Dragon?"

"No sign of him."

That was good, meant he must still be in London. "Put word on the wind to Mighty Dragon's people. I have the real Fortune's Brick. Mighty Dragon has been made the fool."

After leaving Rosemary's, Tom rode the Tube, frequently switching trains, until the system closed down at midnight. No one followed him—he was sure—but nevertheless paranoia kept him to dark streets, occasionally resting in doorways' deep shadows to listen intently for footsteps. Around two A.M., foot sore, he muttered, "This is stupid. Get a bed." He drifted to his bedsit's neighborhood, slowly, cautiously circling, checking cars for watchers, crossing streets to avoid the few people approaching. He worried about damaging Fortune's Brick tucked down the front of his waistband.

He ventured to the corner from which he could see the entrance of his bedsit. The street was deserted. He stepped out. A car pulled from a parking space and flicked on it headlights. Tom dodged into a doorway's shelter. The car passed, the driver indifferent to Tom, if he saw him at all. Still … .

Tom slipped away. Coffee shops would open in a few hours. He'd find anonymity in the early morning crowd until ten, when he'd deposit Fortune's Brick.

He settled down in a hole-in-the-wall eatery to a mash-up of eggs and sausage and toast washed down with sugared tea. His cell phone buzzed. He didn't want to answer; Hong Chen would berate him for withholding Fortune's Brick. Probably threaten to shun him again. Take back the offer to make Tom his heir. Renege on the promise to reach out to Tom's mother. He waited until the fifth buzz in his pocket. Stalemate wasn't a good tactic. He needed to solve the problem of Fortune's Brick, so he answered.

Hong Chen sounded contrite as he invited Tom to afternoon tea. "Come alone. Family only, please."

After breakfast Tom deposited Fortune's Brick in a place as secure as the Tower of London. Smugly satisfied with himself, he went to see Hong Chen.

The butler showed Tom to the sitting room, where Hong Chen waited on the settee, dressed in simple black peasant clothes. He seemed diminished without his stiff silk Manchu robes with heavy gold embroidery, inconsequential, stripped of his haughty authority. "Please sit," Hong Chen said quietly.

Tom took a place one-cushion distance from his grandfather.

Hong Chen poured two cups of tea with the attitude of devoted concentration. "Tea was once reserved only for the emperor and royalty. Its benevolence spread to include the common man. We, too, must become a team." Hong Chen set a teacup before Tom.

Tom did not accept the cup, suspicious of Hong Chen's supposed transformation from haughty overlord to humble man.

Hong Chen raised his teacup with both hands and faced Tom. "It's your duty to give me Fortune's Brick." He kept his eyes downcast, his voice without demand, that of a suppliant. "Duty to your mother. To the family. By fulfilling your duty, you allow me to honor my daughter and the family. As the only son, you succeed me as head of the family. It is important that you assume the responsibility with honor."

"What would you do with Fortune's Brick?"

"Kill Mighty Dragon."

"Hit him over the head with it?" Tom joked, but wondered, in the back of his mind, if he'd be a willing accomplice to murder. Was he that person?

"Bait the trap."

"You assume I have Fortune's Brick."

"I know you have it."

"I don't have it." Tom stood and left.

CHAPTER 15

BETRAYAL

Why not retrieve Fortune's Brick and give it to Hong Chen? That would be a tidy solution. I'd inherit grandfather's money. Mother would have her father back. Hong Chen would put on his fancy costume and pretend to be an emperor. Why not? Tom asked himself.

Mighty Dragon would be just another unsolved crime, probably the victim of a mugging. The police wouldn't suspect the palace intrigue behind his murder.

Am I capable of murder? Even second-hand murder?

Well, I don't have to actually kill Mighty Dragon, Tom told himself as he walked away from Hong Chen's. *Could I do it, kill someone? I don't know. Maybe. Would I experience remorse?* That's like asking would he'd feel love by doing a kind act. Only the doing will tell. *I don't want to murder. But the appearance of collusion may be useful with Hong Chen.*

One thing Tom knew with certainty: he needed Rosemary as a full partner in figuring out how to placate Ow, satisfy Hong Chen, and save Mighty Dragon's life.

Tom called Rosemary on his cell. "I just left Hong Chen. Can we meet? Your place in twenty minutes?"

Her first question when he arrived: "What did you do with Fortune's Brick?"

"I made it invisible."

"You made it into tea?"

Not a bad option. Keep that in mind if things don't work out. Invite all the players to a tea tasting. Can you tell which pot contains Fortune's Brick?

"No, it's hiding in plain sight—if you know where to look."

"So what are you going to do with it?"

"What are *we* going to do with it? Ow wants his money. Hong Chen wants to use it as a weapon."

"What?"

Tom explained Hong Chen's intent to kill Mighty Dragon. He expected her to be repulsed by the idea of murder, given how her friend Geoffrey Milner died. But she was silent.

"This brick of tea," Tom concluded, "this artifact, can be our philosopher's stone."

Rosemary waited for a dubious punch line.

Tom had no idea where this sudden inspiration was taking him. But the concept of the philosopher's stone—transformation of base emotions of greed and revenge into enlightened aspiration, the transmutation into a higher self, an honest man—was so romantic. Turn his base lust for Rosemary into a golden Oscar of love. So Byronic. The Classical Hero, an everyday man with attributes that distinguish him from ordinary people. Harry Potter. Now there's a hero we all can relate to—accessibility, emotional quest, death of old self, and resurrection of new self. Mix in some Marlon Brando/James Dean—moody, defiance furrowing the brow, misery in the heart exposing vulnerability, a humble man capable of strong and deep emotions. A bit absurd, Tom acknowledged.

"We have to convince Ow and Hong Chen that Fortune's Brick is something other than tea."

"Like what?" Rosemary asked.

"An elixir, a rejuvenator of the true self, at least metaphorically speaking. Hong Chen will fall for it. He basically wants Fortune's Brick to make him immortal."

Rosemary burst out laughing at the absurdity. "We're talking about Ow here."

But the possibility of being involved in Mighty Dragon's murder intrigued her. *Why not loan Fortune's Brick to Hong Chen for his deadly deed? Then Ow would reclaim the tea—method at his discretion—and sell Fortune's Brick through his underground connections. He and she would split the money . . . .*

The thought pleased, and appalled, her.

She'd be an accomplice in a murder. Maybe two, depending on Hong Chen's success and Ow's restraint. *How would that feel, having no constraints, no fear of law, not giving a whit about others' opinions? That would be a terrifying thrill. There'd be no turning back. It would be like being ass-over-teakettle in love, completely irrational. Totally insane. But perhaps that state was necessary for a person to realize the best—or worst—of themselves.*

"Tom, really . . . ." She remembered him doing the absurd, but touching, performance in her living room. "Tom, do the swan dance for me."

He didn't get the reference, then his foolish heart came back—their wild dance when Rosemary threw herself at him, wrapped her legs around his waist. Swan, the symbol of love, fidelity, purity, loyalty, and unity. Byron mentioned swans in his poetry, Tom was certain.

He stood from the chair, rose on tiptoes and spread his arms, chin lifted high to elongate his neck. Slowly he swooped low and leapt a good four inches off the floor, trying with every fiber for the grace of romantic love.

Rosemary clapped her hands and laughed. Really absurd. She'd have Tom bring Fortune's Brick back to her. She 'd give it to Howard, the buy-in into his world.

Tom took her laugher as joy. Encouraged, he flapped his arms and cooed, not knowing what a swan sounded like. He arced his arms forward, inviting her into the embrace. This formal declaration of alliance—foreplay to collaboration—was the first step toward his new self, an honest man. A preamble. That's what Tom told himself. A warm-up. Big toe in the water. Serious flirting with hope rather than with a guarantee.

Rosemary stepped into the invitation as if a waltz partner, one hand on Tom's waist, the other extended to his high hand. They held that pose, eyes locked, misunderstood assumptions a shimmering bond, as they moved in an old-fashioned box step, simple, easy to follow, a rhythm from childhood lessons of play. Tom bent a knee to lead Rosemary into a graceful dip. She leaned with him into the turn. He whirled her in circles around the living room with increasing speed, gradually tightening his arm around her back until they were full frontal. He kissed her. She put her arms around his head to hold him in place, her one eye open. Tom had both eyes closed.

The embrace became frottage, heated rubbing to transfer body imprints on each other. The kisses became gulps. Tongue lashings. Heavy breathing formed words. Yes. Wait. They broke apart, but held hands. We have time. Let's luxuriate in this, draw out the moment.

"Shall we have a cuppa?" Rosemary asked.

Tom paced to walk off his erection while she fixed a pot using leaves left over from the fake Fortune's Brick. He was pleased about not jumping her bones. Not yet. *This is it*, he thought, *Romantic Hero winning the day*. Add the idealism of Lancelot to his brooding Brando and the mysterious pout of James Dean—and he'd have the perfect mix to keep Rosemary intrigued.

"Tea's ready," she called out.

He sat opposite her, elbows on the table American style, as she poured. He liked the simplicity of this tea ceremony, straightforward without pretense or theology. "To our good fortune." He lifted his cup in a toast.

"Speaking of fortune, Ow is expecting the payment we promised." Rosemary sipped her tea. "What are we going to do about that? Maybe sell Fortune's Brick? We should contact Rupa. See if she's interested. And there's the loose thread of whoever arranged the auction. We stole tea worth millions and the owner will want it back. What are we going to do about that?"

"That's Ow's problem. Whoever was behind the auction doesn't know we stole the tea."

"And Ow is our problem. I'll call Sandra and see if Rupa has contacted her since the auction. If she's still in town, we should meet with her."

Once Fortune's Brick was back in play, she'd conspire with Ow to steal the tea. A plain, straightforward holdup. Child's play for Ow. Double-dipping. She'd split Rupa's money with Tom. Then, when Ow stole the tea from Rupa and resold it, split that money with him. She was utterly amazed at herself for even thinking of such a nefarious scheme, even more so for seriously considering taking the plan to Ow. *And loaning Fortune's Brick to Hong Chen so he could kill Mighty Dragon—that was being reckless with someone's life.* Stop it, she scolded. This isn't even a fun fantasy.

"And Hong Chen? You don't expect him to sit still waiting for you to deliver?"

"What exactly is Hong Chen going to do?" Tom asked. He had his grandfather by the short hairs. Selling Fortune's Brick to Rupa would seal the partnership with Rosemary, solve the Ow problem, and betray his grandfather. "All right. Call Sandra and see if Rupa is still in town."

Tom had a dilemma: How to make Rosemary believe he'd sell Fortune's Brick to Rupa, while simultaneously avoiding selling Fortune's Brick to Rupa? He was still puzzling over the conundrum when he and Rosemary walked into the Teanamu Chaya teahouse the next afternoon.

Sandra gripped Rosemary by the elbows, a halfway hug, leaning in but not embracing in case there was no good news to celebrate and she had to pull back from the expectation. "You were so mysterious on the phone. Rupa's waiting on the patio."

Tom hung back, hoping for inspiration on how to create an illusion to satisfy Rosemary and Rupa. Rosemary had to be convinced he was working with her for a shared goal. Rupa had to believe there was hope for her attaining Fortune's Brick. That's good magic, he assured himself, the sparkle of life, the fountainhead of faith, the saving grace of sanity. What does truth matter?

The table under the ginkgo tree in the snug high-walled patio had been set for tea. Rupa rose from her chair to greet Rosemary and Tom with a warm smile. "What a welcome surprise to see you both again." Handshakes and cheeks touched to cheeks. "You look stunning as always," Rosemary said, admiring the graceful silk sari, as they sat at the table.

"Do you know that the ginkgo is believed to be one of the oldest living species in the world," Sandra said. "The Chinese cultivated the tree over a thousand years ago. We can make tea of these." She pointed to bright buttery-yellow fan-shaped leaves, then discreetly left.

"I know about black tea and green tea and white tea, but I've never heard of yellow tea." Tom decided not to overthink his dilemma. Keep the conversation light, depend on wit, innuendo, and distraction. Do mental magic with the bean.

"There is also fabled tea and stolen tea." Rupa's sly smile told Tom she expected news about Fortune's Brick.

"The most difficult to procure," said Rosemary.

"Elusive," Tom added.

"Perhaps that's why it's so valuable, if the mysterious, elusive, difficult to procure should miraculously reappear." Rosemary enjoyed the verbal innuendo.

"And dangerous," Tom nodded. "Gunpowder tea."

"Gunpowder is a very fine tea," said Rupa, sensing a negotiation.

"Only you don't want it to blow up in your face, or cup, as it were," Tom chuckled.

"Sounds like an espionage tea," Rupa laughed, "to serve an unsuspecting enemy. A James Bond tea, or CIA tea, or Taliban tea."

"Yes. Stuff you need to keep in a safe and secure place, and handle with extreme care."

Impatient with the wordplay, Rosemary asked Rupa, "How much do you think Fortune's Brick would have brought at the auction, if it hadn't been so rudely disrupted?"

"Depends a great deal on the gentleman from Manila. He has the really deep pockets."

"And you?"

"Fortune's Brick is more a matter of prestige than commercial worth. So I had a limited horizon. And you?" Rupa was now the steely-eyed competitor. "How much were you authorized to bid by the Milner estate, Tom?"

"The bidding was already beyond my brief."

"What if Fortune's Brick became available again," Rosemary bluntly asked Rupa. "Do you think there could be another auction, or a private sale?"

"Then we'd be dealing with thieves," Rupa replied. "A very untrustworthy group. I don't know if I'd put myself at that risk."

"Stolen Old Master paintings find their way into private collections," Tom injected. "Surely there must be honor among thieves. Not that we'd know."

"No, of course not." Rupa didn't know who to focus on, Tom or Rosemary.

"But the thieves, whoever they are, will want to monetize the tea," Rosemary said, nudging the conversation in her direction. "Thieves, like any businesspeople, want to make a profit. So it's not improbable that Fortune's Brick will pop up again."

"Unless the heist was a bespoke order," Tom said, pushing into the opening, "like those paintings stolen from museums for a specific customer."

"The collectible tea world is a very small circle." Rupa recognized a glimmer of possibility. "We know one another. Which is why I was surprised Milner was represented at the auction. The family has a long and illustrious history in the tea business. But Geoffrey"— she gave Tom a hard stare—"he had a different kind of reputation."

"What reputation was that?" Rosemary asked.

"I don't want to speak ill of the dead."

"But do," Tom urged. "My name is linked to the Milner estate and to Fortune's Brick. I need to be fully informed to protect my reputation."

Rupa hesitated, then leaned forward, inviting Tom and Rosemary to lean in also to hear the stain on the dead. "Geoffrey was known to move in the world of stolen artifacts in collaboration with ISIS al-Qaida, and other such groups. Fortune's Brick was valuable as a historical and cultural artifact, not because it was good tea."

This confirmed what Hong Chen had told Tom. He tilted toward Rupa, a gesture of sharing with a confidant. "Could someone from that criminal world have learned of the auction from Geoffrey?"

"Perhaps."

"Would they put Fortune's Brick back on the market, with those of us at the auction as likely buyers?"

Rupa heard the offer of partnership. "Is that why we are at this meeting? You've been approached, but it's beyond your means?"

"If such an offer were made"—Rosemary touched Rupa on the arm, a reassurance—"we'd need a partner. Not saying, but interested in what you'd say. Just saying."

"Very risky," Rupa replied, not moving away from Rosemary's touch.

"And dangerous," Tom added. "But we're friends, like each other, have a common interest. We can trust each other."

Rosemary removed her hand from Rupa's arm. "Something to think about—if you're interested."

Rupa settled back in her chair. "I'll stay in London for a couple days. There is so much to see."

That went well, Rosemary thought as she drove Tom away from the teahouse.

That went well, Tom thought, firmly buckling himself in for another daredevil drive through London traffic. Neither noticed the tailing car, or Ling on the motorcycle following the tailing car.

Tom told Rosemary to drop him off at Hyde Park Corner. It wasn't a far walk to the Victoria and Albert Museum, but far enough so she wouldn't suspect.

Rosemary pulled to the curb. "I'll call you after I talk with Ow. You get Fortune's Brick in hand." She didn't bring the Mini to a complete halt, just slowed enough for Tom to slide out and slam the door shut.

You don't have to play this out, she told herself, pulling back into traffic. Risking an accident, she glanced at the big plate glass display windows of a Boots flush against a building constructed in 1895, according to the date carved in the stone lintel. The three floors above Boots were faced with bluish hexagonal interlaced windows, like pods of crystals. The jewel-like façade twinkled in stark contrast to the dull brickwork of the older building.

The perfect metaphor for me, she thought, *in the gap of clinging to history and flinging myself into a new vision. Well, fuck it, Rosemary, dear, time to make the choice—safe risks or recklessness.*

When she arrived at the Cock & Spur, one of Ow's henchmen waved her into a reserved parking space behind the pub. A perk, she thought, like a CEO.

Ow, wearing sweatpants and a ragged cardigan, his favorite work clothes, sat at his desk, pecking at the keyboard. "Be with you in a moment, Rosie." The sight amused her, this hulking man, intimidating as a hungry bear, her brother the businessman. Ow pushed back from the computer. "I miss the old days when you actually went out on the streets and committed a crime. It was a public statement. Stealing the Bentley, robbing the bank, was showing the flag—the Unfortunates are not powerless." He turned the computer off. "Now I can steal a bank vault with a few keystrokes. No one would know, unless I wanted to crow."

"Crime boss for the masses, are you?" Rosemary sat on the sofa with hands pressed between her knees, chewing her lower lip. "Ow, have you ever killed someone?"

"That might be a bit too personal, even among family."

"I'm wondering if murder, a deserving murder, can be an act of freedom?"

"What are you talking about, Rosie?"

"You live outside the law. Every day is a risk. I wonder how you became so fearless, to take that freedom upon yourself and live it."

Ow came and sat beside his sister and took her hand. "Curiosity, that's what's required to keep fear from scaring you to death. A frightened mind does not seek. A frightened mind cannot kick my demons in the arse, just to see how I'll react when they come roaring at me. My motto, 'Life is grand, if you don't weaken.'"

"I'm afraid to come out of my frightened mind, Ow."

Ow held her hand between both of his, as if to anchor her. "Everyone creates a fiction of themselves as good or successful or whatever. The purpose of life is to discover the fundamental self, and believe in it. That's the angst of life, too, isn't it?"

"How did you get so wise, Ow?"

"By kicking arse."

Rosemary took her hand back. "I'm scared to death to kick my arse."

"It can be very dangerous, if you weaken. What exactly are you asking me?"

Rosemary told him about Tom having the Fortune's Brick from the auction. "He's hidden it somewhere, but he'll bring it to me." She told him about the meeting with Rupa, and her plan of collecting money from Rupa, and collecting again when Ow robbed her and sold Fortune's Brick on his nefarious network.

Ow looked at his sister for a long moment, his hand on hers, not patting or stroking in comfort. Then he tilted his head back and roared with laughter. Rosemary allowed a tentative smile, then a giggle, then all her tension and fear rolled out in a peal of laughter. Brother and sister rollicked on the couch, bonded by clutched hands, by unconditional love.

Rosemary regained control enough to speak. "There's more." She told him about Hong Chen wanting Fortune's Brick as bait to lure his enemy

Mighty Dragon into the open, and then kill him. "We could convince Tom to loan Fortune's Brick to Hong Chen, for a fee. Then take it back after he kills Mighty Dragon. A Rupa/Hong Chen/criminal network trifecta."

"I didn't realize this about you, Rosie; such a devious criminal mind." He studied her for a moment, as if seeing a new possibility. "Hong Chen wouldn't give Fortune's Brick back once he had his hands on it."

"He doesn't have to cooperate. You have ways to take it off him."

"We shouldn't be greedy."

"It's not about greed," Rosemary said, somber now. "It's about kicking my arse to discover my reaction, when it comes roaring at me. Do I have the capability to purposefully cause another's death? An act that will brand me as a despicable outcast, a threat to the very order of society, a person condemned in the Bible and by all laws throughout history. An act punishable by death. I can't think of a better mentor than you."

"Ah, Rosie, that's a big burden you're asking."

Rosemary turned full face to him and pointed to her empty eye socket. "You owe me."

"That's not fair, Rosie. You know it isn't."

"I don't care about fair."

"You could get destroyed in ways you'd not expect. In ways I couldn't prevent. I don't know. Sell Fortune's Brick to Rupa and give me my share. Then we'll consider getting your arse kicked."

Rosemary wasn't the only one considering giving a kick in the arse. Tom, as he walked to the V&A, felt a brooding sense that he had screwed up but didn't know how; too many variables in his plan, too many unknowns to trust.

He stepped into the museum's new courtyard of white ceramic tiles. The boomerang-shaped entrance, white sloping tiled roof above black glass doors, was dramatic enough for him to pause in admiration. In that moment's hesitation, he felt a swift kick in the butt: He'd accept, without equivocation, that he was a criminal. No more beating around the bush. He had stolen the Quan Yin figurine; he had masterminded the Fortune's Brick tea heist; he had conspired with a crime boss, and he had recruited Rosemary to be his partner in crime.

His first reaction was startled recognition, then delighted embrace.

"No more justifying myself with feel-good righting of wrongs, or acting as my mother's white knight in seeking revenge for her honor," he said aloud. "I am a criminal with malicious intent in order to assuage my well-being. I will be a suave criminal; no physical violence, no preying on the vulnerable, but clever planning of audacious crimes, which includes stealing hearts."

How to be a successful criminal, at least in terms of not getting caught? Stay undetected. Be a no-see-um—make the bite felt but don't let the victim see the source of the attack.

With that, he turned on his heel and left the V&A.

CHAPTER 16

PROPOSAL

A white guy, with another riding shotgun, drove the car following Tom and Rosemary from the teahouse, which puzzled Ling. Who were they and why? When Rosemary dropped Tom off at Hyde Park corner, the car had proceeded to the nearby Kensington hotel where Mighty Dragon and Quiet Killer stayed. Odd, thought Ling, tailing on his motorcycle. Quiet Killer's car was parked across the street from the hotel. The white guys paused to check the license plate, and then drove off.

Ling reported the sightings to Hong Chen. The car with white guys was not a puzzle to Hong Chen: Looter had hired a gang to track down people from the auction, set up an attempt to recover Fortune's Brick.

Tom was in danger; they might snatch him and torture him to get Fortune's Brick.

Mighty Dragon was also a target.

Once Mighty Dragon's people in China told him that Hong Chen *does* have Fortune's Brick, he'd come after Hong Chen with vengeance, with Looter's gang right behind him.

Hong Chen didn't like the odds, he and Ling against a gang of hired mercenaries. They'd be outgunned. But that seeming weakness could be an advantage, he reasoned, while sipping a cup of tea in his sitting room. If the enemy is ready, be ready for him. Another common sense and good strategy from *The Art of War*.

Hong Chen finished his tea. He needed an ally. Where to find some firepower?

The only lead was the pub in Peckham twice visited by Tom. Not a place Hong Chen expected Tom to find on his own. The woman, Rosemary—didn't seem like her kind of place either. But she was an unusual woman, the way she flaunted her missing eye. Bit of a rogue. She took Tom to the pub. She knew someone. Hong Chen placed a call to Tom.

"Grandson, I have urgent news." Tom blocked one ear to better hear the cell phone over the street noise. "You are in danger. Bad men are after you. Come to me immediately."

Tom's first reaction was: He intends to hold me hostage until I give him Fortune's Brick. Then: He's trying to save my life. Then: He's fooling with me.

"Bad connection. What did you say?"

"Believe me, Tom. You are in grave danger."

That was the first time Hong Chen had used his name. The simple familial gesture caused Tom to lose his breath. A clot of emotion—longing, thankfulness, relief—blocked his throat. He started to speak, then clamped his lips and took a breath to assert control. "What kind of danger?"

"The painfully dead kind." Hong Chen broke the connection.

Hong Chen stood behind his desk dressed in his Manchu authority robe, not a touchy-feely grandfather but a brisk and stern patriarchal CEO. Tom stiffened to attention, and then resisted, bending his knees and tilting slightly forward, as if poised to jump.

Hong Chen explained about Looter's gang searching for people who had been at the tea auction. "I know the man behind this. He's a ruthless man. His for-hire guns will show no mercy until they have Fortune's Brick."

Preposterous, Tom decided, made up. A Chinese Grimm fairy tale meant to scare me.

Hong Chen added, "They know Rosemary from the auction."

Tom settled back on his heels. He had put her in danger—the "painfully dead kind."

"We need help to save ourselves." Hong Chen softened his voice to invite Tom to join him. "Perhaps"—he made a wave into empty air, a helpless gesture—"perhaps you might have an idea."

"Perhaps," Tom conceded. "I'll check it out."

Ow got an unsettling call an hour after Rosemary left. "Saw your sister recently. Twice, in fact, sussing out tea.

You wouldn't know anything about that—tea—would you?" Ow recognized Jimmy's voice, the quisling who had joined Bogside John's team.

"How you doin', Jimmy? Long time. You still in the circle jerk with BJ?"

"Don't let him hear you say that. Got himself a temper. Especially after that beating you gave his boys. He's not thinking kindly of you."

"You feel me trembling, Jimmy?"

"A friendly call, Ow. I'm on a little retrievable job. Might require a prod and snatch, or not. Seems to be an argy-bargy about some tea. Would you believe that? Tea? You can buy tea in any shop. But apparently this is special tea. I was on guard duty at the auction for this tea and guess who was there? Your sister. Hadn't seen her in years. Scrummy she is, with those perky strawberry creams. Some bold bastards disrupted the proceedings and rudely took the brick of tea. I didn't see them myself, but was told one was a big guy. People are pissed about this, Ow. It's an embarrassment to us, Bogside John's boys. Our client is most upset and made it clear he's not a man you want upset with you."

"You know who he is?"

"Naw. It was a long-distance call-in job. Heard he might be Mr. Wog."

"Why you calling me?"

"Thought you might be concerned about your sister's welfare. It was an inside job, and she was inside. Now she's in our sights. Thought you could be helpful."

"I'll keep my ear to the ground, Jimmy. You on a deadline?"

"Yesterday."

"Give me a number." Ow wrote down Jimmy's cell number.

"Don't make this hard for us, Ow."

Shit. Ow drummed his fingers on the desktop, frustrated at the complication. He reached for the phone to warn Rosemary, but stopped and settled back for a think. It's a chess problem. Move the pieces around, set a trap with the knights, put the bishop in place for a lightning strike, queen for the checkmate. *Shit. It's Rosemary we're talking about,* he reminded himself. *And that fuck Bogside John. He's been trying for years to topple my king, make himself king. Maybe I can kill two birds with one stone, or one brick of tea, as it were.*

Ow enjoyed puzzles. Was good at solving them, be it Rubik's Cube, riddles, Turkish Twist, or what made someone tick. And how to make them stop ticking.

Tom called Rosemary. "Look over your shoulder, both shoulders."

"What are you talking about?"

"Drive fast and come pick me up."

Tom jumped into the car before Rosemary came to a complete stop. "Get lost in traffic." Rosemary rammed her way into the flow of cars. "What? What?" she demanded. Tom nervously glanced in all directions for danger. "They're after us." He explained what Hong Chen had told him about Looter's gang searching out the people at the auction. How they had been followed to the meeting with Rupa. Rosemary sped faster with each revelation, made more daring moves, cutting off cars, taking sudden turns, tasting fear, licking her lips.

"We have to warn Rupa," Tom said. Obviously, Rosemary agreed, with a nod of her head. "Where's the tea, Tom? Let's get it now. Do the deal with Rupa now."

"We'd still have the problem of Looter's gang. We need to get them off the board. Hong Chen wants reinforcements, an ally. I want to talk to Ow."

"Get the brick and sell it to Rupa—now, today."

"They're watching us, watching her, so how are we to do that? They'd swoop in and grab the tea, probably her money too, as a bonus, maybe kill us all to eliminate witnesses."

"Okay. It makes good sense to go to Ow." She immediately set course to the Cock & Spur.

"Drive slower," Tom said. "There's something I want to tell you." His quiet tone made her ease off the gas and pay attention. "I want Ow's help because I'm not a hero. I don't know how to deal with armed men who may kill me. And you. I don't have the physical skills to disarm them. I don't have the mental bravery to be more vicious than they are. I don't have a Superman cape. I don't want to fool you. That could get us both killed."

Rosemary didn't know how to respond. She'd never thought of Tom as a hero. The Fortune's Brick caper had always been a portal through which she could step out of her predictable life, and he had his hand on that doorknob.

Tom took a deep breath. "I want you to know me without my costumes. I want to be in samurai intimacy with you."

Rosemary leaned into the steering wheel, peering intently ahead, as if looking for an opening to dart through. This was a very serious situation, serious as a head-on collision. "I don't understand, Tom. Samurai intimacy?"

"Utter reckless bravery. Sacrifice of the self to a principle that transcends one's own preservation. Loyalty to an ideal beyond the self."

"Tom, I—"

"I want us to collaborate in enhancing each other's lives to the fullest, to force the other to be brave and honest."

Rosemary started to reply. Tom held up his hand to stop her. "No need to mention love. That mystery—and puzzle—is beyond me."

Rosemary stayed silent, focusing straight ahead, both hands gripping the wheel. "Tom." She lapsed back into silence to gather her will. "Tom, I desperately need to find freedom within myself. If I don't seek that now, I'll lose my courage. It's comforting not to look truth in the face, but if I don't, I'll stay tethered to my fear, brittle as glass. I'll break at the wrong moment and shatter happiness. I need to be reckless in my own way."

She fell silent. "Love for myself has no room for another."

Tom let out his held breath, a low soft hiss. Maybe disappointment. Maybe anger. Maybe relief. Maybe acceptance that *I have no choice but to risk loving like this. Loving without possession.*

"I hate you. I love you. I hate you because I love you. Which cup is the bean under?"

Isn't that what dishonesty by omission is all about, sustaining doubt, and in that forcing inquiry? Keep 'em guessing. Keep me guessing, he ruefully admitted. *Well fuck that. If Rosemary has the fortitude and courage to look truth in the face, then follow her lead. Being wrong and in love is better than being in doubt and without love. Who says that love is what you think it should be? Be a samurai.*

"We're in a fight," he said, still not looking at her.

"No," Rosemary began, "we're—"

"In a fight with those guys chasing us, with Hong Chen, with Ow, with the whole idea of"—he wanted to say of winning but he no longer understood what he wanted to win—"the whole idea of staying alive."

Rosemary dropped the Mini into a lower gear and added speed.

When Rosemary entered Ow's back office, he exclaimed, "Just who I've been looking for," and to Tom, "you, too." Without inviting them to sit, Ow said, "There's this gang—"

"Looter's gang," Tom interrupted.

Ow gave him a sharp look, like why's the school kid butting in. "Bogside John's gang. They were the security at the auction. You two have been targeted as suspects in the heist. Their client—"

"The Looter," Tom injected.

Ow turned on Tom. "What do you know about this?"

"The Looter runs this operation from China. He hired Bogside John's gang."

Ow remembered Jimmy's reference to a Mr. Wog.

"My grandfather, Hong Chen, also wants Fortune's Brick. That's why I'm involved. His contact in China told him about Looter."

"Your grandfather?" Ow looked to Rosemary for an explanation, like, *What's this? Why didn't you tell me?*

"My grandfather is also a target. He wants an ally to beat back the gang. Otherwise, we'll lose Fortune's Brick. I thought you would know the best way to go about gang warfare."

"You are a surprise." This new piece on the board pleased Ow, gave him a more complicated game in which to confuse his opponents. "I'd like to meet your grandfather."

Hong Chen had stipulated he and Ow meet alone at his fortified house. They sat in the sitting room, Hong Chen in his Manchu power suit—high-collar, bright vermillion robe with a golden dragon embroidered across the chest; Ow in his stylish gangster best—a wide-shouldered, double-breasted suit with broad wing lapels, weave of silver through the sheen of midnight black, red tie bright as a flame, a dazzling white shirt, a solid gold signet ring on his right pinkie and a ruby ring on his left pinkie. His thick hair was gelled straight back from his forehead, the sides puffed out, a lionized look not meant to be subtle. Hong Chen's walker was nowhere in sight. Ow took his place at the other end of the settee.

"Do you like tea?" Hong Chen spoke without turning to Ow.

"I'm English, aren't I? Although that doesn't mean I like the queen. Nothing personal, just the idea of it all."

"Respect for tea, shown with proper ritual, is shared by our cultures." Hong Chen pulled the tea dolly forward and set two cups on the low table before the settee. "It civilizes us." He poured their cups from a five-hundred-year-old Yixing pot. "I couldn't help but admire the diamond stickpin in your tie. If I may be so bold as to ask how much it cost?"

"Neighborhood of twenty thousand euros, market price. I got a discount."

Hong Chen handed Ow his cup. "This pot of tea is worth more. I paid full price."

"Next time you want some tea, come to me. I have contacts."

"Next time you want quality gems, please contact me," Hong Chen said with a dismissive glance at Ow's ruby ring. "I can get you a discount."

The two men weighed the attitude between them; if they had been snakes, they'd be flicking tongues at each other. Ow was confident he had the upper hand; Hong Chen's emissary had come to him. Hong Chen was confident with an ace up his sleeve: Tom was bound by family loyalty.

"I've had the privilege of meeting your sister in this very room."

"I've met your grandson."

The pawns were in place.

Hong Chen set his cup on the table and, keeping his shoulders straight ahead, turned his head to Ow. "As our countries share histories, so do we share a common concern."

That common concern was fleeting, in Ow's opinion. Other than Fortune's Brick he couldn't imagine sharing anything with this old Chinaman in his fancy dress. Once he had the tea, he'd be done with Hong Chen. But being a polite guest, he asked, "What is your concern?"

"Saving the soul of my country."

That was not what Ow expected. "That's the job of priests, not businessmen."

"No, it's the businessmen who have tattered my country by not honoring the values of our wise ancestors. The same is true for your country, don't you agree? One of your countrymen, John Maynard Keynes, wrote, 'When love of money as possession transcends into love of money as a means of enjoyment, then humans will shuck off the monkey that's been riding us since the invention of the State. We will be free of the deformities the institution of State has wrought upon the human spirit. The high virtues, humans' innate nature, will rise to the top, up through the muck of false values created by self-serving Authority.' Keynes was a visionary. I share his vision."

Ow had never read Keynes, didn't know his economic theories, but he resonated with the quote. To be "free of the deformities the institution of State has wrought upon the human spirit" was his Holy Grail, even if the horse he rode in on was crime. Crime was the enemy of the order imposed by the State. Crime was the outlaw defiantly buggering the State.

"Our countries share a heritage of great literature, yes?" continued Hong Chen. "But writing wasn't invented to compose lyrical songs to beauty, or wooing songs of love, or praise songs to Mother Earth. Writing was devised by accountants. Writing's chief purpose was to compose columns of figures. The first examples of writing discovered in Mesopotamia were tax collectors' accounts. The tax collector—the enforcer for the State, the original oppressor."

Ow liked Hong Chen better with each sentence. But how did Fortune's Brick fit into Keynes, or Hong Chen's, vision? He shifted from buttock to buttock with impatience.

Hong Chen held up a hand, asking for forbearance. "Please, I'm trying to convince you of why we are natural allies. Keynes said that extorting money by self-appointed elites enabled the creation of a hierarchy of power. That segregated society into classes and division of labor and unequal privileges and rights. Our countries have that in common, past and present. But we, in our small ways, can improve on that, don't you agree?"

"What do you want?"

"I want you to kill those who are after Fortune's Brick, our enemy."

"Why should I send my men, risk their lives, to save you?"

"I have asked about you, my English friend. People tell me you are a thug, a cruel man. And you look it." Hong Chen laughed to show he meant no ill will. Much to his surprise, Ow also laughed, his high giggle a delight to Hong Chen. The response reassured him that he had read Ow correctly—a romantic who believed the idyllic lie of Robin Hood. Look how he dressed—like a movie-star gangster.

"But I'm told you have a crusading heart. You have stayed with your people. So you will understand another Keynesian truism: In order to flourish, the State, the base of wealth and power for the few, needs to economically prosper. And how does it do that? Largely by cheap labor. That is the profit driver. That's why we have poor people. Don't you agree?"

"How will I profit by helping you to Fortune's Brick?"

"Because together we can fuck 'em over." Hong Chen slapped his knees as he rocked with laughter. "Yes, yes, isn't that what you really want? Isn't that your satisfaction? For you and I, Fortune's Brick is above money. And once we possess a symbol, greater than money as possession, then we can bring the elite to their knees."

You sly, crafty bastard, Ow thought. Appeal to my heart while you pick my pocket. Well, I've used the rope-a-dope strategy more than once with great success. "Maybe we can find a mutually satisfying solution," he offered. "These bothers you're having, I know them. I'll set the trap if you provide the bait."

Hong Chen bowed from the waist without standing. Ow returned the gesture, thinking it was Chinese etiquette for a handshake. For the next half hour they worked out details and timing.

Then came the toast with teacups.

CHAPTER 17

SHOOT OUT

O w laid out the plan, over a pint, with Rosemary. "It should work out fine. But you can never tell in these situations. Keep the door locked and your head down, and you'll be safe."

Rosemary felt a glob rise in her throat, a big, thick, choking hunk of German- chocolate-cake fear. *Chew it. Chew it. Spit it out,* she told herself. *Shit it out. This is the bill of fare you ordered. You want to shatter your safe world. Now have the guts to pick up the hammer. People may well be killed. And you'll have the responsibility. This is your baptism into freedom. What exactly is that freedom? Being shorn of innocence.*

She had never considered that implication, to no longer have the grace of being good. No longer have a guileless soul. No longer be able to deny her capacity for evil. She could choose to obey or disobey the opposing forces of good and evil, love and lust. Making that choice was the fundamental primordial act of freedom.

"Okay," Rosemary said, and clinked glasses with Ow.

Tom had tea with Hong Chen. "This works only if Looter's gang believes you have Fortune's Brick with you," Hong Chen impressed. "They are watching you. You must show them that you are carrying the tea when you meet with Rosemary."

"They may shoot me on the spot."

"They will want a private place, not on the street. And they may not shoot you. They only want the tea."

Some big assumptions there. As likely to be wrong as right, life as death, thought Tom.

"We will have you covered," Hong Chen assured.

"When will this happen?"

"Tomorrow night."

Tom called Rosemary the next morning. "You okay with this?"

"Yes."

"It's iffy, you know. We're on the front line. Lots of things could go wrong."

"I trust Ow."

Tom wasn't sure he trusted Ow, or Hong Chen.

"Then pick me up shortly before eight."

He spent the rest of the day making up the package.

Mighty Dragon unexpectedly showed up at Hong Chen's an hour before the plan was to go into action, which presented Hong Chen with a quandary: Kill Mighty Dragon right there in the sitting room or not? But the timing was wrong. He wasn't prepared.

Actually, the killing in that moment would be difficult, if not impossible—Mighty Dragon and his bodyguard, Quiet Killer, held guns on Hong Chen and Ling.

"Fooled once, but not twice." Mighty Dragon spoke in his native Han.

"I don't understand your gutter language," said Hong Chen. "Speak English."

Mighty Dragon casually waved his automatic at Hong Chen and said, in English, "When will you learn that you'll never best me? This may be your final lesson."

Hong Chen hung his head. Ling, taking the cue, slumped his shoulders in submission.

"Fortune's Brick. Now."

"I don't have it." Hong Chen's voice was humble.

Mighty Dragon nodded to Quiet Killer. "Shoot him in the knee," he said, gesturing with his chin to Ling.

Quiet Killer smiled at Ling. "Right knee or left?"

"Then if this stupid prick doesn't produce the tea, shoot him in the balls. We can take a long time killing Ling"—Mighty Dragon turned back to Hong Chen—"and a longer time torturing you."

Hong Chen, head bowed, glanced at Ling, who gave no sign of being afraid. He wouldn't give Quiet Killer that satisfaction.

Quiet Killer stepped closer to take his shot.

"Wait." Hong Chen raised his head. "Tell me, did you kill the Englishman Milner just to humiliate me, as if you were taking a shit on my bed?"

"What Englishman?" Mighty Dragon asked. "I don't know any Milner."

"No reason to lie now. Why not take full credit for your superiority? You've always outsmarted me, beaten me down."

"If I wanted to humiliate you, I'd shit on your bed. Piss on your pretentious robes. Leave a note to tell you where to find me, and dare you to face me."

Hong Chen pointed to Quiet Killer. "Ling followed him from Milner's house."

"We were following that messenger you sent around. I had no fight with your man. We warned him away but he foolishly stayed with you. I didn't know for sure he was connected to you until Quiet Killer followed him to your front door. That's why I know you have Fortune's Brick. He was at the auction, your watchdog to make sure the tea was stolen—for you."

"You saw him smash Fortune's Brick right here." Hong Chen pointed at his desk.

"You were being too clever, making me believe your dream had been destroyed. But my people learned about your trick." Then the realization lit Mighty Dragon's eyes. "He has it, doesn't he? Your loyal man is keeping it safe."

Hong Chen's abject posture admitted Mighty Dragon was right. "You can't shoot Ling. He'll take you to the tea." Ling, who knew about the plan with Ow, gave Hong Chen a questioning look.

"You will take me to the tea." Mighty Dragon poked Hong Chen with his automatic.

"I can't. If the people see me, they'll suspect a trap. I would never expose myself so carelessly. You must be quick or you'll miss the opportunity."

Quiet Killer patted down Ling for weapons. Mighty Dragon kept his gun on Hong Chen. "Shall I kill you? Your final defeat?"

"If you do, Ling will refuse to take you to the tea, even if it means his own death."

"Yes, it's better to wait. Then you'll always wonder when I will come back for you, always be afraid." Mighty Dragon laughed. "And I will come back."

He tucked the gun away. "Bring the car around to the front door," he ordered Quiet Killer.

"Better you take my car," said Hong Chen. "If the people see a strange car, they'll drive away." Hong Chen looked Ling firmly in the eye. "Come back safe." Ling nodded his understanding.

Ling, with furtive glances at the car's clock, drove fast. Mighty Dragon sat in front with him, Quiet Killer in the back, his gun nudging Ling's neck. "Where are we going?" Mighty Dragon asked.

"Not far. The man with the tea will come soon, so we must hurry."

Ling turned into Rosemary's mews ten minutes before the trap was to be sprung. He stopped in front of her garage door moments before her Mini turned into the dead-end lane and stopped behind him. Mighty Dragon pulled out his gun and turned to look out the back window.

"That's him," said Ling.

Rosemary opened her car door to berate the driver blocking her garage. Ling edged the car forward. Mighty Dragon waited until Tom emerged from the Mini, then jumped from the car, the automatic pointed at Tom's chest. "So we meet again," said Mighty Dragon with a big smile, "my friend from the auction."

Tom was confused. This wasn't part of the plan. Had Mighty Dragon and Hong Chen somehow joined up to double-cross him and Ow?

"Give me Fortune's Brick now." Mighty Dragon approached Tom. "Then you and Hong Chen will be allowed to live."

Tom held up the book-sized parcel wrapped in brown paper. He had kept it in plain sight for the benefit of Looter's gang when Rosemary picked him up outside his bedsit.

Quiet Killer turned his head to check on his boss's safety. Ling, leaning forward as if to turn off the ignition, reached under the seat and grabbed the pistol always kept there. In one fluid motion he turned and shot Quiet Killer in the head, then leapt from the car.

Mighty Dragon spun at the gunshot. Ling leveled his pistol on the car roof.

Rosemary glanced at her watch. Eight o'clock. Time had run out. "Run, Tom, run!" She hit the garage door opener as a van blocked the entrance to the mews.

Ling shot Mighty Dragon in the head.

Six of Bogside John's gang sprung from the van and ran up the mews, guns drawn. Tom ran to the open garage. Ling dragged dead Quiet Killer out of the back seat and jumped behind the wheel. He executed a fast three-point turn as Ow's men ran from the shadows at the mews' dead end. Rosemary flung the Mini in a sliding turn into the garage as the door came down, nearly running over Tom as he ducked into the garage.

Ling slid down behind the steering wheel and barreled towards the van. He hit two men before they could jump out of the way. A bullet in the shoulder caused him to swerve, slamming into the van's rear quarter and knocking it aside. Ow's men charged forward, guns blazing. The narrow mews was a shooting gallery, with nowhere to hide. Men crouched low, their shots going high into upper story windows. Ow and his men fanned out close to the garage doors, seeking scant protection. The rapid-fire gunshots sounded like popcorn on steroids. The dead sprawled in their death throes; the wounded tried to crawl away.

Ow ran forward shooting anyone in front of him, on the ground or running away or taking a stand. The two surviving members of Looter's hired hands ran out of the mews. Ow surveyed the battlefield; two of his wounded men were being carried toward the mews' entrance and then to the getaway cars around the corner.

Ow stopped next to a fallen man groaning in pain, clutching his bleeding thigh. "Is that you, Jimmy?"

"What the fuck, Ow. You shot me."

Ow reached down and pulled him up. "Come on, let's get out of here before the unwanted show up."

Tom and Rosemary had taken refuge in her bedroom between the bed and the wall, away from the window. Rosemary, trembling, kept her head between her knees. Tom, halfway under the bed, grabbed her ankle to pull her in with him. She remained in a tight ball of fear, unmovable.

After the last gunshots, Tom counted to fifty before he crawled from under the bed. "It's over now." He took Rosemary by the elbows and drew her up to him. She rested her head for a moment on his chest, then took a big calming breath, pushed away, and ran to the window to look out at the mews. Bodies. Dead bodies. She caught a glimpse of a man half carrying a limping man out of the mews. She forced herself to look again at the dead men, seeing if any matched Ow's size.

Tom laid the parcel he had been clutching tightly the entire time on the bed to embrace her in a hug of comfort. She ducked his gesture, picked up the parcel, and ripped off the brown paper cover—to reveal a book the exact size of Fortune's Brick.

"What's your game, Tom? Where's Fortune's Brick?" She had counted on him delivering Fortune's Brick so they could sell it to Rupa—or so Ow could steal it straight away. She had not expected this betrayal.

"Tell you later." Tom glanced out the window at the bodies littering the mews. "Your brother, he's got a mean streak. Gotta go before the police show up."

She grabbed his arm. "Where is it?"

"I'll call." He ran from the room and out the garage door into the mews, avoiding pools of blood and bodies. One man moaned, but Tom didn't want to hear. He hurried to the street, paused to look into the van skewed sideways. The driver had fled. He sprinted to Hong Chen's.

"That bastard; that conniving bastard," Tom swore as he ran hard. Had Hong Chen ordered Ling to shoot him too and take Fortune's Brick? Had Hong Chen planned a double-cross of both him and Ow? Then he'd be empty pockets at the mercy of Ow—not a merciful man. Hong Chen would deny he knew what happened to Fortune's Brick in the chaos of the shoot-out. He'd be in the catbird seat, above the fray of feathers flying as Tom and Ow and Rosemary tore at each other with recriminations of betrayal. Is that why Hong Chen had insisted on meeting Ow privately, so Tom wouldn't glean the plan?

Tom arrived, breathless, at Hong Chen's door. The house was dark. He held the buzzer down while pounding on the door with his other hand. No response. He looked up at the security camera, grasped his side, which was heaving from the run, and mimicking an injury, sagged, as if his knees were giving out.

The door opened a crack. The butler/bodyguard, showing an automatic at ready, peeked out.

"I need help," Tom gasped, and fell heavily on the door to push the crack wider into an opening.

The armed man stepped back and pulled Tom in. Tom pushed past him and bolted up the stairs to the sitting room.

Hong Chen was kneeling on the floor over Ling's supine body, the man's bloody shirt part of the litter of ripped open gauze packets on the floor. Hong Chen, cleaning Ling's shoulder wound, glanced up. "This was not supposed to happen."

The butler/bodyguard, gun in hand, came up behind Tom. Hong Chen ordered the man to go back to the door. "The doctor will arrive soon."

Hong Chen pressed a bandage to Ling's shoulder to staunch the blood. "So you are alive. That's good."

"Shut it." Tom's harsh tone put a gag on Hong Chen. As certain as his name was Tom, he knew his grandfather had ordered Mighty Dragon's death. Coldhearted, cold-blooded murder no matter how draped in the banner of honor. Hong Chen was a despicable man, an unworthy man who didn't deserve the love of his daughter, or his grandson. He was poison in the family well.

"How will you redeem your honor, the 'family' honor, now that Ling has killed Mighty Dragon while you stayed safely away?" he asked with scorn. "How will that earn your daughter's respect? Not even Quan Yin will love you now."

Without turning away from Ling, Hong Chen asked, "You've brought me Fortune's Brick?"

"Fortune's Brick escaped."

Tom left without answering Hong Chen's shouts of "What? What? Where is Fortune's Brick?"

The next morning Rosemary was grumpy, having spent a bad night: ambulances taking away the dead, flashing lights of the police cars invading her living room, hours spent answering detectives' questions. She struck to her story. "I have no idea about the why or who of the gun battle. I was terrified, hiding under the bed." She didn't mention that Tom had been with her.

She had tried to sleep but fought for breath when her throat clogged with dense fear. The booms of gunfire and cries of wounded men echoed in her head. She had assumed all thugs, especially those willing to shoot each other, were tough guys. But one man had kept calling out for his mother, until he fell silent. It didn't sound like Ow, but he had been down there in the shooting alley, taking aim to kill.

She punched in the numbers of Ow's private line on her cell phone. No answer by the third ring, or the fourth ring. Where was he? That Ow hadn't survived was incomprehensible. She was trembling. The possibility of his death, or even being wounded, caused a flush of anguish she couldn't control. No answer on the fifth ring. Her breathing verged on weeping.

He answered on the seventh ring.

"Oh, Ow." She wept a flood of relief. "Ow …" She couldn't get another word out.

"It's all right, Rosie." His voice was a balm soothing her fear. "No harm."

She gulped back a sob. "You're okay?"

"Come see for yourself."

When she entered Ow's private office, he asked, "You bring me good news, Rosie?"

She sat on the sofa, unable to look at him. She had never before imagined the visceral ruthlessness of his world. The gulf between throwing bricks of criticism at architects and shooting bullets at people was so vast she couldn't comprehend the reality.

"What is it, Rosie?"

"How do you do it, Ow? Accept what you do as normal, just doing business?"

"I never said it was normal," Ow said gently. "War is not normal. Firing poor blokes just to increase your profit is not normal good behavior, but it's done all the time. Look around you, Rosie." He was now loud with anger. "People get their arses kicked just because someone can do it. It happens every day in one form or another. That's normal. It's also normal to kick back. Our little business transaction was just normal writ large."

"Because you can do it doesn't mean you should. You shouldn't be ugly because you grant yourself that freedom."

"We all make our deal with the devil. I want to know that devil so I can get myself the best deal possible. It's the devil you don't know that does you in."

"How do you recognize that devil, Ow?"

"By kicking arse. Look, Rosie, there must be evil in order to know good. That's the setup. If there's only good, then you're in la-la land, Lollipop Heaven. You have nothing to push against, no way to understand yourself. If you can't expand your capacity for understanding, then you must be perfect. You are all there is to be. You're God. Or you're vacuous. A vacuous idiot God. Can't have that, can we?"

Rosemary sank deeper into her silence, then rose back to the surface. "I want my freedom to be beautiful, Howard. Does it have to be ugly?"

"It is what it is. How you accept it is your life choice. Now, about Sneaky Tom. Where's the tea?"

"I don't know. He disappeared right after you killed those men. Said he'd call."

"Right now. You go home and stay behind a locked door. I'll get this sorted out. No worries, Rosie. We'll come out smelling like roses." He smiled at his pun, hoping to lift her spirits. She nodded, but didn't seem lifted up.

After Rosemary left, Ow phoned Hong Chen. If she didn't have Fortune's Brick, then Tom must have taken it to Hong Chen. "You were going to contact me, right, honorable partner?" Ow let the sarcasm carry his threat. "Arrange for us to meet and admire our prize?"

"I don't know where it is." Hong Chen sounded dejected, but Ow figured that was a ploy, stagecraft to misdirect him.

"He's your grandson. You Chinese are thick as thieves with family. You shouldn't be fooling with me. You know what happened last night." Ow spaced his words so the menace could be clearly heard. "I know where you live. I expect to hear from you within the hour."

"But—"

Ow hung up. His phone rang immediately. Ow let it go for five rings so as not to appear eager. "Yeah."

"You've gone too far." Ow blinked at Bogside John's voice. "Beating my men was bad enough, but killing five of my best is outside the line. I'm coming after you, you slit of a whore."

"Say you that." Ow, black as a thunderstorm over the suspected double-cross by Hong Chen, was in no mood for Bogside John's puffed-up posturing.

"Ay, I'll—"

"What you'll do is bend over, like to tie a shoelace. Because I'm standing right behind you to fuck you in the arse. You know that don't you, boyo? Say one word, any word, 'Hello,' and make my day, BJ. And I'm keeping Jimmy. He's mine now. I expect you to deliver his car, nicely washed and polished. Just leave it out front with the keys. And send me a thank-you note for allowing you to live." Ow slammed the phone down.

CHAPTER 18

RUPA

Rupa was deeply worried; the Makaibari tea estate's fortunes were under severe stress. A three-year plague of mites defoliated nearly a third of the tea bushes. Then an infestation of root-knot nematodes caused root galling of the mature bushes, with the result of smaller leaves. Acres of the best producing bushes urgently needed to be uprooted to wipe out the pest. Fortune's Brick would have been a gift from the gods, the lifeline that could save her family's business.

Foolish, you are a foolish old lady to have put such hope on a wisp of nothing, she had scolded herself in the days after the auction. She had suspected that Mr. Ocampo would be in attendance, but, despite his vast wealth, he might not pursue Fortune's Brick with ardor. It would be a bauble for him, another collectible to gather dust.

The Chinaman Weiwu Long had been a surprise. Where did he come from? And why? She knew the top-tier tea connoisseurs, and he had never been on the scene. He seemed very determined to win Fortune's Brick, pushing the bidding far beyond the expected price. Now Tom and Rosemary were hinting that Fortune's Brick might be obtainable after all. Dare she hope, again? Criminals were involved. How were Tom and Rosemary linked in? They seemed like such nice people. Tom, very circumspect, had warned of danger in pursuing Fortune's Brick.

However, the possibility of her having secret possession of Fortune's Brick was the best possible outcome. She wouldn't have to sell the tea in parcels, her original plan with Sandra, but could sell it at a much higher price as a rare collector's item. If she could save Makaibari Estates, the risk, whatever it was, would be worth it.

After the meeting with Tom and Rosemary, Rupa had placed a call to her lifelong friend Raj. They had grown up together, their families in the same circle of wealth and status. Raj was now a private banker based in Geneva. A quick trip to see him was essential if Rupa was to be in position for whatever deal Tom and Rosemary might offer.

There was a time, many years ago, in their youth, when Raj and Rupa shared a dream for each other. He was so handsome, with charm that could make Kali dance with joy, the necklace of skulls bouncing on her bare breasts. And Rupa so lithe and gorgeous, her laughter music on the wind, even Lord Shiva would pursue her. As children they recognized each other as destiny, although then they thought only in terms of delightful playmates. Their understanding morphed when their bodies changed, her budding breasts and his first shadow of a beard.

When Raj was nineteen, and Rupa sixteen, their love for each other was so obvious that the parents plotted against the sweethearts. Raj's family claimed a distant connection to royalty, and had aspirations that their son marries a princess. Rupa's family had no sons, so her father groomed her to assume control of his tea business. The children were told that family took priority over starry-eyed romance. To escape the fate of separation, Raj and Rupa planned to run away together. But their fathers sniffed the musk of desire on their children. Raj was sent to England to study. Rupa's father made a deal with a tea distributor who had an unmarried son ten years older than Rupa—perfect union, tea producer and tea distributor.

But Raj and Rupa had kept in touch through all the years, using business as their channel of communications.

"Raj, I need to talk with you," Rupa said in the phone, her tone businesslike. After all these years, even with Raj being long married (not to a princess but, in defiance, to a Swede) and Rupa a widow, it was important to keep the personal damped down.

"Be glad to, Rupa."

"In person."

"Ah." In person always meant serious business, like renegotiating Rupa's outstanding loan, her land as collateral.

Rupa appreciated his discretion. "I'll fly to Geneva. Can we meet tomorrow?"

"Yes, I'll be free late afternoon. Perhaps dinner after the meeting?"

"Very good. I'll call from the hotel."

That night, after making plane reservations online, Rupa stayed in and ordered room service so as to have time to work out how to explain the situation to Raj. Especially her plan. It's good business, she told herself. He will understand that. It was the only way she could repay the loan and save him the embarrassment of repossessing her estate.

Other concerns worried her late into the night. Why had Tom and Rosemary approached her? Because of the personal connection? Her accessibility? The criminals who had stolen Fortune's Brick were a dark cloud. Were Tom and Rosemary part of the criminal gang? They liked her, she said to soothe her restlessness. They wouldn't harm her.

The tea business could be a rough trade. Smuggling tea to avoid taxes was a big and profitable business. Damn near wrecked the Pakistani economy at one point. A police captain in China had been executed for running a tea smuggling ring. She had successfully fought off competitors who, when seduction failed, changed their caresses into a hard slap. She countered bribes with better bribes to hold off the cartel formed against her. She armed her workers to stop the marauders from burning her tea trees, and paid them well for their loyalty. When the neighboring cur hijacked her tea bound for market, she met him face-to-face with a softly spoken ultimatum: Return my tea or I'll burn down your mansion.

Fortune's Brick was nothing like that. It was a game for rich snobs. I grew up with rich snobs, she reminded herself. Some are my best friends. She couldn't imagine why anyone, especially criminals, might follow her. Nevertheless, she didn't want to lead danger to Raj's door. Prudence, even paranoid prudence, would be her watchword.

The next day, on her way to Heathrow, Rupa tried to remember spy movies. What would James Bond do? Use gadgets. She had no gadgets. Jason Bourne? He ran around a lot, and fired guns, and drove fast cars, and looked threateningly serious. Not her style.

At the airport, Rupa told the cab driver to drop her at the domestic terminal. She entered without glancing around, towing her carry-on. Inside, she slipped into the crowd, then sidestepped to sit out of the flow, where she could watch for anyone searching for her. Nobody suspicious. She took the bus to the international terminal, once disembarking to wait for the next bus to see if anyone stayed with her. She had no idea how to spot someone tailing her.

In Geneva, Rupa checked into the Hotel d'Angleterre. Discreet, intimate—if a bit of a fussy dowager—the hotel was expected of a woman of her status. The room had a view of the fountain—The Water, as the Swiss called the plume spurting out of the lake. She liked the Swiss for their practical side. Perhaps she and Raj would dine at the hotel's restaurant, famous for its food. But first came the business. She was nervous: it might be a serious miscalculation to ask her old flame to risk millions of dollars for her sake.

She made the call and Raj's secretary put her straight through. "Glad you've arrived safely, dear Rupa. Is four o'clock here convenient for you?"

Tall, handsome, suave, and impeccably dressed, Raj bore his age well. He rose from behind his desk to greet her, stepping forward with a spring of eagerness he couldn't disguise, didn't want to disguise. He took both her hands in his as if they were in a garden and held them. "Such an unexpected delight to see you." Rupa saw the joyous little boy in his eyes, and, for a flash, the smoldering young man she was still in love with. The charge between them never failed, even after all these decades. "Would you like tea?" he asked, directing her to the sofa with a view of the mountains.

"I've come to talk about tea." Rupa kept her eyes decorously down, so he wouldn't see how vulnerable she felt, not because of her economic straits, as dire as they were, but because she was with him. "I have an opportunity to solve my problem, but I need your help."

Raj listened attentively as she explained Fortune's Brick, the auction, the heist, her disappointment, and now the unexpected resurrection of hope.

"Bold boys, weren't they?" he said of the robbers.

"Confident," she agreed. "They had guns."

"Are they the ones selling the tea?"

"A definite possibility," she nodded, "seeing as they stole Fortune's Brick."

She told him about Tom and Rosemary. "I don't understand how they figure in," she admitted. "They were tied up like the rest of us. How would they know the criminals?"

Raj was an experienced man of the world, especially about the ways of money; as a private banker, he knew firsthand the wiles of crooks. "Are they dangerous, these men with guns?" Rupa repeated Tom's veiled hint of danger. "How much do you trust this Tom and Rosemary?" Raj asked with concern. Rupa shrugged. "I don't have a choice."

Then she explained her business plan. "I'm sure I can get Fortune's Brick at a discount. I know eager buyers who would pay full price. Bidding at the auction had reached six million."

People like Mr. Ocampo in Manila, who collected rare tea as art, not art to be looked at and admired but as a live connection to the earth, to the women who picked the delicate leaves, to the culture that treasured the connection to the gods. Mere mortals did not drink such tea. They put it in a place of honor on altars to be revered as a worthy old soul.

The conviction in her voice persuaded Raj to risk his money. Not the bank's, but his. He'd become Rupa's silent partner. That would be a bond to her, a show of good faith and trust—and love. A legitimate bond they could discuss openly, a reason to schedule business meetings. And the even greater allure—a secret to be relished. The perfume on the flower of their love. Raj had written love poems to Rupa, which he never sent, during his long years of exile while earning his degree from the London School of Economics. She'd be at risk of her father's punishment if he discovered Raj's heart paeans. Now he would write poems to her again, on the palimpsest of contract language.

"How shall we do this?" he asked.

Rupa hid her tears of joy under a quip: "With cash. We're dealing with crooks, after all."

"Will you dine with me?"

Rupa asked if his wife would be joining them.

"Monica is in the Caribbean with friends. I image the not-so-secret Rafael is there too."

"I'm sorry, Raj."

"I'm thankful."

Rupa had planned to return to London the next day, and contact Tom and Rosemary to close the deal. But she dallied in Geneva. So she didn't read or hear about the London "gangland" shoot-out.

The shoot-out was big news for two days—shouting headlines, breathless television accounts, police solemn in their press conferences to assure the public this was not a terrorist attack. Behind closed doors, the police brass was content. Let the slime balls kill each other. A gangland war was a good war. Orders given down to keep on the job asking questions, police procedure and all that—but allow time and space for retaliation so the pests clean out the foul nests for us.

When Rupa did check back into her London hotel, she found an invitation to a "tea event" at the Teanamu Chaya for the following evening.

She took the timing as the gods smiling on her. She would be able to save her business and avoid the shame of failure on the family name. And she and Raj would have many occasions to meet "for business."

CHAPTER 19

SWITCH

Tom had called Rosemary and asked her to arrange for the teahouse to be closed Thursday for a private event at eight P.M.

"Ow's a bit testy," she reported.

"Bring him with you. Tell him to have his boys at hand but out of sight. Looter's gang might show up and we don't want them to interrupt our tea party."

Tom phoned Hong Chen and left a terse message of place, time, and date for a "special tea ceremony."

Rosemary contacted Sandra with the request. "Is this about the special tea?" Sandra asked.

"Yes," confirmed Rosemary. "We'll be having a tea ceremony." That's all Tom had told her.

Tom placed chairs before a plinth upon which sat a box under a black cloth, similar to the original auction. Hong Chen arrived first, with Ling, arm in sling, hovering to assist with the walker if necessary. Hong Chen told Tom in a whispered conservation: If Tom kept Fortune's Brick in the family, he would give a blood oath to contact his daughter. He was willing to go on bended knee in asking for forgiveness if necessary. Tom pointedly ignored him.

Ow and Rosemary walked in together.

Nodding to Hong Chen, Ow said to Rosemary, "That old fox might try something yet. He's as crooked in his heart as I am in mine. I would have taken the tea from him. I think he took it from me. No proof, of course, the sign of a master thief. But then, I don't always require proof to validate my gut feelings."

She patted his arm. "Are your men in place?"

"Well hidden," he assured her. "Ready to spring a surprise if called on."

A bustle at the door caused them to turn around. Two of Ow's crew roughly shoved Bogside John, one on each elbow, to Ow. "Got my special invitation, I see," said Ow. "Have a seat." He patted the chair next to him. "And behave yourself if you want to see your boys safely home. Right, mates?" he said to his men. "All's under control," they confirmed.

Rupa arrived a few minutes late, bursting with expectation that she'd save her tea plantation. The presence of the three unknown men surprised her. Had Tom and Rosemary brought in competition?

"Who are they?" she whispered in Rosemary's ear, nodding to Hong Chen, Ow, and Bogside John sitting in a row as politely as if at a Christie's sale.

"The big guy is my brother and the old man is related to Tom. The other fellow is an associate of my brother."

A shadow of betrayal flitted across Rupa's face. She expected to obtain Fortune's Brick with minimum fuss at friend's price, then sell it on in her circle of tea collectors to pay off her tea planation's debt and live happily ever after.

She made quick assessments of Ow and Hong Chen. The big guy stirred a familiarity; he reminded her of the Russian at the auction. The Chinaman in old-fashioned Manchu robes? He looked like an actor from central casting. The third man appeared a ruffian. Maybe they were ringers planted by Tom and Rosemary to bid up the asking price.

Rupa settled in a chair at the end of the row, to state her separation. The set of her shoulders, her face stern and eyes snapping, said, I've stared down worse. Tea auctions in India for the year's crop were a cockfight compared to these poseurs. Besides, she had Raj's backing as the ace up her sleeve. Whatever the bidding, she'd top it. Six million. Seven million. Raj would put his entire fortune behind her if necessary. She was sure of it after their time in Geneva.

Tom, standing next to the plinth, cleared his throat for attention. "I have asked Dr. Jeremy Jessel, a curator at the Victoria and Albert Museum with a doctorate in art history, to tell us about Fortune's Brick. Dr. Jessel."

A tall man stepped from Sandra's office to replace Tom next to the plinth. "It's my pleasure and honor to speak to you about such an important historical subject." Dr. Jessel's accent was plummy, rich with culture, but he smiled easily and moved in a relaxed manner.

"I was thrilled when Mr. Edelson brought me Fortune's Brick. The fable was real, if this was truly Fortune's Brick. How to confirm its authenticity? That's my job, as an Asian cultural expert at the V&A. The images imprinted on the tea brick correlate to Chinese art and technique of the mid-1800s. So at first glance, I was very encouraged. I sent shavings of Fortune's Brick by express to colleagues at the Tea Research Institute at the Chinese Academy of Agricultural Sciences and to the Hangzhou Tea Research Institute. They both performed a chemical forensic analysis. Their reports stated that wild foods contain a proper mineral balance not influenced by select breeding or other human intervention. All tea plants contain fluorine, and old tea accumulates large amounts of fluorine, which is a poison in concentrated levels. If consumed, it deteriorates bones and teeth."

Dr. Jessel paused to let the information sink in. "Their conclusion"—he took a folded piece of paper from his suit pocket and dramatically snapped it open—"is that the tea in Fortune's Brick was unnaturally high in sugar and starch, and devoid of proper mineral balance. In their judgment, the tea did not come from wild plants. Tea leaves reserved for Chinese emperors came from the wild King Trees in Yunnan. Also, Fortune's Brick did not contain high levels of fluorine, as would be expected in tea dating back to 1850.

"In their opinion,"—he whipped off the cloth covering the box to reveal an ornate brick of tea in the glass cube from the auction—"the Fortune's Brick is an exact duplicate of the memorial commemorative brick of tea made for the coronation of Xianfeng, the ninth emperor of the Qing Dynasty. We've determined that the Menghai Tea Factory in Yunnan, which specializes in historical reproductions, produced it within the past decade. It is with great sorrow that I must pronounce Fortune's Brick a fake."

Rupa's face collapsed, then she pulled her composure back into place before anyone noticed.

Tom stood. "But all is not lost." He removed the tea from the case. "We are privileged to be the select few who will drink the infamous Fortune's Brick." He smashed the slate of tea on the plinth and gathered a handful of shards. "Sandra, would you be so kind as to boil up a pot. Who will join me?"

Ow declined. He never knew tea contained a poison. To drink a cup would be the same as eating the poisonous fugu fish, in his opinion; he wouldn't know the death sentence until it was too late. He leaned heavily on Bogside John's shoulder, lips on his ear, and whispered, "Game's over. Take that back to your paymaster. If you ever come near my sister, or Jimmy, or anyone here, I'll gouge out your eyes and smile while doing it, you understand?"

Rosemary hesitated, then nodded her willingness to join Tom.

Hong Chen rose from his chair with the creakiness of an old man in defeat and shuffled on his walker towards the door. He stopped and reached out to Tom. "Give me your arm."

Tom, not feeling mean towards the father of his mother, extended his left arm. The old man gripped Tom's bicep to get his attention with pain. "Where is it?" he hissed. "I've seen this trick before."

Tom bowed his head so Hong Chen would hear clearly. "It will never be yours."

"It's the reason I live."

"Poor choice."

Rosemary watched Tom leaning nearly cheek-to-cheek with Hong Chen. She mistook Tom's gesture as one of consideration.

Ow escorted Bogside John to the door and, with a smile and hearty clap on the back, as if seeing a pal off, said, "If you or your boys ever come into my territory, you'll be with the fishes."

Bogside John tried to turn with a scowl, but Ow's hand on the back of his neck kept him moving forward. When Rosemary came alongside, Ow gave Bogside John a push, not enough to make him stumble but firm enough to carry the message.

"So, Rosie dear," Ow hooked his arm in Rosemary's. "Did you know about this?"

"No. It's a total surprise."

Ow nodded at Hong Chen as Ling helped him to the car. "Him and Tom, blood is thicker than loyalty. I think we may have had our arses kicked. What do we do about it? Do we kick back?"

"It's a question of character, isn't it?"

Ow laughed and gave her a squeeze. "You know my character, Rosie. I like to kick arse. Great satisfaction in that."

Rosemary stepped away from Ow. "I need to talk to Tom. I'll meet you back at the Cock & Spur."

Rupa tugged on Rosemary's elbow. "You've not been kind to me. Why have you treated me so cruelly?" she asked, her voice dropping in disappointment.

"I didn't know what Tom was up to," Rosemary replied sincerely. "I truly didn't. I'm so sorry this didn't turn out as I had planned."

"I'll be leaving London now. I don't expect we'll see each other again." Rupa wasn't entirely dismayed that her salvage plan had been wrecked. Raj had pledged his backing. Perhaps he would extend his agreement on different terms.

Dr. Jessel stopped to give Tom a quick handshake. "Been a pleasure, Mr. Edelson. I've enjoyed our brief time together."

Rosemary pulled Tom aside. "What was all this about?" She was furious that he had not told her about the V&A testing. Now Rupa no longer thought of her as a friend. Yet, her gut intelligence nagged that there was something more to be discovered, and that beguiling possibility intrigued her.

"Hiding the bean under a cup," Tom replied.

"And which cup is the bean under now?"

Tom shrugged. "Don't know if I could say. I've given up on magic."

"And mystery?"

"Always a fascination. If a mystery is revealed, then it can be manipulated, corrupted, bent to purposes it wasn't created for. Shall we have that cup of tea?"

"Will you tell me the truth about Fortune's Brick?"

"It could be recklessly risky to reveal that mystery."

Risk and recklessness together might scare me out of my mind, Rosemary thought. Worth the try.

They sat on the back patio while Sandra prepared the tea. "I have a confession," Rosemary said, a tentative move toward recklessness.

Tom sat straight, hands on the table, fingers steepled, pretending to be a church in an effort to be calm. His breath fluttered. He remembered her body against his, the foolishness of his swan dance, her wild rush towards him. He wondered if she had found her freedom.

"I've had this fantasy," Rosemary began, "about murdering someone. What do the Catholics say: If you think of committing a sin, it's the same as doing the act? I always thought that rubbish, but now I'm not so sure. It might be the necessary preamble to finding your freedom."

Tom uncoupled his hands and laid them flat on the table. "I have killed someone." He saw no shock on her face, which gave him courage. "At least metaphorically. Fortune's Brick was my weapon. I used it to stab my grandfather in the back. I have no regrets, a little sorrow maybe for what could have been, but he is dead to me."

"What will you tell your mother about her father?"

"I'll give her his phone number."

They sat quietly while Sandra served the tea, then exited quickly, intimidated by the solemnity hovering over the table.

"What now?" Rosemary asked.

"Collaborators in committing the improbable?" Tom ventured. "To discover how far we'll push each other"— he looked at her until she held his gaze—"beyond what we thought possible."

"The blind leading the blind."

"At least we'd be moving forward." He leaned towards her, one hand raised. "There is something I've always wanted to do." He slowly moved his forefinger to her empty eye socket, tenderly felt the bone beneath the eyebrow, caressed the rim of her cheekbone, pressed deeper to touch the skein of skin. "Tell me about it."

"It's a long story."

"Then let's take a long weekend."

He took a sip of tea; she took a sip of tea.

Rosemary motioned with her teacup. "Is this Fortune's Brick?"

Now was a moment of truth for Tom. The test results on the Fortune's Brick that Dr. Jessel had sent to China were his long shot come home. Tom had made a private agreement with the V&A man—Dr. Jessel would report the alleged Fortune's Brick on the plinth a fake, as indeed it was, purchased from the Menghai Tea Factory. In return, Tom entrusted to him the authentic Fortune's Brick on the condition that the Victoria & Albert not announce its latest acquisition until after Hong Chen's death.

"Yes." Then full disclosure. "One of them."

"What's the risky recklessness?" Rosemary asked.

"Looter knows Fortune's Brick is the real thing, and that I've hidden that bean by this charade. He'll want his bean back. It may be beyond risky into recklessness to collaborate with me. More than either one of us bargained for."

Rosemary licked her lips.

Tom thought she was being salacious. Big grin. Heroic grin.

She tasted for fear. Sherbet. Cool, tasty, zesty lemon sherbet. She liked sherbet.

CHAPTER 20
LOOTER

Tom's long weekend with Rosemary extended to a sabbatical. He and Rosemary discussed finding a place together, as her mews apartment was too small and he had a temporary bedsit. But the cost of London real estate, even suitable rentals, was astronomical. So their residential hunting was dilatory, which was all right; they were together a great deal and could retreat to private spaces when necessary.

Rosemary decided to practice what she preached—design architecture for positive emotions. Her test subject was the Cock & Spur. Ow, the owner, agreed when she promised to include large flower boxes in the design. She faced the problem of all urban architecture: how to combine security with a welcoming embrace, especially in Peckham.

"I must start with a blank slate," she told Ow. "Filling that may be expensive."

"Don't worry, Rosie. I'll steal the crown jewels, or someone's jewels. I'm expanding into cybercrime. Keeping up with the times. Aren't you proud of this old dog, Rosie, and his new tricks? Found myself a gang of pranksters, smart lads who believe in playing while they work—and getting rich."

Rosemary spent her time sketching and envisioning and researching new building materials. If Ow was going high tech, then she'd design a complementary Cock & Spur. She was the happiest she'd been in her life. She had the freedom to express herself through her work that would influence by example rather than academic harping. Her contribution to changing her childhood neighborhood for the better would give hope and optimism to young Rosemarys and Ows that they could create harmony in their lives.

And she was working in partnership with her brother—without being a criminal.

Tom continued his research to identify common values in Chinese and American business cultures, and then translate them into an understood language businesspeople could apply to joint ventures. He spoke with his mother once a week. He never asked about Hong Chen. Once, she queried if he had contacted his grandfather.

"He's on my Christmas card list. I never send Christmas cards."

Fortune's Brick was never mentioned.

The tea escapade faded into yesterday's news for Tom, until one of his research sources, founder of an import/export firm, casually mentioned a growing market in China for anything with an English provenance related to the Opium Wars. "You have any ideas about that?" he asked Tom over a working lunch.

Tom replied that being an American he wasn't knowledgeable in such memorabilia. "What exactly do you have in mind?"

"Anything connected to the East India Company, like old authentic stationary or rubber stamps relating to opium or tea. I've heard scouts from China are in town looking for such items. Seems like a business opportunity to supply that demand."

Tom thought back to his search for the East India archives, and the Wardian case at Tregothnan—and Fortune's Brick. Was Looter looking for his bean?

The possibility of a Looter retaliation gnawed at him. While out walking, he'd scan for Asians approaching. He glanced behind himself so often he got a crick in his neck. His paranoia grew to where if he saw an Asian, male or female, he'd cross the street or dodge into a shop. Once he saw two young, well-toned Asian men walking towards him holding hands. He feared they intended to ensnare him so cohorts in a car could snatch him off the street. He turned and fled in the opposite direction, breaking into a brisk trot.

His growing distrust became such a distraction that Rosemary asked if something was bothering him. No, no, all's well, he assured. No need to raise a red flag, he told himself. No reason to infect her with my jitters.

Fear overwhelmed him one afternoon in a pub. He was at the bar with a glass of bitters, taking a pause from public exposure. An Asian man, about Tom's age, wearing a business suit, stepped up next to him with a friendly nod. Tom gave him a nervous glance and a cold shoulder. The man politely asked if Tom could recommend ale, as he was visiting from Hong Kong and didn't know English beers. Tom calmed himself, explained that he was American and not very familiar with English beers. He immediately realized his mistake in identifying himself as American. That put him in the target range: Looter was looking for an American.

The man introduced himself as Harp. Harp? What kind of name was Harp? Obviously a fake name. The man offered his hand, which Tom shook by the fingertips so Harp couldn't get a good grip and haul him down. Harp made innocuous comments to get a conversation going. Tom responded with a word or a shrug. He detected feyness about the man, like a visible lisp. Perhaps it was his sweet cologne or the lavender shirt, which Tom, in his heightened paranoid state, suspected as camouflage for a thug. He abruptly left the pub, leaving his half-full glass of bitters on the bar.

Ten steps down the empty sidewalk he heard the man call after him. Tom picked up his pace. He heard Harp's quickened footsteps. He could smell the man's cologne.

"Excuse me." Tom felt Harp touch his arm. "You left this—" Tom lashed back with an elbow, catching the man full in his nose. Harp fell back, both hands to his face. Full-blown fear-panic surged through Tom. He dropkicked the man in the balls. Harp doubled over with a HUMPH, ah-ah-ah, gag-gag and fell to the sidewalk. Tom kicked him in the head. The skull sounded like a peanut shell cracking. The blow felt fatal, as if he had stomped on a bundle of kittens.

He saw his cloth cap beside Harp. The man had been trying to return his cap. At least that was the pretense, the excuse to stop him, disarm him with the thoughtful gesture, and then capture him. He snatched up the cap. Two men emerged from the pub. Tom sprinted away to his bedsit.

Had the two men seen his face? Would the bartender remember the American and the Asian talking at the bar? Could his clothes identify him? Tom spent a restless night scaring himself. In the morning he scanned the *Daily Mail* for a headline of a fatal beating. There was a small article about a gay bashing outside a pub. A tourist from Hong Kong was in hospital with a fractured skull.

Tom was certain that Looter's men would now double down on him, kidnap him, torture him in revenge and for information about Fortune's Brick.

He was equally certain he didn't have the balls to be a real criminal.

He phoned Rosemary and told her about the threat on his life.

"Are you all right?" She sounded worried.

"No harm, but you and Ow and Hong Chen might be in danger."

He told her about his suspicion that Looter's men were in London probing for Fortune's Brick. She should alert Ow. He'd warn Hong Chen—maybe, although he didn't let her hear that ambiguity. His grandfather had ordered the death of Mighty Dragon, so maybe leave that dishonorable old man to his fate.

"I'll come pick you up and we'll go see Ow." Rosemary was excited. This could be risky. An opportunity to be reckless. She imagined willfully letting Looter's men find her and Tom, and engage them in a car chase. She'd give full rein to her inner rally car driver, execute dare-devil maneuvers she had never attempted, double back so she was the pursuer, and run them off the road into a smashup. There, take that, you amateurs. You get the message, Looter? We're not to be messed with. Her imagined movie so overtook her that she nearly caused two accidents by careless driving on the way to pick up Tom.

Ow met them in his secret office in the back of Cock & Spur. He was stiff with Tom but cordial for family relation's sake. Ow had never seen his sister so delighted, and he didn't want to put his heavy thumb on her happiness.

Tom told his story, how he had beaten Looter's man to the punch and put him in hospital. "Today's *Daily Mail* has a small item," he said, as if offering credentials.

"Do you know for certain that was Looter's man?" Ow asked.

"When a dog bares its teeth, you don't ask it to verify that it's mean. You kick it away." *That was good,* Tom thought. *The misdirection wasn't exactly dishonesty by omission, and it had a ring of truth.*

Ow heard the bravado dodge but decided not to challenge Tom. No need to belittle Rosemary's squeeze in front of her. "I'll call in Bogside John for a confab," he said. "If new men are on the scene, he'd know." He loved the idea of intimidating his nemesis. Salt to wound, he'd send Jimmy to deliver the command for Bogside John to present himself for a "tea ceremony" at the Cock & Spur.

Plus, he might learn something that would enable him to snatch Fortune's Brick. What a pleasure to out-fox Hong Chen.

"What about your grandfather?" questioned Ow. "He could be behind this as well as Looter. He's one sneaky bastard. Must run in your family."

Rosemary pinched Tom under the table as a warning not to throw a verbal dart.

Tom said he'd give Hong Chen a call.

"You must see him in person," insisted Rosemary. "He's family, too. I'll drive you there now."

"All right," Tom agreed. His mother would never forgive him if he deliberately left her father to the wolves.

Tom and Rosemary's unexpected appearance caught Hong Chen completely off guard. But he couldn't turn Tom away; the visit must have something to do with Fortune's Brick. Why else would Tom come see him?

He didn't have time to put on his mandarin robe so received Tom and Rosemary dressed in a simple cotton cheongsam buttoned from neck to ankle. "To what do I owe this honor?" he asked, unsure of Tom's status. Grandson? Enemy? Betrayer? Still a possible ally?

"Looter is back on the attack," Tom said. "His men tried to kill me."

Rosemary raised an eyebrow at the new highlight. Hong Chen saw her surprise.

"You might also be in danger," Tom added.

"We thought your contacts in China could be helpful in calling off, or thwarting, Looter," Rosemary said.

If Looter was making such an effort, then good chance the Fortune's Brick was genuine, reasoned Hong Chen. Why else spend so much money trying to recover it? That meant Fortune's Brick was still in London. And Tom knew the location. Maybe he could broker a deal: He'd save Tom from Looter if Tom gave him Fortune's Brick. At least give that impression. He had no pull with Looter.

"I am glad you are still alive, grandson." The truth of that sentence struck Hong Chen as a thunderclap: he was humbly thankful Tom was alive. "I have spoken to my daughter. She may come visit. Perhaps . . ." He gestured to the tea set on the table, leaving the invitation unspoken.

Tom made no acknowledgment of the olive branch. "Right now we have a Looter problem. Ow is putting out inquires to find Looter's new men. If you can pull strings in China, please lend a hand."

Hong Chen realized Fortune's Brick would be truly lost if Ow seized the prize. "I'll have my friend jiggle his web and see what might fall out."

"My mother cannot come to London as long as this danger is around us," Tom said, to give Hong Chen extra incentive.

As they drove away, Rosemary asked, "What next? How do we protect ourselves? How do we deal with Looter?"

Tom liked the "we." Team We, he and Rosemary looking out for each other. But to take on Looter could be fatally reckless. "I don't have a plan," he said, and immediately a plan began to form. "Ow and Hong Chen have bodyguards, and guns. They can take care of themselves. We should leave town, perhaps a romantic holiday in Paris. I've always wanted to take the Chunnel." He wagged his eyebrows. Rosemary laughed and licked her lips.

In the morning, Tom made an appointment with Dr. Jessel at the V&A. "Immediately. This is an urgent matter," he insisted. Dr. Jessel said to come to his office.

Tom explained the life-or-death situation. "We can prevent bloodshed," he told Dr. Jessel, "and the V&A will come out smelling like roses."

"How's that? This whole thing is a criminal enterprise, and I put the museum right in the middle." Dr. Jessel tried to put on a stiff upper lip; his actual upper lip twitched with tension.

Tom laid out his plan. When he stopped speaking, Dr. Jessel stared into space, his fingers nervously tapping on his desktop "Maybe," he conceded. "It will certainly win the museum points with the government—always helpful." *And,* he thought, *helpful to my career.*

On Tom and Rosemary's second day in Paris, the Victoria and Albert Museum announced, with very public fanfare, that Fortune's Brick, a historical and cultural treasure, would be returned to the Chinese people and displayed in the National Museum of China on Tiananmen Square.

"Isn't that nice," said Rosemary when she saw the television report. She rolled on top of Tom in their hotel bedroom, straddled his hips, pinned his shoulders with her hands. Tom thought she was ringing the bell for another round of joyous lovemaking. But she wasn't smiling. Her one eye snapped anger. "If you ever *ever* again are not fully honest with me, this collaboration is over. Understand? I will not recklessly give my heart if you don't leap with me."

Tom saw the determination in her face. So that's what a true samurai looks like.

He started to defend himself: Only *I* had the solution.... only *I* could make it work.... *I* could do it quietly so we wouldn't be connected to the V&A or Fortune's Brick. Only *I*.... Only *me*.... He bit his tongue so the pain stopped the words from being spoken.

This was it, Tom's death. Suicide by love.

"Sorry. Never again."

He lay flat on his back, palms down.

Rosemary straightened up, his hips firmly under her. She put one hand on his heart and one hand on hers. "Help each other achieve the possible no matter how improbable."

Tom placed his hands over hers. "Drive that stake into my heart."

She leaned forward with all her weight on the hand over his heart, and kissed him.

This was going to be exciting, he thought, two criminals lying dormant in seemingly ordinary people—waiting for a kick in the butt to pull off the next caper.

DoneFB

www.ingramcontent.com/pod-product-compliance
Lightning Source LLC
Chambersburg PA
CBHW071311170626
46809CB00001B/404